twin motives

BY MARK ROBINSON & PHIL KEMP

twin motives
DECEPTIVE HEARTS. DARK SECRETS.

Tate Publishing & Enterprises

Published by Tate Publishing & Enterprises, LLC
127 E. Trade Center Terrace | Mustang, Oklahoma 73064 USA
1.888.361.9473 | www.tatepublishing.com

Tate Publishing is committed to excellence in the publishing industry. The company reflects the philosophy established by the founders, based on Psalm 68:11,
"The Lord gave the word and great was the company of those who published it."

ISBN: 978-1-60696-263-3
1. Fiction: General: Suspense
01.15.09

DEDICATION

To our wives, Rita and Muriel, for the many
years of happiness, sacrifice, and love

1

CHAPTER

"Medic!"

The scream tore through the jungle smoke and dust. Somehow he heard the plea above the constant crackle of automatic gunfire, exploding mortar rounds, and officers' orders. The young combat medic, a marine corporal, raced up the hill. It seemed the wounded were everywhere. *Dear God, there are so many! Too many!* he thought.

"Medic!"

"On my way! Keep yelling!"

WHAM! The earth shook as another mortar round landed all too close. He dove headfirst alongside a shattered tree trunk. Rounds from the AK-47s and Chicom 56s were cracking limbs overhead. The medic was exhausted but pushed up the hill anyway. His left arm clutched the bag that carried the drugs and supplies necessary for treating the wounded and, if possible, saving lives. *Where was this guy?*

He could not see through the thick haze. He ran in the general direction of where he thought the screaming came from. It was almost impossible to filter out the chaotic noises around him as he tried to locate the anguished screams of the unknown soldier ahead.

"Corpsman!"

This time the young medic zeroed in on his quarry. He

was about fifty feet up the hill and to the left. Pushing off a boulder, the corporal stumbled out from the safety of the trees, keeping his head low. His knees nearly bashed into his chin as he ran. The medic thought, *There he is! Finally!* As he approached, the corporal could see that the wounded soldier was not alone. There were six men under a rim of rock running perpendicular to the hill. He slid in beside the wounded man. *Sergeant Branch!* He immediately recognized his patient as Sergeant Kyle Branch, only in Nam for a few weeks. *Oh God, the arm!*

"Vanhouse! Help! I'm dying! Don't let me die!" Sergeant Branch screamed. He writhed in pain. His right arm appeared to be nearly severed just above the elbow.

Crack! Ping! Automatic rounds ricocheted off the rocks and snapped off limbs just above their heads, showering them with dirt and debris. Vanhouse covered Branch with his own body. Chunks of rock bounced off the medic's helmet and tumbled down the hill.

"I gotcha, Sarge! Try to relax!" *Geez, how many times have I said that today?*

The young medic concentrated on treating the shattered arm.

"Sarge, try to stop moving! I need you to stop rolling around!" *Oh God, this is not good! Gotta stop the bleeding first! The bone was destroyed, and blood was spurting into the medic's face. Pressure ... apply pressure!* He wrapped a tourniquet around the bicep just below the shoulder. He inserted the rod and twisted, cranking down on the blood vessels to stop the massive stream of blood. Vanhouse snapped open a vial of precious morphine and tore open a syringe pack. Minutes after the injection, the sergeant passed out.

—

CLANG! Doctor Robert Vanhouse popped open his eyes. Was that another round? Was that real, or was it just an echo from his past? A dream relived. It was so dark. Another battle? Lie still.

BLAM ... WHAM ... CLACK!

"Freeze, police! On the ground *now!*"

Vanhouse jerked up, pushing his six foot four inch frame off the leather couch. The fog of sleep rested heavily on his mind. *This is real,* he thought. *Where am I? Oh man, where did that come from? I gotta stop working doubles.* Rubbing his eyes he slowly recognized his surroundings. He listed things in his mind: *cluttered table and chairs, smell of old coffee, microwave. Oh yeah, the lounge.*

The doctors' lounge had provided a welcome escape from twenty-six hours in the chaotic emergency department at Hall Park General Hospital. A sprawling suburb of Norman, Oklahoma, Hall Park was a place where twenty thousand people could live in the country but still be close to the events and shopping of a college town like Norman. This two hundred-bed facility served not only Hall Park but also the surrounding rural communities.

Another scream broke the momentary silence.

"You'll pay. You'll all pay for this!" *CRASH!* Shattered glass striking the floor added to the mixture of sounds.

With the door closed, Robert could not see what was happening in the hallway. He stumbled over to grab his white coat. Still drowsy he grappled with the right sleeve while fumbling with the doorknob. Vanhouse stepped out into the hallway to find papers strewn all over the hall and an IV stand sticking through a broken window. *What happened out here?* he thought.

Police were everywhere. As one of the ER nurses rushed by, Robert asked, "What's going on? Did we have a weekend special on coffee and donuts?"

"Not funny, Robert. Not funny at all," the nurse responded. Looking back over her shoulder, she added, "That new nurse, Wyatt. I think he was arrested."

"Oh, sorry," he said. "This kind of stuff isn't supposed to happen in small-town Hall Park, Oklahoma. That's why I chose this place," he groaned to himself. "I need a cup of coffee." He pivoted abruptly and headed for the nearest vending machine.

"Dr. Vanhouse." Robert closed his eyes in disappointment. *Great. Another day in paradise. Now what?* The charge nurse handed off a clipboard. "An old man in room three may have a fractured hip. You need to see him ASAP."

Robert clicked his heels and raised his arm in a Nazi salute and blurted, "Heil Spitler!"

Nurse Spitler looked back on her way down the hall.

"Sorry, Robert. We're short on help. Can't you ever be serious?"

"Hey, the only thing I'm serious about right now is my sleep," Vanhouse said. "This is my last case for the day, then I'm headed home for some sack time."

—

Across town another war was in progress.

The emergency vehicle zipped through the residential neighborhood, narrowly missing cars parked along either side of the street. The ambulance lights pulsed out from the unit, dancing across house fronts, treetops, and cedar fences. Eventually the big station four rescue vehicle slowed to a stop in front of the corner house, the Duncan house. Now the red, blue, and white lights visited the living room walls. White chasing red and blue.

"Finally," Ken mumbled while hurrying to the front door. Patricia's husband yanked open the entry door and shoved hard on the screen. The screen door swung open wide then sprang back. It caught his elbow on the recoil. A few mild expletives spewed from the stout 230 pound construction worker. He grabbed his arm, grimaced, and did his best to rein in his temper. He angrily threw his shoulder against the frazzled screen door, grabbed one of his cement crusted work boots from its overnight resting place on the front porch, and jammed the toe tightly underneath the frame.

"This will fix you," he said as if the door were prepared to argue. Curious neighbors peered through partially-drawn curtains and half-opened front doors. The children across the street stopped their hide-and-seek game and sat down on the curb. Drawing their knees to their chests in the cool night air, they sat huddled shoulder to shoulder, watching the excitement. The red, white, and blue lights flashed across their faces.

"Ken!" Patricia yelled from the couch. "What in the world are you doing?"

"Honey, for cryin' out loud, would ya calm down! The paramedics are here."

"Don't tell me to calm down, Ken. This all started because of you! If you'd paid the phone bill instead of buying beer, we wouldn't … oh!" The pain came again, this time sharper, stabbing, deep. Patricia buried her face in the sofa pillow and doubled up in agony. Ken would not back down. He stomped back inside and continued his verbal assault.

"Don't blame this on me!" Ken exclaimed. "You're the one who didn't get the house payment in on time. Cost us a one hundred dollar late fee! How are we gonna pay for the ambulance? This is gonna cost me a fortune! And now you pull this!"

"This is no stunt, Ken. Something's wrong. You should be concerned. You should be helping me! The baby's not due for another eight weeks!"

Sean, a husky, barrel-chested man jumped into the fray.

"Okay, folks, is there a problem here? I think you guys need to calm this down and relax."

Ken's jaw tightened as he considered the man's words. He noticed the tears trickling down Patricia's cheek. Still, he could not contain himself.

"Don't give me any excuses," he fumed. "It's your fault we're in this mess, and now … and now this stupid baby's coming!"

"Don't call our baby stupid!" Another cry of pain escaped through Patricia's clinched teeth.

"I'm scared. Something's wrong. It's not supposed to happen like this!" she exclaimed.

Then he began to vent his frustration on the paramedics. "What took you idiots so long anyway? Don't just stand there. Help my wife!"

The two men ignored the comment. Jim, six feet tall and thinner than Sean, steered the bed into a position parallel to the couch. There was barely room to work. Sean pushed aside the coffee table in an attempt to give them more space.

Before he began treating his patient, Sean addressed Ken.

"Listen, buddy. You need to either go sit in that chair and do as I tell you or go to the local bar and drink this one off."

His partner gave him a cautious glare.

"Don't worry," Sean responded. "I've seen his kind before ... all mouth, no help." He knelt beside Patricia. Ken, startled at the paramedic's resistance, grudgingly retreated to the corner of the living room.

"Hello, ma'am. What's your name?"

"Patricia," she responded. "Patricia Duncan."

Jim slid a blood pressure cuff around her arm. He could hear her labored breathing.

"Hi, Patricia. My name's Jim. That big fella behind me is my partner, Sean. So, what has happened here tonight? Why'd you call us?" asked Jim. He placed the stethoscope tips in his ears and began taking Patricia's blood pressure. "One sixty over one hundred." Sean wrote down the numbers on his clipboard. Jim gently took her wrist between his fingers to get the pulse rate. "Pulse, ninety-two. Temp, ninety-nine-point-one." Again, Sean wrote the numbers down in the chart.

"She passed out, for God's sake. I thought she was going to die," Ken answered from across the room. He leaned on the wall with his arms crossed. "Might have been better that way," he scoffed just loud enough for everyone to hear.

"Sir, I asked the lady." Jim stared Ken down. Suddenly the room was quiet. For a brief eternity no one spoke. The aquarium hummed.

Patricia broke the silence when another cramp started.

"Oh, please!" she screamed. "I think my water broke!"

Jim's voice was soothing. "All right, just try to relax. Did you have any prenatal care?"

"I've taken good care of her," Ken interrupted.

"No, I mean have you regularly seen a doctor?"

"We don't need a doctor. She's a nurse."

"Do you remember your breathing training?"

Patricia lifted her head and nodded affirmatively.

"Okay, then concentrate on that."

Patricia started a series of short, shallow breaths.

"Good. That's it." Jim and Sean both noticed the wet stain on the couch and on Patricia's jeans.

"How far along are you?" asked Jim.

"Almost eight months, I think."

"Did you pass out?"

"I may have."

"Well, Patricia, we need to get those jeans off. We need to check on that baby." Sean placed his stethoscope on Patricia's stomach. A few moments passed.

I can't find a fetal beat, he thought.

Jim put his scope onto her stomach and moved it around, searching intently for precious signs of life. Patricia watched as a slight smile replaced his intense stare. He had picked up the familiar rapid *lub-dub, lub-dub, lub-dub* of a fetal heartbeat.

"There ... got it."

"Let's get the ER on the radio," Jim said. Sean quickly made contact with Hall Park General.

"Okay, we have a hot one here," Sean began. "Twenty-three-year-old female. First stages of labor. Water broke, but judging by the amount of fluid, I think it's more of a slow seepage. The membrane must be torn but not completely gone." He paused for another question from the ER. "Dilation, only a two," he answered.

Patricia screamed and clamped down on the seat cushions.

"Breathe, breathe … good," Jim coached. Ken stood in the corner with his arms crossed.

"Negative. I think she needs to be transported. It looks like there are complications with both the mother and baby. Elevated blood pressure and a syncopal episode. Baby is viable but unstable. Please advise."

"Affirmative. We are on our way. ETA, eighteen minutes. They began packing up their equipment. Looking up at Ken, Jim said, "We are taking her to the hospital. You are welcome to ride with your wife, or you can follow in your car."

"Great," Ken grumbled. "I guess I'll ride with her." He sighed.

Jim was not impressed with Ken's lack of concern. "Okay, make sure you get your wallet with some identification and your keys."

"Oh, yeah. Thanks," Ken replied. He ran through the house locking doors.

The medics gently lifted Patricia onto the gurney. They moved it quickly but cautiously out the front door toward the ambulance.

"Please hurry!" Patricia said, arching her back off the gurney.

"Try to breathe, Patricia. Breathe and relax." Jim was trying to comfort her while loading the gurney into the rescue vehicle. Once in the ambulance, Sean stayed in the back with Patricia. He ripped open several sterile packages of IV lines and needles. He immediately started a drip. Ken stepped up into the rear of the ambulance. Jim slammed the back doors and scrambled into the driver's seat. Once Sean had the IV. secured in Patricia's arm, he yelled, "Okay, let's roll!"

The vehicle lunged in reverse as the big ambulance backed out of the driveway. Jim slammed it into drive, and the ambulance took off, quickly reaching cruising speed, the siren and lights warning all in its way.

"Relax ... breathe. You're doing great," Sean reassured Patricia.

Not wanting to talk, Patricia clamped her jaws tight and pursed her lips. Her fingernails dug deep into the gurney's mattress.

"I've done this several times before, Mrs. Duncan. I even delivered my own son in our living room. Everything's going to be fine."

2

Ding, ding.

The elevator doors parted. Doctor Keith Murdock, the slightly balding, overstuffed hospital administrator strode into the ER battle zone.

"Lieutenant Steele!" Murdock motioned for the police detective to join him. "Looks like I may have missed out on some excitement."

"Well, your nurse got a bit irritated when we tried to arrest him."

"Where is he?"

"A couple of my officers have him subdued in one of your exam rooms. He needed a little cooling off time before we take him downtown. Do you want to talk to him before we go?"

"I don't think it's necessary, unless you think it would help."

"Well, maybe we should let it slide. It might stir him up again, and we don't need that." Lieutenant Steele walked over to the exam room turned holding cell. Murdock stayed a step behind. Steele pushed open the door.

"It's time to go, gentlemen."

Wyatt sat on a metal bench, his hands cuffed behind his back. His thick red hair was disheveled. He had a small cut on his nose. His green nurse's scrubs were in disarray and torn at the v-neck, evidence of the skirmish just a few minutes before.

"Let's walk," commanded one of the officers in the room. Wyatt held his position, emotionally as cold as the metal bench he sat on. He stared at the floor, pretending not to hear the order. "Come on, buddy, let's try and make this a pleasant trip."

He tugged on Wyatt's arm. Wyatt jerked defiantly, tightened his jaw, and dared the officers to move him. Two officers each grabbed an arm and forced him to his feet. As the trio moved beyond the exam room door, Wyatt caught a glimpse of Murdock. Once they had moved a few steps down the hall, he looked back over his shoulder and yelled like a mad man, "You'll be sorry! I'll be back, and you'll pay! You'll pay big time!"

One of the officers yanked Wyatt's arm. "Not smart, buddy. You're in enough trouble already. Now you've made it worse by threatening people. Keep your mouth shut!" They hurried Wyatt out of the ER and into the waiting squad car.

Lieutenant Steele remained behind with Murdock.

"Well, we ran a background check on your nurse. For a young guy he has a pretty good rap sheet. Minor drug charges mostly, but he did have an assault and battery on the list. Those concerns you had about him were valid. I'll keep you posted on how all of this develops. We've got a solid case against him. I wouldn't worry about the threats. He's not going anywhere. He sold morphine to one of our undercover guys. He'll be doing some significant time for theft and distribution. I just have one question, Dr. Murdock. How did this guy get hired in the first place?"

"That's a great question. We didn't do the full background check because he did his clinical rotations here and performed well," the embarrassed hospital administrator answered. "I guess I learned my lesson."

—

The dramatic exit of Wyatt and the familiar sound of the intercom signaled an attempted return to normalcy. That is, if there is such a thing as normalcy in a hospital emergency department.

"Dr. Shircliff, Dr. Elizabeth Shircliff, please report to the emergency department! Dr. Shircliff."

Dr. Elizabeth Shircliff rounded the corner at a fast walk but slowed when she gazed across the damage caused by the Wyatt arrest. The head nurse on duty greeted Dr. Shircliff with the news of the coming emergency as soon as the good doctor reached the nurse's station.

"What's all the mess? It looks like world war three around here."

"Man, you missed it," the nurse began. "The police arrested one of our people for stealing drugs. It was quite a show, a little scary for a while. Anyway, everything's okay now. They just took him away."

"You're kidding me. One of the doctors?"

"Nope, it was a nurse. Wyatt I think was his name. He was a new hire that just finished his clinicals. I worked with him in the ER a couple of months ago."

"Don't remember him. Was that why I got summoned here?"

"No, we've gotta hot mama on the way in."

"A hot mama?" Shircliff questioned the term and chuckled.

"Yes," the nurse replied, "seems that they've picked up a mom, seven or eight months along, in the first stages of labor. The paramedic team suspects the mother may have had some type of trauma or illness and that the baby is in distress. We made the decision to bring her in. Anyway, here is what we know." She handed Shircliff the typed printout.

Shircliff scanned the sheet, folded it, and put it in her coat pocket. She was a perfectly manicured, middle-aged professional. After graduating from the University Of Oklahoma School of Medicine and a five-year stint in a Colorado Springs emergency medicine department, Elizabeth landed back in this small general hospital in Hall Park, Oklahoma, as a highly trained and experienced specialist in obstetrics and gynecology. Two months ago she was appointed chief of the OB/GYN department.

"What's in progress now?" she asked the nurse.

The nurse reviewed her chart. "We have a DUI in six with minor cuts and scrapes. He ran head on into a parked police car. That's the reason for the guard outside the room. There's an eight-year-old with an asthma attack in four. She's been treated and is ready to go home." She flipped to the next page. "We have a couple of kids with flu-like symptoms and, last but not least, an eighty-six-year-old man with a fractured hip who fell at the nursing home. Dr. Vanhouse is currently handling that one. Of course we have a few less critical cases waiting. That's it. You're now up to date."

"Busy night," commented Shircliff. She smiled and shook her head. She was beginning to regret offering to fill in for the night, but she owed a favor to another doctor who had covered for her last week.

Elizabeth's smile faded as she thought about the pregnant woman soon to arrive.

"I don't have a good feeling about this one coming in." There was a short pause while she studied the communication records. "When she arrives let's put her in five. Let's get everyone advised. We may have a possible C-section. Get prepped accordingly. Advise neonatal ICU we have a pending critical situation. Also contact that response team and have them start a D5W IV if they haven't already done so. Who else did you say is supposed to be on duty?"

"Vanhouse was working on the hip fracture. I think he still might be in the building," the nurse replied.

"Have somebody page him," Shircliff ordered. "We're gonna need some help."

—

Patricia writhed in pain.

"Oh, the baby moved! Oh … it hurts! Oh … "

Sean, the paramedic riding with her, tried to calm her down. He grabbed her hand.

"Short pants, short pants, relax now." He looked at the monitor and saw that the contraction was subsiding. "There we go. It should be coming down now." Almost immediately another contraction started. Patricia jerked. Sean looked over at Ken in the corner of the ambulance. "You need to help me here, sir."

"What do I do?" asked Ken in an uncharacteristically timid voice.

"Just comfort her as best you can. Help her with her

breathing. Hold her hand. Talk to her. Rub her shoulders. You know her better than I do."

Sean continued to monitor the contractions and Patricia's vital signs. He spoke to Jim, who was driving, and they decided to pick up the pace. Ken grasped his wife's hand in both of his.

"Oh, it hurts, Ken. I can't do this!"

—

The quiet was deafening. Night had fallen on the Vietnamese hillside. The smell of gunpowder and death had settled over the jungle, a reminder of the earlier battle.

"Vanhouse." Branch had come to.

"Yea, Sarge? Whisper, will ya?"

"Am I gonna die?"

"Naw. You're gonna be fine. I'll see to that." *Yeah, right,* Vanhouse thought. *I'm about out of morphine. Lots of blood loss. His heart rate is up, respirations are shallow and labored.*

"What about the guys? Did everybody make it?"

"You bet," Vanhouse answered. *Another lie. I've been working on them since I got here. Smith and Mitchell might make it. Beaumgartner, George, and Riley are dead.*

"I don't hear gunfire," Branch said as he fought to ask a few more questions.

"The firefight died down about an hour ago."

Branch tried to change positions and yelled out. The pain of even the smallest movement tore through his body. The shock was too much for the sergeant, and he fell unconscious again.

Robert's mind raced. *Geez, he's in trouble. And what about the others? What am I gonna do? I can't just leave 'em, but I can't do this alone! Where are the medevac choppers? I called for help hours ago.*

One of the wounded men was delirious. "Oh man, Danny. Danny! No, not Danny! He got it!"

"Shut up, Mitchell!" Vanhouse scolded quietly between clinched teeth. It wasn't necessary. The soldier quickly quieted back into the slumber of the dying. Robert was left with only his thoughts in the quiet. *It's so dark. I can't see a thing. Where is everybody? What's that? Voices! VC are close! Gotta be quiet. They will eventually move in and kill us all! Footsteps!* He reached for his .45.

Someone scrambled out of the darkness and dove under the ledge. He rolled onto his back, panting heavily. He drew his medical bag to his chest, pushed the helmet back into place, and looked over at Robert.

"David?" Robert could hardly believe it. His identical twin brother was beside him. He knew David's unit had been in the area, but this was unbelievable.

"Robert!" They stared at each other in astonishment. Then they slapped each other's arm in excitement.

David spoke first.

"We're in big trouble," he said, still catching his breath. "Our platoons have pulled back down the hill. The VC are on our flanks. Pretty soon we'll be surrounded and in the open. It'll be a turkey shoot."

Robert responded by shaking his head toward his fallen comrades.

"Look, I have these six guys to take care of. I can't leave 'em." A few silent moments passed. "Hey, let's surrender. They won't kill us. We're doctors."

"Don't be a fool." David was irritated at his brother's

naiveté. "We're the enemy." He sat up and started rummaging through his medical bag.

"What are you doing?" asked Robert.

"Look, these guys are in bad shape," David whispered. "We'll never get them out alive. But *we* can survive. Sometimes it's survival of the fittest." Robert watched in shock as his brother injected Sergeant Branch. The sergeant took a deep breath and gave a little cough within minutes. Death came quietly.

"Robert, get between this guy and the next one there."

Robert gave a confused look but did as his brother commanded.

"Listen closely. As soon as I put the last one down, pull a couple of the bodies over you. I'll inject you with two cc's of this morphine then do the same to myself. Hopefully when the enemy storms this position, they will assume we're all dead and go on their way. It's our best hope. You're already covered in blood anyway. If it doesn't work, well, at least we won't feel anything."

"David, this isn't right."

"Sometimes right is negotiable."

"I don't agree," Robert said as he pulled Sergeant Branch's body across his legs.

"It's our only chance. Remember, we can wait on each other until the meds wear off."

Robert felt the needle entering his arm. He slid down under the body of his comrade. Before sleep overtook him, he heard footsteps and voices all around him. Man, the Sarge is heavy … he's squeezing my shoulders. Sleep finally came.

—

"Dr. Vanhouse, sir." Robert heard the voice. He felt pressure on his chest. No, it was his shoulder. Was he safe? The voice spoke English. He rolled onto his side and shoved blindly, mumbling, "Don't ... please ... this isn't right."

No man left behind. They came back for us. Robert struggled to wake up. He shoved the weight off his chest and sat up.

"Doctor, are you okay? I've been trying to wake you." The nurse chuckled as she said, "You kept pushing my arm away and mumbling, saying something about a safe or being safe. Anyway, you're needed right now in the ER. Sorry to wake you."

He wiped his hands across his forehead and looked at his hands. "Well, no blood, just sweat. I must have been dreaming again. I've had some crazy ones about my brother and the Vietnam War recently."

"Is your brother as handsome as you?" The nurse smiled. "More importantly, is he single?"

"He's still single, but he's not your type." Robert ran his fingers through his hair. "What am I needed for?"

"Dr. Shircliff needs your assistance with an emergency C-section in room five."

"What time is it?"

"Nearly midnight."

"This may sound silly, but what day is it?"

"Friday, sir."

"Thanks. Tell Dr. Shircliff I'll be right there."

—

Seconds before Patricia's ambulance arrived, a worn out station wagon driven by Brent Wells sputtered to a stop under the emergency room car port. Brent heard a siren shut off, so he knew an ambulance would soon pull into the empty space next to them.

He glanced at Rebecca, his wife of twenty years. "Just our luck, an incoming ambulance. I'd better move."

Brent turned the ignition key and was greeted with a soft *click* but nothing more. He tried again. Still nothing. About that time the ambulance rumbled up next to their car. The diesel engine clacked rhythmically. Brent turned to talk to Ryan, his thirteen-year-old son sprawled across the backseat and in obvious pain.

"Ryan, looks like we're going to be here awhile. That ambulance needs to unload."

—

Swoosh! The automatic glass double doors at the emergency entrance parted. Dr. Shircliff led the way as a parade of medical staff swarmed around the rear of the ambulance. Jim, the ambulance driver, got out and trotted to the end of the vehicle.

"Wow, what a reception!" he said in amazement.

"Best service in town!" quipped Shircliff. "We're ready to take her off your hands. We've given her priority. Stick with me for a bit if you don't mind."

"Will do," replied Jim.

The troupe worked its way to ER room five. The smell of diesel exhaust from the ambulance gave way to the faint pine cleanser odor inside. A male nurse guided the bed; another nurse walked alongside, carefully listening to Dr.

Shircliff exchange information with the paramedics while at the same time trying to keep the intravenous line from being torn away from Patricia's wrist during the transfer.

"Coming through," yelled a nurse as they approached a small group of onlookers in front of the entrance to the treatment rooms. The people scattered.

"Ken!" Patricia cried. He had become separated from her side when the large group funneled through the emergency entrance.

"I'm here," he replied reassuringly.

It only took moments to get Patricia situated onto the hospital bed in room five. Shircliff started asking questions while a nurse assisted with preparations.

"Hi, I'm Doctor Shircliff." She snapped on some latex gloves. These are a few of my closest associates, and we're gonna get you and your baby through this. Have you ever been pregnant before?"

"Help me!" Patricia yelped, turning her head from side to side. She blurted out, "Two abortions!"

Ken corrected her from the corner of the room. "Two miscarriages. She means two miscarriages. It has been hard for us to stay pregnant."

"No, no," moaned Patricia. She then sorrowfully confessed, "I had two abortions in high school."

Ken shook his head and smiled knowingly. "She's delirious. She means two miscarriages, not abortions, and not in high school. She just doesn't know what she is saying right now."

"So this would be your fifth pregnancy?" asked Shircliff.

"Yes, yes," Patricia cried. "It's true!"

Ken was stunned at the revelation. "Who was the other guy, or was it guys? It sure wasn't me. Oh man, this is too much. You lied to me! You said I was the first!" he shouted. "I married a—"

"*Knock it off!*" Sean, the barrel chested paramedic was still close by. He turned to Shircliff and said, "They've been going at each other all the way here."

Shircliff glared at Ken. "Watch your mouth, sir! I'd like you to be here with your wife, but I have no problem having you removed."

"Help me! Please, help me!" Patricia continued her cries for help through her pain.

Shircliff leaned over Patricia and spoke calmly. "You know what? I think your little one is very close to full term. That's good, so don't worry. You just need to try and relax. Everything will be alright."

3

Ken reluctantly stood at Patricia's bed side. There was a blur of activity. Ken breathed deeply and tugged at his mask. Sweat poured down his forehead.

"Are you okay, sir?" asked an attending nurse as she rushed to Ken's aid.

Ken nodded his head slowly. His sunken eyes and pale expression did not support his response. The nurse wiped his forehead with a towel and then gave it to him.

"Sir, you'd better sit down on this stool and put your head between your knees," she suggested. She started to assist Ken, but her focus shifted back to the birthing table when Patricia shrieked once more.

Dr. Shircliff was still uncomfortable with this case. She gathered her staff and whispered, "I would prefer a few things be different, but we better go with a natural birth. A Cesarean is out of the question. With her rising blood pressure and other symptoms, I just feel that it is much too risky. Natural has its drawbacks also, but I think it's our best option now. The baby is well into the birth canal."

Then the doctor turned and addressed her patient. "We are going with a natural delivery. Patricia, you need to follow all my instructions. You just relax as best you can. Take slow deep breaths."

The staff took their positions around Patricia. Dr. Shircliff placed Patricia's legs in the stirrups and quickly finished prep work.

"Patricia, your baby is coming fast. So, listen to what I say. Don't push just yet." The doctor looked over at Ken. "Dad, if you're ready to get back in the ballgame, she could sure use your encouragement." Ken moved closer to the bed. Patricia's screams came at short and regular intervals, coinciding with her contractions. The baby seemed determined to come forward. She wasn't dilating fast enough.

With the exception of Patricia's screams and wiggles of discomfort, there was very little movement in the room. Suddenly the doctor leaned forward.

"Okay … " Shircliff's tone became more intense. "Now I want you to really bear down with this next contraction. Okay … push … you have to … this is it!"

The baby's head crowned and soon fully appeared. Shircliff whispered new instructions to a nurse. The baby was a grayish blue, not the expected pink color of life. Something was wrong.

"Once more … push once more. I need those forceps handy. Push hard now."

There were a few seconds of silent anticipation. Then the baby's shoulders appeared. Ken heard a slurping sound as the tiny body slipped quickly through the birth canal. The child was born.

"Hey … here he is … a boy." Elizabeth Shircliff cradled the baby. She quickly counted the boy's fingers and toes and noted that everything seemed to be in the right place. She cut and clamped the umbilical cord. "Suction bulb," she ordered.

Nurse Chalmers, a veteran of hundreds of births, already had the rubber bulb in hand. She gave it over. Immediately Shircliff used it to remove mucus and any obstruction from the baby's nose and mouth. She watched as the baby began to draw his first precious breaths. But the breathing was labored. The tiny infant's color was not changing like it should. A quick thinking nurse stepped between mother and child.

"Better get him to the neonatal intensive care unit."

Dr. Robert Vanhouse, gloved and masked, had just entered the room to offer assistance. He overheard Shircliff's request.

"I can take the baby," he offered.

"You?" Nurse Chalmers questioned.

"You bet," he answered. "You're needed here, and I've got the time now." He quickly wrapped the baby in a blanket and exited the room with the newborn cradled in his arms.

"Great. Thanks, Robert," said Shircliff as she turned back to the table to deal with the placenta and begin the task of repairing the damaged caused by a nine-pound baby coming through a very small opening.

There was no time to waste. The situation was critical for the infant. Vanhouse rushed to the "medical personnel only" elevator that was located between the treatment rooms. He waited impatiently at the elevator door. He swung his stethoscope around and listened to the baby. *Ding!* The doors parted. Robert stepped inside the empty carrier and pushed the button. The elevator went up to four. He had pushed the wrong button. An elderly couple attempted to get on.

"I'm sorry. I have an emergency here. This is for medical personnel only," stressed Vanhouse. The couple yielded to his plea. As the doors closed, the doctor carefully punched the proper white button for floor two.

Neonatal ICU was fully prepared, but by now the child was blue. Robert held his stethoscope on the child's chest and did not detect a heartbeat. He knelt, placed the child on the floor, and began CPR. The elevator doors slid open, and Robert handed the baby up to a member of the neonatal team.

"Hope I'm not too late."

—

Brent left his family in the waiting room and searched for the admitting office. He followed the signs and found the office mostly empty. Two receptionists were on duty. There were four cubicles, more than enough to handle the load on the busiest evenings. The two women were completely caught up with their workload and thoroughly enjoying the lull. They were in the middle of a laugh-filled conversation. The younger one looked up and quickly hid her soda pop can when Brent entered the room.

"No waiting on aisle one," she said. And both women giggled some more.

Brent walked over to the first cubicle and sat down. He smiled at the young brunette as he pulled his chair closer to the desk so he could sign the numerous forms he knew would be coming.

"How can I help you?" asked the brunette. She kept talking before Brent could respond. "Are you ready to answer some questions?" she perked. "Do you have a living will?"

Brent smiled and replied, "I have a will to live, but hold on. I'm not the patient. It's my son. I think he broke his leg."

"Oh, I'm sorry." The young clerk blushed as she realized her mistake.

"Yeah ... he's sorry, too."

The woman smiled. "Has he been a patient here before?"

"Sure. He was born here. All of my children were."

"Great. He should be on file. This will take just a second. We just got these new computers. This sure beats those electric typewriters over there." She clicked a few keys as she spoke. "They call it a 286 or something."

Brent just smiled.

"Okay, give me his full name."

"Ryan Lee Wells."

"Age?"

"Oh geez. My wife should be doing this. Uh ... thirteen ... fourteen ... no, it's thirteen."

"Does he have a social security number?"

"There is no way I'm going to know that."

"No problem. I can get that information later."

"And your name, sir?"

"Brent Allen Wells."

She typed it in, hit the enter key, and said, "Oh yes. Here you are. Do you still work for the state?"

"Yes."

"Any changes in insurance?"

"No. They just cover less and less each year."

She ignored his editorial. "All your information is complete. I just need you to read and sign these two forms. The receptionist printed the second form while Brent signed the first one. He signed the second one. She collected the forms and said, "Okay, we are done. Have a seat back in the waiting room, and somebody will be with you shortly."

—

Vanhouse stayed on to assist the intensive care team. Despite their best efforts, the baby could not be resuscitated. Elizabeth Shircliff managed to make it into the room where they were tending to the newborn infant. She arrived just as Vanhouse was discussing any remaining options of treatment.

"I think we have done everything possible," he said.

Elizabeth was shocked. "You mean we lost this child? I knew he was struggling, but I certainly did not expect this. What happened?"

One of the nurses spoke up. "I think we were just too late. Dr. Vanhouse said he began CPR on the way up. He was searching for a heartbeat when he came off the elevator."

"They're right. I was under the same impression as you, Elizabeth, but I think the child had already expired before I could get him up here. Anyway, we have got to sign off on the cause of death. Elizabeth, if you will sign off on the death certificate, I will go talk to the father. You were the first attending physician."

"This is the part of the job I really hate," she said. Elizabeth was obviously shaken.

"Hey, you can talk to the father if you would rather," countered Robert.

"No thanks. I think you would be better this time. Let me warn you, though. He has a real temper." Elizabeth looked at the big round white clock on the wall. "Time of death, 12:15 a.m. Cause of death, failure to thrive and respiratory failure." Most of the team members quietly pulled their masks and gloves off and threw them into the hazardous waste bin.

"It's never easy to lose a little one," mumbled one of the nurses.

"You're right about that," replied Robert. He would have said more, but it was more important that he talk to the father. Vanhouse lowered his mask, tossed his gloves away, and walked out of the room in search of Ken Duncan.

—

Ken was asked to leave the room when the baby was taken upstairs. Vanhouse found the young father pacing back and forth in front of the vending machines in the waiting room, an empty plastic cup in his hand.

"Are you Mr. Duncan?"

"Yes. How's my son, my wife?" quizzed Ken anxiously.

"I thought I would find you here. Would you like another drink?"

"Oh, no thanks." He walked over to the trash can and threw away his cup. Ken was expecting to be reunited with his wife. "How's my son?" he asked again. The idea of having a son had begun to appeal to him.

Vanhouse looked around the crowded waiting room.

"Mr. Duncan, let's go over there, and we can sit down and talk." They walked over to the only unoccupied area and sat down on a pair of dark blue overstuffed chairs in the corner of the room. It provided a space where they could have a more private conversation.

Dr. Vanhouse didn't say a word. He just studied Ken's face. Ken feared that he was about to receive some bad news and fumbled for words. Something was wrong. He finally broke the silence.

"Just level with me, Doc. Just tell me what has happened. My son . . . where is he? Patricia . . . she's okay, isn't she?"

Vanhouse looked Ken straight in the eyes.

"Mr. Duncan, there is no easy way around this conversation." Ken squirmed uncomfortably in his chair. Vanhouse, tactfully, and with all the dignity of his profession began, "Sir, I will do as you requested. I'm just going to shoot straight with you. Your wife had a rough time with this delivery, but she will be fine. Your son also had problems, serious complications, including respiratory difficulties. He passed away at 12:15 this morning. He is dead."

Ken's face went blank. Vanhouse continued. "I want you to understand that the delivery was complicated from the start. The paramedics had concerns when they first diagnosed the situation. I also want you to be confident in the fact that we did everything within our abilities to help the child to survive."

Ken was in shock. "Then how? Why?"

"He was born in a condition doctors call 'failure-to-thrive,' and we were unable to bring him out of it. A newborn just does not have the stamina that is sometimes needed. The birth process is stressful and physically demanding for both the mother and child. Some newborns just don't make it. There are times we just don't know why. Medical science, despite all the technology and rapidly advancing knowledge, still does not have all the answers. I don't have anything to add. That is as simple as I can explain it. Your son suffered respiratory failure, but we don't know the exact reason or cause. Do you have any questions? Would you like me to call someone?"

Ken slumped back in his chair. He looked lifeless for a moment. He looked up at the ceiling. Then he stared at the floor. Then he covered his face with his hands. There was no place to run with the feelings. Vanhouse just watched. Finally Ken sat up, his back straight, his eyes red, and he managed a fake little smile.

"Thanks for trying." Ken struggled to speak. "I'm numb. I don't know what to say."

Vanhouse felt maybe Ken wanted to continue talking. "Children are so precious."

"I know. I didn't even get to hold him. This is the worst day of my life."

Vanhouse made an effort to be compassionate. "I heard somebody once say in a situation similar to this that you can always hold them in your heart."

"That's good, but it's just not the same. I will try to remember that, though." Ken just stared at the floor.

After a short pause, Vanhouse spoke again.

"I am very sorry, but I have to ask you something else, something very unpleasant. Have you any funeral home preference? It is a decision you will have to make very soon. I don't believe your wife will be in any condition to handle such a tough issue. I would suggest that you make the arrangements and just keep her out of the matter if possible."

"Oh, I had never even considered a burial. My wife and

I don't even have plots. What do I do? We don't even have family nearby to help."

Dr. Vanhouse rested his elbows on the chair arms and clasped his hands together as he thought then said, "Well, we have people here who can answer some of your questions. There are three mortuaries in town. I've heard that Flanders Funeral Home is reasonable and does good work. If I'm not mistaken, they offer special services in a case like yours. But my concern was not to recommend a place but rather to make you aware of the coming decision. I just know that you will have to decide immediately, and I wanted to prepare you for the task."

"Thanks again. You have been so kind." Ken cried.

Robert moved a tissue box close and patted Ken on the shoulder.

"I'm so sorry that this has happened. I've got to return to my duties. Somebody from the chaplain's office will be here shortly. Take some time to talk with him. It will do you some good." Vanhouse walked away, leaving Ken alone to grieve.

———

Ryan Wells struggled through the X-ray session with the help of his parents and a very gentle technician. They were assigned to examination room two and felt they were finally making some progress.

Robert had just returned from the second floor.

"Dr. Vanhouse."

Robert turned to see a nurse headed his way with a chart in hand. *Will this day ever end?*

"You're the only one available to see this patient in

two." She handed off the chart and escorted him down the hall to meet the Wells family. The long day was weighing on his eyes. He closed them briefly, breathed a heavy sigh, and tapped politely on the door before entering the room.

"Hi, I'm Dr. Vanhouse." His outstretched hand was met halfway by Brent's.

"Brent Wells, this is my wife Rebecca, and my son Ryan is your patient."

"Hmm. I see we have had some pictures taken." The doctor slid the X-ray into the clips on the opaque viewing screen on the wall and quickly discovered Ryan's fracture.

"Okay, let's hear the story. What happened?"

Ryan hurt too much to give details. "I was jumping a flight of steps on my skateboard. Ten steps, and I only cleared nine."

"Ah, and presto, this is the result," piped Vanhouse. He pointed out the fracture line to the parents. Then he maneuvered Ryan's leg, making mental notes of the most painful positions. "There is not much we can do. As I have shown you on the X-rays, he definitely has a fracture of the tibia, but the swelling is too great to apply the cast. What we will do for tonight is immobilize it with a temporary splint. The only other thing I can do for him is prescribe some mega pain killers."

Brent was trying not to sound irritated. "You mean we have to come back?"

"No, I wouldn't come back to the hospital. You need to take this young man to your personal physician or a specialist and let them set his leg in a permanent cast."

Brent and Rebecca started to collect their belongings

while the doctor wrote the prescription for Ryan. Rebecca bent down to pick up her purse.

"Ahh!" She grabbed her side and froze in a half-stooped position.

Vanhouse rushed to her side and grasped her elbow. "Ma'am, you all right?" Just as he touched her, she went faint, her body limp. She fell to her knees and would have fallen flat on the cold tile floor had Vanhouse not been there to break her fall. Brent grabbed her other arm.

"Sir, let's stretch her out on the bed. I might as well look at her, too. Let's move you over to the chair, son. Let your mom have the bed." Ryan painfully complied.

Rebecca immediately recovered and reluctantly went along with the instructions.

"Just lie still for a moment."

She protested the pampering.

"I really feel fine. The evening has just been too stressful."

Vanhouse pressed gently on her abdominal area with his right hand.

"It's probably just all the stress," repeated Rebecca.

"Have you ever had pains like this before?" asked Vanhouse.

"I did not have a pain. I felt a little flutter, like my baby was kicking. And then I went faint."

Vanhouse pressed firmly now. Both hands worked in tandem. He explored a larger area. He was very quiet. He worked. He plugged his ears with his stethoscope and listened. He thought.

"Ma'am, I don't want you to be alarmed, but I am really

concerned about this little episode considering where you are in your pregnancy. I want you to see your personal physician as soon as possible. Yesterday would be great. In fact, what is your doctor's name?" He produced a small spiral notebook from his jacket, opened it, clicked his ball point pen, and jotted down the information and some helpful reminders.

"Our doctor's name is Charles Crawford," she replied.

"Old Chuck, the last of a dying breed. He still make house calls? He is a good doctor and a great guy."

Vanhouse pressed one more time. "Does that hurt?"

"Well, it's not a stabbing pain, but it sure doesn't feel good either.

With his hand still on her abdomen, he said, "Breathe for me." Vanhouse reached across her and grabbed the blood pressure cuff off the wall. He wrapped it around her arm and pumped it up and continued talking. "All right. You be sure and see your doctor. I will call Dr. Crawford in a few days and confer with him. And again, I don't want you to be alarmed, but your situation needs further investigation." He measured her blood pressure and replaced the cuff in its holder on the wall.

Dr. Vanhouse turned to leave. "I am going to call it a day." He paused at the door, looked over his shoulder at Rebecca, and said, "You can leave, too, soon as the nurse sees you. She will get your blood pressure again, along with a blood and urine sample. Might as well check some chemistries since I have you here." He looked at Brent. "You'll have a few forms to fill out for your wife. I'll talk to the desk on my way out and explain what has happened. Anybody have any questions?"

—

Not long after Brent had left the admitting office, another man had entered the room, his shirt partially untucked. His eyes were puffy and red. He had been crying. It was Ken Duncan. Everyone in the admitting office focused their attention on this troubled man. Both receptionists quickly transformed into a more somber mood. He sat down and waited to be called. The two women on duty stared at each other. Each one hoping the other would volunteer to help the distraught man. Finally, one clerk volunteered, "I guess it's my turn." Grudgingly she spoke out, "Sir, how can I help you?"

Ken stepped up to her cubicle and began to speak. "My wife came into emergency; she was pregnant. I think they are sending her up to a private room. My son ... " he cleared his throat, struggling to speak, "did not survive."

"I see. I'm very sorry." She pushed a box of Kleenex toward Ken. "What is your wife's name?"

"Patricia Duncan."

The clerk typed in the name. "Has she been previously admitted?"

"We were planning on having the baby here, so we had all the admittance forms filled out."

The woman completed a few computer key strokes and confirmed what had been said. "Well, Mr. Duncan, everything is in order, but you will have to tell us what funeral home will handle your child's arrangements. Have you made that decision?"

Those were hard words to hear, but Ken responded. "That has been taken care of. Flanders Funeral Home will handle everything. I had a talk with the chaplain, and he agreed to notify them."

"Very good. I'll indicate that on your paperwork, and you'll be set. Is there anything else I can do for you?"

Ken was staring into space.

"Sir?" The clerk tried to gain his attention.

"Oh, sorry. What was your question?"

"Never mind. Your filing is complete. Your wife will be assigned a room momentarily. If you'll have a seat in the lobby, we will notify you when she is settled. Be sure and let us know if we can help you in any way."

Ken took the papers and walked away. The two clerks looked at each other and sighed.

"Poor guy," whispered one of the women.

4

CHAPTER

Patricia's nursing studies had taught her standard procedure for delivering babies, and what had just happened was not in the textbook.

"Hey, what's wrong? Why didn't my baby cry?" She aimed her anxious inquiry at the closest nurse. The nurse was busy assisting Shircliff. She initially responded without looking at Patricia.

"Everything is going to be okay." She turned to Patricia and softened her voice. "Don't worry. The baby was not breathing as well as we would like, so the doctors are being very cautious."

Patricia was not satisfied with the answer. She turned her questioning toward Shircliff. "What do you mean, cautious? There's more to it than that, isn't there? You're not telling me everything. I'm almost a nurse. I know how this should work, and this is not it! Why did you leave the room? You were gone for a long time. What's going on?" Patricia's voice was rising to a higher pitch now.

Shircliff tried to calm Patricia down. "Mrs. Duncan … Patricia … please. We are doing all we can to help you and your son. If you are going to be a nurse soon, you should know that we don't take these sorts of precautions without good reason. I am sorry you didn't get to hold him immediately, but I thought it best to get him up to intensive care as soon as possible."

"You messed it up, didn't you? Something is very wrong here." Patricia worked up to an even higher pitch. "I want to see my son! Bring him back... now!" She began cursing at both the nurse and Doctor Shircliff.

The tirade continued for several minutes. Shircliff excused herself and left the room. She needed a minute alone in the hall to regain her composure. There was no bringing her son back, and there was no telling Patricia what happened, at least not now. Elizabeth was trying her best to remain calm in the midst of the verbal assault. Once her strength returned, she re-entered the room and began barking out orders, ignoring the continuing bombardment.

"Sedate her! Ten milligrams of valium, IV, *right now!* We have enough to deal with around here without having to listen to this junk!"

—

Robert staggered out to the doctors' parking lot. *Man, I thought this day would never end,* he thought. A cool wind felt refreshing, yet he realized his eyes were puffy tired, swollen with exhaustion. He unlocked the driver's side door and slid into the bucket seat of his latest purchase, like-new 1957 Corvette. He sat still for a few moments. Life had been good to him. He made enough money to take care of his mother, his twin brother, David, and still had more than enough to live comfortably himself.

"One last stop," he said to himself and sighed.

Robert drove to his mother's house, the house where he had grown up. An old white two-story wood-framed farm house that had been in the family for generations. White paint curled away from the slat siding. One faded green shutter on an upper-story window dangled from a single screw. Once lovely rose bushes now wrestled with weeds and grass for nutrients in their piece of earth. The house struggled to exist. New additions squeezed in on all sides, encroaching on its territory. Once planted in the center of 160 acres, the well-worn homestead clung to only two acres framed by mighty oak trees.

Robert parked in the gravel circle driveway, hurried to the front porch, and dropped an envelope through the mail slot in the front door. He took a deep breath, stepped aside, and rang the bell. He only waited a few minutes. *I can't do it. Not yet.* Robert retreated to his car and drove away.

Robert's brother, David, had been back now for about six weeks. Yet Robert still couldn't talk to him. Vietnam was traumatizing. Robert couldn't deal with what his brother had done that day on Hill 239. On the other hand, he couldn't let anything happen to his brother. He was family, so Robert made a deal with David. David would be confined to the farmhouse. He could live out his days in seclusion as an AWOL medic. His sole responsibility was to take care of their mom. In return Robert would manage the financial needs of his family and of the waning farmhouse.

Robert surveyed the front of the house as he drove away. He thought he might have seen his brother peek out of a second-story window.

———

Two orderlies came wandering down to the emergency area and approached the nurse's station. They handed some paperwork to a nurse behind the desk, and one of them said, "We are here to pick up a Patricia Duncan."

The nurse chuckled. "Oh yeah. She's a mess. She's going up to 216."

"Got it."

Patricia was so heavily sedated that she didn't appear to know she was in motion as the orderlies rolled her bed down the hall. Upon entering the elevator, the preoccupied workers accidentally bumped her up against the back wall. Patricia's head flipped to the side, and her eyes opened wide but then immediately closed again. She settled into a deep sleep due to the combination of sedatives, her emotional outbursts, and the physical exertion of labor.

They were a little more cautious when they moved her out onto the second floor.

"Room 216 … is that the room at the end of the hall?" asked the orderly in front who was guiding the bed.

"Yep. How many years is it going to take you to learn the layout?"

"I always get turned around on this ward for some reason."

"You must be one of those same folks who goes the wrong way on a one-way street."

"Hey, if I'm so bad with directions, then how come you're following me?"

The orderlies dropped their conversation and got Patricia to her destination. She was wheeled into a room well away from those assigned to new moms.

"Man, she is out cold," noticed one of the orderlies.

"We should be rejoicing about that, according to the

ER folks. They said she was a real tiger. Just delivered a baby and then was ready to get up and spar with Doc Shircliff."

"Would never have guessed by her looks."

—

The Wells trio was finally able to go home. Brent put his arm around Rebecca's waist.

"Well, I sure wasn't planning on spending the evening like this."

They followed an orderly, who pushed the wheelchair transporting their son, Ryan, to the exit. Rebecca spotted some vending machines.

"Honey, would you mind getting me something to drink?"

"Sure. Let me get you two loaded up, and I'll run back inside."

Brent returned to the vending area only to see a very distraught young man fumbling through his pockets, looking for change.

"Can I help you, man?" asked Brent.

"Oh, I've had a horrible night, and now I don't even have change. Life stinks."

"Let me turn things around," Brent responded, reaching into his jeans. "What do you want?"

"Just a Coke," answered Ken.

"How about something to go with it?" Brent said, glancing over to the snack machine.

Ken was taken aback by the stranger's hospitality, but he could see Brent was sincere. "I could sure use a candy bar. By the way, my name is Ken Duncan. Why are you doing this? What are you selling?"

"Well, you never know when you might be entertaining angels. By the way, I'm Brent Wells."

Ken gave a puzzled look.

"Brent, I appreciate this, but believe me, I'm no angel."

"Oh, that's just a reference to a Bible verse. I hope your day gets better. Why are you here, anyway?"

Ken bowed his head. He tried to keep his voice from cracking.

"I lost my newborn son in the middle of the night."

Brent put his hand on Ken's shoulder.

"I'm so sorry. I'll be praying for you."

"Hmmpf. That's a line if I ever heard one."

"I'm a man of my word. I believe in prayer," Brent said. "Sometimes God allows us to experience lows so that we can soar to new heights."

"Thanks for the snack, but I don't need no Sunday sermon." Ken walked away.

Brent followed him a few steps.

"Hey, I didn't mean to come across that way. God bless."

Sure. God bless me, Ken thought. *God cursed me is more like it!*

—

Jimmy Wyatt was booked on several drug charges. He'd been read his rights and placed in a holding cell. Now he paced back and forth between the bars and the bunks. He had placed a call. He felt good having low friends in high places. His attorney owed him big time.

The familiar hollow click-clack of the guard's shoes

on the concrete floor could be heard coming down the hallway.

"Wyatt!" the guard scoffed.

Wyatt gripped the bars at shoulder height and pulled up flush to the cell door.

"Did you need something, your holiness? Leave my door unlocked, and I'll make it worth your while."

"I'll bet you would. I'll bet you'd fix me up so well that we could have adjoining jail cells for life. Forget it, man. You aren't gonna buy off anybody today."

"We'll see about that! Did you just come to harass me?"

"Nope, stand back. I'm taking you down the hall. You've got some lawyer who wants to see you."

Wyatt was escorted into a room with one glass wall.

"Move over to that first cubicle."

"Yes, your holiness," said Wyatt as he sarcastically bowed.

One corner of Wyatt's mouth curled up in a one-sided grin. "Well if it ain't Stephen Willis, attorney at law."

"Wipe that grin off your face, Wyatt. You are in hot water this time."

"Yeah? Well, you better change all that, egghead. You owe me big time."

"Hush, you fool! Whisper! I'll get you out of this deal, but do exactly what I say or this will become your permanent mailing address."

"You owe me at least a grand for the weed I've been supplyin' you with."

"I said lower your voice, or I'll walk right out of here," Willis whispered.

"Okay, okay. What's the plan?"

"I can get you out on bail, but you've got to behave yourself. I can call in a favor or two and post bond. You can walk free until your trial. But they catch you doing anything wrong, and you'll do time for sure."

—

The shift change on the second floor had begun. The charge nurse coming on duty flipped open Patricia Duncan's chart.

"Do you know any particulars on this new patient in 216?" she asked the nurse going off duty. "It looks like Shircliff left orders for this lady to remain isolated and under close observation. Looks like she's scheduled for some psychological testing. How come she is even on this ward?"

The nightshift nurse responded as she stood up and stretched. "Her baby died after delivery ... respiratory failure, I think. They told me she was one angry lady, cussing like a barroom bully. I don't think you'll have to worry about her for a while. That gal is out like a light. She was heavily sedated before they brought her up. I'm not expecting her to wake up until late this afternoon. I hope she is in a better mood when she wakes up. Hopefully you'll get to see Shircliff before you have to deal with her."

"That's going to be something to look forward to. Is there anything else out of the ordinary that I need to be aware of?"

"Nope, pretty routine evening except for that one lady. From what I've heard, if she ever wakes up, she will keep you plenty busy."

The night shift nurse finished filing her paperwork.

"Good luck." She smiled and walked away.

—

Robert punched the remote garage door opener. He had it timed perfectly. The car cleared the door by inches. Any onlooker would've thought he'd taken out the door for sure. But Robert always knew what he was doing. He shifted into park and punched the remote again. The door clattered down the track. The garage light was burned out, so when the door closed, it squeezed out any remaining light. It was dark as a cave.

Robert was tempted to just recline where he sat, but he needed a good rest. He climbed out of the car and entered his house. He unbuttoned his shirt. It trailed off his body to the floor. He slipped out of his shoes, unsnapped his pants, wriggled free one leg at a time, and kicked them off against the wall.

He smiled. Maybe he was happy just to be a free bachelor, able to live as he pleased. Maybe he was relieved that he no longer had to care for his mom all of the time. Or perhaps it was because he would finally have uninterrupted sleep. He turned off his pager. He was asleep as soon as his head hit the pillow.

—

Muffled voices. That is what he heard. Muffled voices and the clanking of metal on metal close by. Robert opened his eyes. He was at a field military hospital, a mobile army surgical hospital, or MASH unit as they were called. The metal on metal sounds were coming from instruments and utensils being dropped in pans as the wounded were being treated. As Robert scanned his surroundings, he saw doctors and nurses scampering about, looking after their charges with the utmost care.

Suddenly a voice came from over his bedside.

"Can I get you anything?"

Robert looked up and saw a pretty face. Her smile lit up the huge drab green tent. She was the prettiest thing Robert had seen in three years.

His mouth tasted like sawdust.

"Well, I think I'd like a drink of water. Where am I?"

"You are at the 1086th MASH. You got here last night. You are in pretty good shape, just some exhaustion and a little dehydration. Sounds like it was pretty awful out there. But you have no wounds to speak of. Sounds like you'll be getting out of here in no time."

"What about my brother?"

"I didn't see your brother. Was he with your unit?"

"Yes, we were together on the same hillside."

"Hmm ... I'll check on him. It could be that he made it out all right and has returned to his unit. I'll go get you some water right now."

"Yes, please check. And thanks."

"You bet." She smiled and walked away. Robert melted.

"Hey, buddy," another voice whispered from his left. Robert turned to see another soldier in the bunk next to his.

"Yeah."

"I saw your brother. Vanhouse, right?" the soldier asked to confirm the name. "He ran off into the jungle with two other guys. They were getting out of there but quick. Man, are they in trouble. Leavin' like that."

"Where were they going?"

"I don't have a clue, but wherever it was, they were getting there in a hurry."

"Thanks."

Robert turned back and closed his eyes to consider what might have happened. Where could David be? Why did he run off and leave Robert behind? He said he was going to inject himself and they would wake up under the ridge together. Was he okay? Was he AWOL? Sleep returned.

—

The dreams had been with Robert Vanhouse since his tour of duty in Vietnam. But since his brother returned home a little over a month ago, they seemed to visit him more often. They were disturbing, haunting. They were reminders of the evils of war and of terrible sights he wished he had never seen. Drinking used to provide some relief from those past images. Now they were stronger and more frequent.

I think I'll go by and see Hibbitts, he thought.

Jeff Hibbitts was a psychologist on staff at Hall Park General. They were closer friends a few years ago, but their careers had taken off, and even though they worked in the same building, they rarely saw each other anymore.

Robert sauntered into Jeff's office. Jeff was totally absorbed by some paperwork and didn't hear Robert approach. It was a nice office with soft autumn colors and leather furniture. It almost felt like a living room instead of an office. Pictures of the wife and kids stood on the desk.

"Hey, shrinky-dink," Robert began.

Hibbitts chuckled as he looked up. "I haven't heard

that name in a long time." Jeff stood up and smiled as he removed his glasses. "Where you been hidin' yourself?"

"It's good to see you, Jeff. We should grab lunch sometime and catch up on life," replied Robert. "But I guess that's why I haven't seen you. I can't seem to catch up with life."

"I know what you mean," said Jeff. "I always feel like I'm running behind."

"Say, I really did have a reason for coming up here. I was hoping you might answer some questions for me."

"Sure. I'll give it a shot." Jeff sat in his desk chair, leaned back, and interlocked his fingers behind his head. "What's on your mind?"

"That's a great line. Do you use that all the time?" asked Robert. Robert shook his head and pointed to his own brain. "It's more like what's in my mind. I've been having dreams. Flashbacks of my time in Vietnam mainly. I'm not sleeping well. It bothers me."

Jeff lowered his arms and rested them on his desktop as he leaned forward. "Well, I know that Vietnam was a tough time for you, as it was for a lot of guys and gals. If I'm guessing correctly, you'd probably like to erase that segment of your life."

"Exactly. So what can you do for me, short of a lobotomy?" Robert asked.

"Robert, I would suggest trying some sleep aid and see what happens. Start with something mild like an antihistamine. If that doesn't work, then come back to see me, and we'll get you some valium. It could be that the stress of you job and the long hours might be contributing factors to the frequency of the dreams. Maybe take a day or two off."

"Okay, I'll try that. But I would really like to ask you some more questions when you have time. Do you know much about dreams?" Robert inquired.

"Well, I'm no expert," Jeff said. "But I did some research into dreams and hallucinogenic drugs like LSD. Drugs were big when I was in college. I could get you some information. I'll have it for you when you come back."

"Great. I'll talk to you later," Robert said.

5

Beep, beep, beep!

Robert Vanhouse reached over to the nightstand and pressed the snooze bar of the clock radio. *You have got to be kidding me,* he thought. *It can't be 6:00 a.m. I just went to bed!* The numbers on the digital clock remained the same despite the wishful thinking. Robert swung his feet over the side of the bed and ran his fingers through his hair. His body was begging for more sleep, but it was Sunday morning. He was due back at the hospital at 7:00 a.m.

The hot water felt so good. Robert let the shower engulf his body as he stood there, immovable. He mulled over the patients he needed to see and his schedule for the next few days. *Maybe someday I'll actually have a social life.*

Robert finished dressing and headed to the kitchen. Dirty dishes had the sink surrounded. Work had not allowed for such menial labor as housekeeping. *I need a good woman to take care of me; that's all there is to it.*

He slugged down a glass of milk, a breakfast bar, and a banana. He rifled through the mail on his kitchen table. Nothing exciting caught his eye. Grabbing his keys he scrambled out to the car and reluctantly headed for the hospital.

—

The drugs had begun to wear off. Patricia was groggy, but she was beginning to recall the tragedy of her son's death. She kept repeating the same statement, her eyes staring at the wall, cold and fixed.

"They killed my baby."

Ken did not accept Patricia's accusation.

"Pat, Dr. Vanhouse explained what happened. The baby was just not in good shape from the get-go. I think he called it failure to thrive."

Patricia was not listening.

"They killed my baby, and I know it. They will pay," she said, still staring at the wall. Her impatience was growing. "When can I go home?"

"They say you may be able to check out by the end of next week," said Ken.

"I guess we need to make funeral arrangements for him," she said.

"Babe, I already handled that myself. You were sedated, and the staff felt it would be too much for you to have to make those decisions."

"Oh, so you let other people make my decisions." Patricia's jaw tightened. Her sneer grew colder. "They killed my baby. The autopsy should prove that."

Ken tried to speak in a loving tone. "Pat, they didn't do an autopsy. Dr. Vanhouse said that the cause of death was respiratory failure and failure to thrive. There was no reason to do an autopsy. That's what I've been trying to tell you."

Pat grew angrier. "Why are you taking their side? They

just want to be able to pull a good cover up. That woman doctor screwed up!"

"We have been over this several times now. It was nobody's fault. I talked with Dr. Vanhouse and the hospital chaplain myself. They were both very kind, informative, and told me exactly what happened. We have to grieve and start moving on with our lives. You can't keep being this angry."

"Angry? Angry?" She raised her voice higher and higher. "Have you forgotten? I am a nurse. I know what a botched delivery is! It was that woman, Dr. Heathcliff!"

Ken lowered his head then pushed himself out of the chair. "Dr.Shircliff, not Heathcliff."

"Where are you going?" she snapped.

"To get a cup of coffee." He sighed. "You want anything?"

"I want answers! Get me that baby-killing doctor!" she screamed as Ken slowly left the room.

—

Rebecca put on her pajamas and brushed her hair. She was worried about Dr. Vanhouse's suspicions regarding her health. She sat down on her side of the bed.

"Brent?" she said. He was already in bed on the verge of sleep.

"Hmm?" he answered reluctantly.

"I'm scared. That doctor suspects something serious. I could tell by the expression on his face. He was talking to me, and then all of a sudden his face just went blank. He didn't have to say anything. I knew something was wrong."

Brent turned on his side and faced her. "Honey, I did

not see that at all. You are jumping to conclusions." He reached across the bed and touched her arm. "He gave you no reason to worry."

"Well, you must not have seen his face."

"No, but I listened to what he said, and you just need to relax. You're getting all keyed up and blowing this way out of proportion. You don't even have one piece of information on which to form an opinion. Look, tell me what happened when you saw Dr. Crawford."

"He didn't really say much. He took my blood pressure and asked me some questions. He mainly treated Ryan. I didn't want to bother him about my condition since it was the weekend. He wants to see me next week though."

"There you go. That should dispel some worries. Just wait and see what happens after you talk with Doc Crawford next week after he has had a chance to examine you more thoroughly and have your blood test results. He knows you better than anyone. And besides, if he thought this was anything serious, he wouldn't have waited until next week to see you. Right? It's going to be okay." Brent gave her a kiss and rolled over.

The conversation was no comfort to her. "I guess."

—

At the hospital Dr. Vanhouse got out of his car and grabbed his stethoscope from the front seat. He walked through the brisk morning air toward the hospital employee entrance with his white coat draped across his shoulder.

He pulled open the door and thought, Here we go again, just another day in para... Before he finished his

thought a man came barreling out the door, almost collid-
ing with Vanhouse.

"Sorry, uh, excuse me," said the man as he scurried by.

"Sure." Robert leaned against the wall to let him by.
"What's the rush?" Vanhouse noticed the white coat but
could not make out the name on the ID badge. He was
impressed by the thick head of red hair.

—

Ken returned to Patricia's room that evening. He was sitting
next to the wall with his head leaned back, staring at the
ceiling. Patricia was in bed, looking at the television but not
really watching it.

"So, what do we do now?" she asked.

Ken responded calmly. "Well, they will be letting you
out of here before too long, and we will go home to live our
lives."

"And just forget what happened here? Forget about our
baby?"

"No, of course not. We won't forget the baby. There's just
nothing for us to do but keep livin'."

Patricia turned to face Ken. Her blood pressure was rising. "They killed our baby, and you're just going to let it go."

"Look," Ken said, "you and I have to work through this.
The baby is not the only issue here. We have more to deal
with than the loss of the baby."

"What other issues could be more important than our
baby?"

"Well, for instance, I would like to know more about the
past. I didn't realize you had been with so many men. I didn't
realize I married a woman who had been passed around."

"Okay. I made some mistakes. I slept with a few guys."

"Well, what about the abortions? No wonder we had so much trouble conceiving." Ken knew he was going too far, but he could not help it. "How many times have you been pregnant? How many guys have you slept with? Every guy you dated?" Now his voice was rising.

"Oh, come on. You're not exactly a saint! Let's talk about your character!"

"Oh sure, shift the blame to me." Ken was standing over her bed now. "Yeah, let's do talk about my character. Cause you sure don't have any!"

Patricia was sitting up in bed now, ignoring any pain.

"You … !" She grabbed the metal bedpan and threw it at him. Ken was able to avoid the missile, and it clanged against the wall.

"You can't deal with it, can you?" he shouted. "You can't deal with the fact that you may be the cause of our baby's death. Maybe those abortions were the problem. Maybe your body couldn't take care of him right!"

"*Stop it! Stop it!*" Patricia threw the plastic water pitcher, missing him, but water splattered everywhere. She put her hands over her ears to shut out what he was saying.

Dr. Vanhouse burst into the room.

"Hey, what's going on in here? We can hear you clear down the hall!"

Ken slid past him.

"Nothin', I was just leavin'. I think I've seen who my wife really is, and I don't like it."

"I think you leaving might be the best thing. Come back in the morning when things have cooled down."

"That's it, leave! Run away!" Patricia screamed.

"Mrs. Duncan! Cool it! I will medicate you if I have to!" Dr. Vanhouse was trying to get things under control. Two nurses came to assist and were now in the doorway.

Ken pulled his wallet from his back pocket.

"Here, take twenty bucks and call a taxi when you are ready to go home!"

"Fine, when the going gets tough, you just get going. *Go!* You would have been a lousy father anyway!"

Ken stepped into the hallway. That comment had stung, but he could not go back. He hurried toward the elevator to escape.

Vanhouse turned back to Patricia. He checked her condition. Everything seemed to be okay.

"Mrs. Duncan, you need to calm down now. Can we get you anything? Nurse, could you get someone in here to clean up this mess?"

"Leave, just leave, all of you!"

Not wanting to stir her up anymore, Vanhouse and the nurses backed out of the room.

"Holy cow," one of the nurses said. "That was some fight."

"Yep, they've been at it ever since their baby died," Vanhouse replied. "Keep an eye on her. I'm going to the lounge for a power nap. I'll be back later."

"Yes, Doctor."

Room 216 was quiet. In the dull glow of the hospital lighting, Patricia fell back onto her pillow. She was frustrated, confused, angry, and now, very much alone.

—

Mary's Bar was smoke filled and stuffy. You almost had to cut your way through the smells and smoke to get inside. There were a few soldiers at the bar, but most of the people occupying tables were Vietnamese locals. The music was local as well with a piano and a less than beautiful young lady in a red dress providing the vocals.

Corporal Vanhouse could not understand a word she was singing. He had strolled into the establishment alone, hoping to have a drink or two and enjoy some company. Who knows? He might get lucky. *What a lovely place,* he thought, *right out of Casablanca. I wonder when Humphrey Bogart will arrive.* He looked over at the stage at the singer and piano player. *You can barely hear her for all the talking going on. They're just ignoring her. Poor kid.*

Vanhouse made his way to the bar.

"Beer please!" he yelled to the barkeep. Soon the bartender was placing the obligatory paper coaster and beer glass down in front of him. Yum, yum... lukewarm beer. Nuttin' better. The young medic looked up and down the bar. To his left there were three GIs huddled around a small Vietnamese woman. They were laughing and appeared to be having a good time. To his right... wait, could it be? His line of vision carried beyond the end of the bar. There in a smoke-filled booth was a face he recognized. The man was sitting alone, a drink with a little paper umbrella sitting in front of him. No way! But why is he in civilian clothes?

Corporal Vanhouse eventually made his way over to the booth after being bounced around by several partying bodies. He felt fortunate to still have his beer in hand.

The stunned young corporal spoke first.

"David! I can't believe it! How did you get here?"

"Shut up! Sit down, you idiot!" exclaimed Corporal Vanhouse's twin brother. "I'm AWOL, remember?"

"I tried to find out what happened to you, but no one seemed to know," Robert said. "I've been looking for you since that day on the hill. Are you all right?"

David was not in the mood for small talk. "I'm fine, but you have to help me. I need to get home somehow, some way."

"Well, I'm due to go home in a couple of weeks. I'll see if I can arrange something."

"Look, I need more than maybes here. I need solid answers."

"Okay, okay. I'll get you home. Let me know where you're staying. I'll contact you next week."

David grabbed Robert's shirt with a trembling hand.

"I'll be waiting on you. You gotta get me out of here. Don't let me down. If you don't follow through, I'll take you down with me. I'll tell them you helped me go AWOL. In fact, I'll go one step further and tell them you helped me put down those guys on the hill."

"I'll get it done." Robert's voice was quivering. He had no choice.

—

In a dimly lit hospital room at the other end of the second floor, Bonnie Rowden slowly opened one eye.

"Are you a doctor?" she whispered. "My throat really hurts. I hurt all over." She was unable to see clearly much of anything in the room. Her vision was blurred as a result of the accident. The tissue around her eye was swollen, a mixture of pink, red, blue, and green tones. Most of the right side of her head was bandaged. Her right arm was in a cast from just below the shoulder, making a forty-five degree turn at her elbow and ending slightly beyond her wrist. Her left leg was in a cast and in traction. Her stomach was still big, round, and firm.

"Doctor," she whispered in a raspy, weak voice. "Is my baby okay? I don't remember how I got here. Was it a wreck?" There was no response to the question.

"Doctor. Are you a doctor or a nurse?" the injured woman asked. She was only able to see a blurred figure in a white coat. "Are you a doctor or a nurse?" She struggled to form the words. Her mouth was dry and her tongue swollen.

Finally the figure responded in a soft, soothing voice, "Which do you need?"

"I am really hurting. Can I have something for the pain?"

"That is why I am here." The white figure reached into the hospital coat pocket. "We knew you would be waking up soon and would want something for the pain. You were in a terrible wreck. The highway patrol said that you and your baby were very fortunate to have survived. Your car was more banged up than you, if you can imagine that."

"So you will help me?" pleaded Bonnie, shifting her position ever so slightly.

"That's my duty." The person prepared the injection. The syringe needle squeaked as it was jabbed into the vial and the assembly was turned upside down to draw out the liquid. Air bubbles were removed with a flick of a finger on the syringe barrel.

"I will give this injection into your IV tube. You won't even have to feel the stick of the needle. It should start working almost immediately, and soon you and your baby won't feel a thing."

Bonnie gave a feeble smile as she looked forward to the relief. The clear fluid was administered. Almost as quickly as the plunger was depressed, Bonnie's eyes opened wide. Her face was not one of peace but one of fear and shock. Her expression screamed with pain, and her chest felt like it would explode. Her body shuddered for a few seconds, and she made a desperate clumsy attempt to push the button for the nurse's station, but the mysterious figure moved the control only inches beyond her grasp. Her head rose from the pillow, and then, just as the figure had promised, she felt no more pain. She never felt anything again.

The white figure placed the vial and syringe back into the coat pocket. The fluorescent bulb above the bed cast a pale glow over the deceased. A flash of light dashed across Bonnie's body and was gone just as quickly when the intruder opened the door and disappeared down the hall.

6

CHAPTER

Keith Murdock held a doughnut in one hand, a cup of coffee in the other, and had a smile on his face.

"How are you, Wanda?"

"Good morning, Dr. Murdock," replied his secretary.

"Any news for me?"

"Seems to be pretty quiet for a Monday morning."

"That's what I like to hear." Murdock shoved his office key into the lock and gave it a turn.

The red signal light was flashing on his phone. *An urgent message demanding my immediate attention, no doubt.* There was a note lying on the floor next to his desk. Setting down his morning snack, Murdock stooped to pick up the note. It was a notification of the death of Bonnie Rowden. Murdock shook his head.

"This is not good. The board is already on my case."

Murdock continued to read. *Oh great! She was pregnant, expecting any time. That will technically be three unexpected deaths in a week at this facility. I guess I need to be proactive on this.*

He punched the intercom. "Wanda?"

"Yes, Dr. Murdock."

"Would you please page Dr. Shircliff? I need to speak with her as soon as possible."

"Yes, sir."

The page went out. Murdock grabbed his coffee, punched the phone recorder, and eased back in his chair to listen to the news.

"Lieutenant Steele here. I just wanted you to be aware that Jimmy Wyatt was able to post bond. I don't think he'll cause any problems, but you never can tell about some of these guys. Logic is not their strong suit. Anyway, don't hesitate to call if he shows up at your facility." *Beep.*

"You just ruined my morning," Keith Murdock blurted back to the answering machine.

"And a good morning to you, too," replied Elizabeth Shircliff from the doorway.

"I'm sorry. I was just venting a little frustration over a message on the recorder."

Dr. Shircliff stepped up to Dr. Murdock's desk.

"This is not the way I like to start my week. Usually when I have to see you on short notice, it's about a problem with an employee or a patient. So which is it this time?"

Murdock skirted the question.

"Dr. Shircliff, thank you for dropping by my office so quickly. We just need to talk." Shircliff settled into one of the chairs in front of Murdock's desk.

"I must say that the board of directors was very excited to appoint you to your current position. It is not that often that a candidate fits the job description so perfectly. Not only do you have the education and experience, but you have a unique quality of authority with compassion. You are able to keep the staff underneath you content and very productive. You even brought in that research grant to study how toxins affect the placental transfer of nutrients last year. That is a remarkable achievement for the short time you have been at this hospital. But ... " He paused.

Somewhat apprehensively, Shircliff said, "But what?"

"Now, I'm speaking to you as an employer, as the hospital administrator." Murdock eased back in the cushioned chair. He rubbed his balding head, not knowing exactly how to continue. "Have you noticed the alarming rise in the mortality rate over the past few months around here?"

"Well, I certainly am aware of the deaths, but I wasn't keeping score," Dr. Shircliff replied.

"Now I realize there are ups and downs. People live, people die. The disturbing thing is, we have no explanation. Emergency room admissions have been about average, no major catastrophes. It does not add up. Anyhow, I am being pressured to find out if there are any systemic problems that might explain it and trouble shoot if needed. Jobs could be in jeopardy, including mine and yours. The resulting publicity could really damage this institution. I don't want that to happen. I love this job, and I take pride in this hospital."

"Does this have anything to do with the loss of that baby the other day? Was it that Patricia Duncan that started this? I hear she's been complaining about malpractice on my part and saying all kinds of ridiculous things."

"Her complaints only brought more attention to the matter. The problem already existed," explained Keith. "I will be talking with all the department heads to make them aware of the concerns. That's why you're here this morning."

"Well, I'm sorry that this has happened. I'm sure it's nothing more than the natural ebb and flow of things. I will certainly keep an eye on it. Keep me posted of any further developments. If the problem is in my area, I'll do whatever is necessary to take care of it."

"Thanks, I know you will. I have full confidence in you."

As Shircliff rose to leave, Murdock opened a manila folder and added, "Do you know anything about this Bonnie Rowden death? She was a forty-one-year-old pregnant woman involved in a terrible auto accident, pretty serious injuries, but actually we thought she was out of the woods and would be fine. She was found dead this morning of unknown causes. Thought is might be a pulmonary embolus, but the autopsy done later in the day was negative. We lost her baby, too."

"I haven't heard about that one."

"Of course, toxicology studies are still pending and will take two or three weeks. Well, as I say, this is a big concern for the hospital, Elizabeth. I have got to give the board of directors some indication that we are on top of this."

"I'll make it a priority and keep you abreast of anything I come up with."

"Thanks. I appreciate it. Say, do you know if Dr. Vanhouse is around?"

"I think he is," she replied. "Nobody knows this place better than he does. He would be a good one to talk with."

"That is exactly my intention," said Murdock. "If you see him, send him my way, would you?"

"Of course." Dr. Shircliff left the office, mulling over

the problem as she walked back to the nurse's station on her floor. The ward seemed to be operating smoothly, so she checked out. Before she left she stopped at the doctors' lounge to get a bottle of juice and quench her thirst. Dr. Vanhouse was relaxing on a couch.

"Hey, Robert, Keith Murdock wants to talk to you as soon as possible."

"Where is he?"

"In his office."

"Oh man, I'm pretty comfortable right here."

"I'm not kidding. He needs to see you. It's urgent." Shircliff decided to reveal the reason for the summons. "Apparently the higher-ups are pressuring him about the unusual number of deaths occurring around here, particularly pregnant women."

"Hey, didn't you just get here? It looks like you're leaving."

"Yes and yes," Shircliff responded. "I've got a speaking engagement this morning. See ya this afternoon." Shircliff waved goodbye and disappeared through the door.

Vanhouse put down his monthly journal, got up, and made the walk over to Dr. Keith Murdock's office. The door was open, and Murdock was sorting out his remaining work in the order that he would attack it the remainder of the day.

"I quit reading a perfectly enthralling medical research article on "Pig Livers, Our Hope for the Future" just so I could talk to you. This better be important," said Robert, grinning.

"Have a seat," commanded Murdock. "You know any time I request your presence that it is an urgent matter."

"So you want me to take your cousin to the football game again?" Robert joked.

"You won't ever let me forget that, will you?" said Murdock and laughed. "I wish it were that simple this time. The hospital has developed a problem. At least it is perceived as a problem. It is serious enough to draw the attention of our board of directors. Since you have been at the facility for several years now, I value your insight into the situation and your analysis of the problem."

"I will be glad to share my insight as soon as you tell me exactly what I am supposed to be looking at."

"It is the hospital mortality rate," Murdock revealed. "We have too many people going out our back door covered by a sheet, if you know what I mean. The trend has been higher than the board would like to see, and they want me to look into it. I realize it could be caused by factors that are beyond our control, but if we have become lax or careless in some area, then we need to rein in the problem and bring the numbers back down."

Robert could tell by the look on Murdock's face that he was being pushed for answers. "How long has this trend been noticeable?"

"The stats show about a year, but the alarming rise has been over the last few months. The problem is that we have had no major disasters or epidemics during this timeframe, so I have no obvious answers staring me in the face."

"What about personnel? Any big changes that coincide with the trend?" inquired Vanhouse.

Murdock thought for a moment.

"We've had the usual number of hires and fires, I guess."

"Say, what about that nurse that tore up the ER when he was arrested? I think his name was Wyatt. What do we know about him?" asked Vanhouse.

"He was a drug addict caught stealing meds from the floors," Murdock responded. "But now that you mention it, he did his clinical rotations here, and we hired him right away. That puts him here at the hospital at about the right time. You can't predict what a drug addict will do. Maybe he could have come back. I was just told he is out on bond."

"What does he look like?"

"Well, he's pretty average, about five foot ten. But the most obvious feature is his thick red hair."

Vanhouse uncrossed his legs and scooted forward in his chair, recalling the brief encounter with the red-headed doctor who almost ran over him. "I think he may have been back to see us, but I didn't get a very good look at him. He was in quite a hurry."

"I'll alert security. Better to be safe than sorry."

"Is there anyone else you can think of?" asked Vanhouse.

"Well, the only other person I can think of is Elizabeth Shircliff. She was hired awhile ago."

"I don't guess all of this started when she came on board, did it?"

"What kind of a question is that? Do I detect a little jealousy?" Murdock was smirking.

"Hey now, that is a low blow," Robert said. "You know I

was well qualified for a promotion around here. But I guess the best man, or in this case woman, got the job. I am sure the board had to fill some minority or female job quota."

"Aw, come on, Vanhouse, your time will come. You are good at what you do. We would be hard-pressed to find a surgeon with your skills. And like it or not, it is a little more politically correct to have a woman in charge of the OB/GYN floor."

Vanhouse pushed himself up and out of the chair.

"I am about ready to call it a day. I'll look things over and give it some thought. It is probably just a coincidence about Shircliff, anyway. But that Wyatt guy might be worth checking into."

"I think you are right," said Murdock. "Hey, thanks for stopping by on such short notice."

—

Patricia Duncan was fidgeting through last Sunday's paper for the third time. Now she was down to reading the obituaries and the weather report. A nurse was checking her vital signs.

"This is nuts," Patricia scolded. "There's no reason for me to be here. I'm fine. Could you see if I can go home anytime soon?"

"I will check, Mrs. Duncan. The doctor has made no mention of it to me, but I can check your chart to see if there are any notes about releasing you."

"Thank you. I'm going stir crazy." The nurse left the room.

A few minutes later there was a knock at the door. The six foot four inch frame of Dr. Vanhouse entered room 216.

"I hear someone in here doesn't like our fine facilities here at Hall Park General."

Patricia looked at him with contempt. "Just get me out of here."

"Well, everything is looking pretty good at this point. Barring any unforeseen problems, I think we can get it done pretty quickly."

"Great," said Patricia emotionlessly.

—

Tuesday morning Dr. Shircliff met with the intern and staff psychiatrist assigned to monitor Patricia Duncan's progress. Shircliff had removed herself from the Duncan case, feeling that it would be best with all the furor surrounding it. She stayed connected from a distance, avoiding the violent outbursts from the patient. It was better all the way around.

Shircliff started the discussion.

"This Mrs. Duncan is an unusual case. We have many different angles of treatment to consider. Since I removed myself from any contact with the patient, I am going to rely on the information that the two of you supply before I approve any decision to release her. Bear with me while I review the information, and I'll seek your opinions." Shircliff paused long enough to get an affirming nod from both doctors.

"When Mrs. Duncan came to the emergency room, we had already suspected complications. Just as we anticipated, it was a difficult delivery, and the baby died of respiratory failure, a failure to thrive situation. Naturally she was distressed and unfortunately became extremely violent. We sedated her for her own safety, as well as that of the staff.

During the entire labor and for at least the next few days, her blood pressure was oscillating dramatically, and her blood chemistries were slightly off. Now I would like your updates."

The doctors exchanged glances, and the young resident began reviewing his notes out loud.

"Mrs. Duncan remained physically and emotionally unstable for the first few days. No doubt the stress of the entire ordeal played a role. I began to notice a change today. We cut back her meds, and she seems to have stabilized."

Shircliff looked over at the psychiatrist. "Good to hear. How about her psychological profile?"

"She is a very angry young woman and is having problems dealing with her grief. In addition, she is experiencing a great deal of post-partum depression, for which I ordered a light regimen of paroxetine. I have counseled with her, and she has other problems besides just dealing with the death of her child. Her husband has apparently abandoned her, which is not that uncommon after a tragedy like this. I would recommend release from the hospital and follow-up with treatment and a local support group."

"All right, it sounds as if she is in pretty good shape physically, and we will work on the emotional issues as an outpatient. Let's keep her one more day, and if everything remains status quo, we will discharge her. Maybe we can get her home pretty soon. Thanks, guys."

—

Rebecca was able to see Doctor Charles Crawford Tuesday afternoon. She returned home. It was already lunch time. She paid the babysitter and sent her on her way. She plopped down in the recliner in the den. Her daughter immediately appeared. Four-year-old Kara scrambled into Rebecca's lap with her fists full of paper.

"Mommy."

"What have you got there?" Rebecca asked.

"It's a present I made for our new baby. It took me a long time to make."

Rebecca reached out and tenderly received the gift.

"Mommy, you open from this side." Kara pointed to the starting place and then began talking about her creation. "They are paper dolls, and there's one of you and of daddy and of all of us. I even made Ryan with a broken leg." Kara watched Rebecca's face closely. She was eager to hear and see her mother's reaction. When a little time had passed without comment, Kara asked, "Do you like them, Mommy?"

"Oh yes, sweetie. You did such a wonderful job."

Kara's eyes sparkled with pride. She was so excited. She blurted out a request she had been keeping to herself for just the right moment.

"Mommy, I hope you decide to have a baby sister. That's what I really want."

Rebecca placed her hands on her stomach. She cried as she moved her hands around to feel the flutter that would reassure her that the baby was okay.

"Mommy, why are you crying?"

"I'm sorry, sweetie. You just got me to thinking about our baby, and I was just wishing that I was holding her in my arms instead of inside my tummy."

Kara jumped up and down. "Her...you said her. Yippee, it's going to be a girl!"

Rebecca wiped her face. "Not so fast, sister. Mommy doesn't know if it'll be a boy or a girl. And I really think that you would enjoy either one. Come here and let me give you a great big hug."

—

Dr. Vanhouse walked down the hospital hall and tapped on the door frame to Murdock's office. Murdock was on the phone but motioned him to be seated as he concluded the conversation.

"Yeah, okay, but I have got to have it here by Friday. Go ahead and ship it two-day delivery with UPS just to make sure the shipment arrives on time. Okay, thanks!" Murdock hung up and sighed. "I hate fixing goof ups." He turned to face Vanhouse.

"What do you need, my good Doctor Vanhouse?"

"Well, it has to do with our previous conversation," Robert replied. "You know, the one we had earlier about our little problem."

"Oh yes. So did you come up with some pearls of wisdom or perhaps some new information?"

"A couple of things have come to mind. I've heard through the grapevine that this Jimmie Wyatt guy made some threats. I don't even know the dude, but—"

"Well, we are a little concerned about him," Murdock interrupted. "As we talked about Monday, we don't know what he is capable of. Drugs can really drive a man to do strange things, don't you think so?"

Robert's thoughts flashed back to his dream on the hill

in Vietnam. *"Just push the plunger down. We'll meet up after the drugs wear off."*

Murdock repeated the question. "Don't you think so?"

Robert stuttered, "Yes … yes … absolutely." He gathered his thoughts.

Murdock slid a file folder across the desk. "You asked what Wyatt looked like. I retrieved his personnel file. Take a look at his photo."

Vanhouse shook his head as he examined the photo. "He nearly ran me down coming out of the hospital. But if I didn't know any better, I'd say this is him."

That spooked Murdock. "Where … what time do you think you saw him?" Murdock asked as he picked up the telephone. "I am calling Lieutenant Steele. He wanted to be on top of this thing should Wyatt show back up."

"It was about 6:45 in the morning. I was just coming on," Vanhouse said. "Listen, if you're done with me, I'm headed home for some shut-eye."

Murdock waved. "Great. Thanks for the information. I'll see you later." He swiveled the leather office chair around.

After the conference with Dr. Murdock, Robert Vanhouse headed home. *Man, some weird stuff going on at the hospital. Shircliff, a murderer? Na, not a chance. Wyatt? Maybe.* He tried to put all the pieces together.

On his way home, Vanhouse swung by his mother's home. The grass was high, and there were two newspapers on the front lawn. Robert was irritated. He bore most of the responsibility for his family. He had set up David with a cushy job. All David had to do was take care of the yard, look after their mom, and occasionally type a few reports.

Robert sat in his car and stared at the house. *I guess I should go in and check on things.* He grabbed the car door handle and bowed his head. *I just can't.* He drove on.

Maybe later.

7

CHAPTER

The following day Dr. Morgan, a young resident assigned to Patricia Duncan's case, strolled into her room as he was perusing her chart.

"Well, Mrs. Duncan, looks like you'll be getting out of here today. I just need to ask you some questions."

"Whatever. Fire away."

Patricia's response annoyed Dr. Morgan.

"Do you understand what we want you to do about follow-up appointments and treatments?"

Patricia rolled her eyes and sighed. "Yes."

"What about medications? Do you understand how to take them and what they are for?"

"Yes, yes." Patricia's patience was running thin.

"Do you have any questions for me?"

"Nope," came the terse reply. "I just want to go home." She turned away annoyed. "But getting there may be a problem. My loving husband has not shown his face in a while. I guess I'll have to call a cab." She made no attempt to hide her frustration.

"Let us know when you've called the cab, and I'll have one of the nurses wheel you down for the pick up."

"Fine. Now if you don't mind, I would like to get dressed."

81

"Sure. I'll get out of your way." The doctor left, and Patricia immediately dialed information, who connected her with Hall Park's lone cab company.

"I need a taxi to pick me up at Hall Park Regional Hospital. Yes, the front entrance will be fine. My name is Patricia Duncan. Can you dispatch one immediately?"

"Yes ma'am. We'll have one there within fifteen minutes."

"Great. I'll be waiting." Patricia hung up and turned to get dressed.

—

Rebecca Wells uneasily dialed Doctor Charles Crawford's office number. A cheerful voice answered, "Good morning. Doctor Charles Crawford's office. This is Lisa. How may I help you?"

"Hello. This is Rebecca Wells. I am inquiring about the results of the blood testing I had done."

"Yes. What did you need to know?"

"The results!" replied an overanxious Rebecca.

"Of course. I am sorry, ma'am. I meant was there any particular thing you needed to know. Did you need to consult with the doctor? Oh, I see, there is a note here in your file. Could you please hold for just a moment?"

Rebecca's anxiety was not helped by the silence. After the long pause, the receptionist came back on the line. "Mrs. Wells, sorry to keep you waiting. Doctor Crawford does need to speak to you personally. I can either put you on hold, or I can have him call you back later this afternoon, probably after 4:00 p.m."

Rebecca tensed. "It must be something serious."

"No, ma'am, I don't think so. I think he just wants to counsel with you and give you some special instructions."

"Put me on hold. I will wait." Rebecca pulled out a chair and sat down at the kitchen table. She placed her hands on her stomach and automatically felt for the baby's movements. The wait was awful. She felt like her nerves had been yanked from her body, placed in a blender, and turned on high. It was almost too much to bear. The soothing background music with soft stringed instruments coming through the phone receiver even agitated her as she waited. Just then two of her children came running through the room, ducked the phone cord, and ran out the back door, letting it slam behind them.

"I need to pray," she said to herself. Rebecca blocked everything out of her mind. She became oblivious to the tune over the phone line. Her lips trembled. She was scared. "Oh Lord, if it be your will, please let this report be good news. Dear God, please allow me the privilege of bearing another child. Give me strength in whatever happens. Calm my fears. Please give me peace and a healthy child." She had to hurry through the last few words as Dr. Crawford picked up the phone.

"Rebecca?" She did not answer. "Rebecca?"

"Oh yes, I'm here. Sorry, Dr. Crawford. I was just thinking."

Crawford began, "I looked over the results of your tests. I was wondering if you have ever had any other dizzy spells. In fact, I would like to know if you have had any type of symptoms uncommon to your previous pregnancies. Any different pains or light-headedness and such?"

"Well, you know me. I'm hardly ever sick. You treat my husband and children a lot more often than me. I've only occasionally seen the inside of your office as a patient. I guess the only reason I come see you is … " They both said in unison, "when I'm pregnant." They both laughed out loud.

"How true," Dr. Crawford said. "But, Rebecca, you did not answer my question."

There was a pause in the conversation.

"Rebecca, it is very important that you are honest and that I know everything if I'm going to find anything and be able to choose the proper treatment."

"Well, I have been extremely tired with this pregnancy," she said. "There have been some mild dizzy spells other than the hospital episode. I guess I just thought it was all part of being pregnant and a little older and having several little munchkins to care for. It takes a great deal of energy to keep up with everybody."

"I'm sure it does," replied Crawford. "Rebecca I have given this situation a lot of thought. I want to recommend that you go to the hospital and spend the final few weeks of your term there. I have spoken with Dr. Robert Vanhouse, the doctor who attended you in the emergency room. We compared your test results and his observations, and we both think we need to be careful. What you just told me about the fatigue and dizzy spells just confirms my suspicions. Your blood sugar levels and blood pressure are just too high, and I believe that we need to get a handle on it. If we don't, we could be in for some pretty serious problems. We don't want to compromise the health of the littlest Wells or his mother. If you were to experience another situation and it went unattended for too long a period, then the baby could be in serious peril. So, as soon as you can arrange to get the rest of your family cared for, I suggest you check into the hospital. How about today?"

"Could I just get bed rest at home?" Rebecca asked, already knowing the answer. "I would rather do that. The kids have things going on at school, Brent is completing a big project at work, and I—"

"Rebecca, listen to yourself. You have just proved my point. You have five children. I understand your desire to be home, but I mean you must relinquish your motherly duties temporarily. I am afraid that fixing dinner, vacuuming the carpet, maybe even something less strenuous could induce one of these spells."

"Could I at least spend Memorial Day weekend at home? How about I check in the Wednesday after Memorial Day?"

"I forgot about the holiday. I guess I can compromise on that, but you must understand that I am very serious about resting. You have to be very cautious."

"Thank you so much. I promise not to do any strenuous work. And I'll report to the hospital first thing Wednesday morning."

"All right, stay on the line, and my nurse will give you additional information and help you get checked into a room."

"Okay. Thanks, Dr. Crawford. I'll do as you say."

—

Patricia stood silently in front of her house. Newspapers were scattered across the lawn, and a bright yellow advertisement flyer twisted around the front doorknob in the Oklahoma wind. Other than that everything outside the house appeared just as she had left it a few days ago. The fallen leaves from the maple tree were still gathered against the front porch steps. She walked slowly toward the porch, stepping over the old green water hose that snaked across the yard.

She put her key in the slot but noticed that the door was unlocked. *Oh my gosh! How long has my house been open?* she thought. Cautiously she pushed the front door open.

"Hello!" she yelled, hoping for no reply. *Well, at least they'll know I'm coming in,* she thought bravely. Slowly she entered. At first glance everything appeared to be just fine. The mirror and coat rack were in their usual place in the entry, and her old gardening hat hung from its hook. She noticed one thing missing: Ken's oil-stained cap.

The house had an unfamiliar, stale smell. She turned the corner and discovered the source. Last week's cereal dishes and leftover food scraps from other meals had combined in the sink to form an almost gagging odor. The refrigerator compressor cycled on. She gasped, twisted around, and her skin prickled.

"Okay, Patricia, let's be sensible here," she whispered to herself. There was nothing to fear in this room.

Patricia struggled to keep her composure as she walked down the hall to the bedroom. The door was partially open. She gave it a shove. "Oh my gosh." She put her hands to her lips. The room was in a shambles. A wooden rocker was piled full of laundry. The closet had been ransacked. Clothes were scattered everywhere. The top dresser drawer hung precariously from the casing. The bottom drawer was empty and upside down in the middle of the bed. She ran back into the living room to call the police, but the phone was gone. It was then she noticed the nineteen-inch color television was missing, along with the stereo system. About half of her cassette tape collection had been hijacked.

"All right, what about the bathroom. Um... also a mess." Ken's hair brush, toothbrush, and electric razor were nowhere to be found. It was then that it registered. Only Ken's things were missing. Well, what a gentleman, she thought. He took only the things that were rightfully his. It then became a game to find what he took and what he left behind. If it was something they shared, he left it, like the deodorant stick still lying open on top of the bathroom counter.

It was in the kitchen that the game became reality. Ken had left a note on the table. She stopped short. Her throat tightened. She sunk into the kitchen chair and picked up the note. Her hands trembled as she started to read.

Patsy,

I'm sure you won't be too shocked to find me gone. I'm sorry for not being with you these past few days, but I could just not bring myself to see you again. Your anger has changed you. I don't even know you anymore. I just cannot love a woman I don't know and obviously never knew. I'm angry, too. I can't forgive you for the past few days. The disappointment and heartache has cut too deep. You left me with some good memories, but finding out about your past and seeing this hateful side of you made me realize I need to just go. After you read this, you'll discover I've only taken my stuff. I've left you plenty. You have the house and all the bills that go with it.

Patricia was numbed to the soul. He knew she hated the name Patsy. *The jerk,* she thought. *He didn't even sign it.* She rose from the table, crumpling the note in her hand.

"Couldn't face me in person, could you?" she said. "Never were good with confrontation."

She opened the door to the garage. It was as cold and empty as her heart. Ken had taken all the tools and their only vehicle, a 1968 Ford pickup. It made sense. Without the equipment he could not make his living as a concrete finisher and brick mason. She stood in the doorway with her arms crossed and began thinking out loud again.

"I wonder what he is doing right now. Aw, this is nuts. Why should I even care?" She glared at the twisted note in her hand. "I hate you, Ken. What am I supposed to do for transportation?" She crumpled the note again and unceremoniously chucked it in the trash. She slammed the garage door. The ironing board hanging next to the door crashed to the floor. She left it there.

Exhausted from the stresses of the day, Patricia made her way to the couch for a much needed nap. She laid down on her side, placing one pillow between her knees and another folded, just right, under her head. It did feel good to be home. She was soon in an unshakable sleep, and all the events of the past few days replayed vividly in her dreams.

—

Wednesday morning at the Wells home, Brent was already dressed when he walked back into the bedroom and heard the alarm blaring. It was 8:30 a.m. He had pre-arranged to arrive late at the office. So, for the moment, he turned off the alarm, sat on the edge of the bed, and spoke softly while he massaged his wife's shoulders.

"Honey, it's time to get going."

Rebecca laid in bed and stretched her arms and legs.

"I am not looking forward to this. I'm going to be so lonely."

"I'm not looking forward to this either," he said, "but I know this is the right thing to do. I would rather have you safe and sound at the hospital than take a chance of something happening here at home that might put you and the baby in danger."

"It is just going to be so hard not being with you and the children," she lamented, "especially at the start of summer vacation. I'm going to need to do something to help the time pass. I hate crossword puzzles. Maybe I can make something. I can't crochet. Maybe I could hook a small rug. Gloria did one. It was beautiful. She said it was easy, but it just took lots of time. Right up my alley since I'm going to have plenty of time."

She got up from the bed and put on her robe while she waddled down the hall toward the living room. "It's too quiet. Where are the kids?"

"You won't believe this, but I got them all up, dressed, fed, and out the door without waking you. Mrs. Marsh took them all for the day."

"And some say miracles don't happen. I must have been

exhausted not to hear anything. Of course, I didn't get to sleep until sometime after three a.m."

"Well, I promised each of them a dollar if they could get everything done without waking you."

"Free enterprise."

"It worked, didn't it? Hey, I'll go even one step further. I will give you a dollar if we can make it to the hospital before quitting time. You only have an hour and a half before you are supposed to be there." Brent held up his wrist watch and tapped the crystal face as a reminder to his wife.

"I'm scheduled for 10:00 a.m., right?"

"Yep," he said and popped her with a dish towel.

"Okay, okay. I'm going! Give me thirty minutes. Can you fix my breakfast while I shower?"

"I would rather shower with you, but I guess I could cook some eggs in the kitchen instead of cooking something up in the shower."

"Oh, you fiend. My mother told me about men like you." Rebecca blew him a kiss and headed for the bathroom. Brent moved to the kitchen to fulfill his promise of breakfast.

Thirty minutes later the couple sat at the dining room table. It was a quiet time. Brent sipped a cup of coffee and simply watched his wife eat her breakfast. Normally Rebecca would have commented on Brent's stare, but she was thinking about her hospital stay and wishing she had seen her children one more time. Her thoughts were everywhere except at that table. Finally, Brent said, "Babe, we gotta go."

Rebecca started to clear the table. She picked up her plate, but Brent guided it back to the table.

"Honey, leave the mess. Get your things. I can clean up later."

She reluctantly accepted the offer and went to finish packing. Within minutes they were driving to the hospital. The quiet was deafening.

The check-in went surprisingly quick.

"This beats our last excursion to this place," said Rebecca.

"Oh man, that was a trip we'll never forget," replied Brent. "Let's go see what sort of wonderful accommodations you'll have. Maybe you'll get a room with a view. Hopefully you won't have to stare at a clunky looking air conditioning unit on a rooftop."

A nurse on the second floor guided them to the room. She checked Rebecca's identification bracelet.

"Okay, Rebecca Wells, you match the chart, so this is your room.

It looks like this will be your home away from home for a while. What do you think? Never mind, I know what I would think if it were me."

"There's no place like home," Rebecca said.

"I won't argue that!" replied the nurse. "I'll let you get settled in. I'll be back in a little while." She left the couple and returned to her station.

They allowed Rebecca the luxury of wearing her own pajamas for the moment, so she changed clothes and got into bed. Brent sat down, but it wasn't long before Rebecca insisted that Brent leave her and go to his office.

"Honey, there is absolutely nothing you can do here except watch doctors and nurses come and go."

"I guess you're right. I'll tell you what. I'll stop back by on my way home from work." He bent over and kissed her on the forehead. "See you tonight, my love."

—

Patricia slowly awoke. She rolled onto her back and realized she had moved to her bed from the couch. *I needed a good night's sleep.* Her thoughts turned to the future. *Well, I'm on my own now. I'll have to find a job pretty soon.* She got up from her bed, put on a robe, and walked outside to the mail box. It was over flowing with a variety of materials. She flipped through each item as she returned to the house but stopped when she noticed the University of Oklahoma School of Nursing logo on the corner of a large envelope. She tossed the rest of the mail on the coffee table. A letter from Ken went unnoticed as it skimmed across the glass tabletop and hit the floor. Patricia carefully opened the oversized envelope and slid out the cardboard holder containing the prized sheet of thick stock paper. She held it at arm's length and began reading aloud:

> This certifies that Patricia Ladonna Duncan has completed the required course of study and is therefore awarded the degree of Bachelor of Science in Nursing.

Her thoughts were happy for a change. *Awesome! This is suitable for framing. Now let's see, where do I put it?* She looked around the room. A large wooden-framed picture of her and Ken hung on the living room wall above the book case. "Perfect!" she said. She took out the photograph and replaced it with her diploma and then hung it back on the wall. The photograph, now on the floor, crinkled under her feet. She stepped back to admire the new masterpiece.

"I am a new woman!" she exclaimed. "Patricia LaDonna Duncan, RN!"

Patricia walked to the bathroom and stood in front of the full-size mirror. She brushed her hair slowly and began to think of her situation. *Great. What do I do now? I have to start all over.* She leaned over the bathroom counter, touched the reflection of her face. She then spoke to her image. "Well, if I am starting a new life, I might as well start from scratch. I need a full-fledged makeover. I want to look completely different for my new life."

Patricia took her long blonde hair and folded it under. *Hm, that would be a great start!* she thought. She pulled open the cabinet drawer, pushed some hair brushes to the side, and withdrew a pair of scissors. She marked her new hair length by holding it between her middle finger and fore finger and cut several inches of hair at a time, paying little attention to the jagged edges. The long locks of her hair floated to the floor. One snip followed another until a golden nest formed at her feet. It didn't really matter if her hair looked perfect at this moment. Refinements could be made later. She reached back in the drawer, drew out a curling iron, and plugged it into the wall socket next to the sink.

Another idea began to form as she waited for the curler to heat. *My face should change, too.* She focused on her eyes, particularly the lack of color surrounding them. Patricia fumbled through the drawer for eye shadow and her eyebrow pencil. She went with a heavier eye shadow, and with the pencil in hand she completely encircled her eyelids. She had beautiful brown eyes, and her handiwork really drew attention to them. As a finishing touch, she used the pencil to enlarge the tiny mole on her cheek. *How cute! A rather sexy beauty mark if I do say so myself.*

The curling iron was hot, so she began curling the uneven ends of her freshly-barbered hair toward her face. In a matter of thirty minutes, Patricia had achieved a strikingly different appearance. A turn to the right, back to the left. Something was familiar about this new look. She continued to fine tune the hair with the scissors, smoothing out the rough ends and trying to get a more professional-looking style with the curling iron.

She realized that she now resembled a person she had known or seen in the past. Patricia became engrossed with her new image. Patricia stared in amazement at her reflection. *I don't believe it. If I dyed my hair red I would look just like her. Shircliff! That witch, Shircliff!* Her mind raced with thoughts of revenge. She laughed as she turned off the bathroom light and muttered, "I know where I'm looking for a job! Move over, hag, that hospital's too small for the both of us!"

While the thought was still fresh in her mind, Patricia scooped up her purse and walked to the corner drug store to buy red hair dye.

8

CHAPTER

The lingering smell of incense barely covered the odor from the marijuana Jimmy Wyatt had smoked before falling asleep in his recliner. Now he was awake, and there was no place to go. He paced nervously around the living room of his apartment, still wearing the wrinkled clothing from the past two days. He was oblivious to the television crackling in the corner. A forest of empty beer cans stood on the coffee table. Bowls and glasses were scattered around the room, as were a number of old pizza boxes and potato chip bags. Two cockroaches were enjoying a feast of half-eaten pepperoni slices.

Withdrawal from his drug addiction was gripping every thought. *Man, I gotta get somethin' quick. I'm dyin'.* He was addicted to prescription pain medications with a preference for morphine. He could get drugs on the street, but his nursing career provided easier access to many pharmaceuticals, including morphine, his favorite, or two of his alternates, hydrocodone and ketamine. Wyatt stared at his trembling hands. *Stop!* He crossed his arms. The knuckles of his hands turned white as they clamped down hard on his elbows. *Oh God, please!* He doubled over in pain, collapsing on the brown sofa. A white doctor's coat and green scrubs crumpled under the twisting body. His stomach felt like it was being squeezed in a vise.

He picked up one beer after another and tipped them up over his mouth. All he got were drops of hot beer. He retrieved a precious piece of a marijuana joint from the ash-tray on the end table. Wyatt re-lit it and took long slow inhalations. He held his breath for as long as he could to allow as much of the drug to enter his body as possible. He kicked back in the recliner, hoping to be whisked away from the symptoms of the opiate withdrawal. It didn't help.

That's it. I've gotta call her. Wyatt picked up the phone. It was a fight to keep his hands steady enough to dial and hold the receiver.

"Hello?" a voice on the other end said.

"Hey, I've got to get somethin'. When can I come get some of your inventory?"

"I told you not to call me here!" the person responded, straining to keep their voice low.

Wyatt's temper flared. "I don't care what you told me! I need some now! Now! When can I come get it?"

"I'm in the middle of something right now. I can't just drop what I'm doing."

"Then when?"

"Never! We're done! You've got a real problem. I'm not going to risk everything for a low-life like you." *Click!*

—

Having showered, Patricia sat at the breakfast table in her blue cotton bathrobe. She was halfway through a bowl of cornflakes. The clock radio alarm in the bedroom came to life.

"Good mornin', neighbors! It's 8:15, and traffic and weather are just around the corner. You're listenin' to the 1080 KIKK, the Kicker."

Patricia closed her eyes as she realized she had not reset the radio alarm. *Blast that stupid country junk! Why Ken likes that stuff is beyond me.* She pushed her chair away from the table, stood up, and raced down the hall to the bedroom. A steel guitar was just beginning its loud refrain when she marched in the room and sharply slapped down on the Off button. "I've got to remember to find some good old rockin' roll," she muttered on her way back to her bowl of cereal.

Before she sat back down, she reached over and turned on her tabletop five-inch black and white television perched on the end of the kitchen counter. She turned to her favorite station and caught the last few minutes of the local news update. The weatherman concluded his portion of the broadcast with, "It will be a warm and beautiful day. So enjoy it! We will be right back."

A commercial followed from the big Methodist church in town. A man's soothing voice beckoned viewers to come worship this month of May and offer special thanks to God for His blessings. There was an opening shot of a family playing kickball at a park. As it faded out, an elderly couple appeared strolling arm and arm together down a picturesque street on a summer afternoon as a breeze swirled green leaves around them. Then in the final scene, a young mother and father appear in the foreground, peering over the edge of a crib, making faces and cooing at the newborn child. All of this happened with the hymn Amazing Grace playing in the background. The commercial closed out with the announcer providing one more invitation. "Won't you give thanks with us this Sunday?" The address and time of the services faded into the picture.

Patricia compared flashbacks of her past few weeks of life with those rosy scenes in the church's commercial. She despised her circumstances and envied all those people. She promptly and deliberately turned off the television. The pains of jealousy remained. Patricia looked up to heaven defiantly.

"Worship God? Please! First you let my baby die, and then my husband leaves. Thanks for nothing!"

She glanced at the microwave clock and thought, *Almost 9:00. Great, that is all I need is to be late for the first interview.* She scooped up one last bite of cereal and chased it down with a few swallows of coffee. She dressed in a hurry while her curling iron warmed up on the bathroom counter. She looked glamorous in the gray suit she had pressed the night before. By 9:15 she was looking for her purse and trying to decide which pair of shoes would be the most comfortable for her walk to the bus stop.

"The black leather low-heeled pumps will do." She rolled the shoes left and right, comparing their color to that of her dress. "So, what do you think?" she asked the fish in the aquarium. "Well, I don't have time to wait for the answer." Patricia yanked a light jacket out of the entry closet and put it on as she maneuvered out the front door. "Brrrrr! I knew I should know better than to believe the stupid weatherman. Warm and breezy, my foot." She quickly pulled the collar of her jacket up around her neck and then checked her watch. *Good,* she thought. *I can make it to the bus stop in five minutes.*

The sun had begun to dissolve the clouds by the time Patricia reached the hospital entrance. She entered the double doors at the main entrance where a few days ago she had waited for a taxi to take her home. In the center of the main lobby there was large information directory mounted on a black marble base. The maze of diagrams confused her. She glanced at her watch and then looked around for assistance.

An elderly woman in a pink smock sat behind the information desk on the other side of the lobby. It was unusually quiet for this time of day. Patricia's footsteps softly echoed when she walked over to the counter and asked the hospital volunteer for directions. The old woman was busily involved in a needlepoint project and didn't notice Patricia approach the booth. Patricia leaned over the counter.

"Excuse me, ma'am, where would Dr. Murdock's office be?"

The old woman finished her stitch, looked up, and pointed across the street and said, "There are doctors' offices over there."

"I'm sorry," she spoke louder. "I need the hospital administrator, Dr. Keith Murdock."

"The hospital's minister is at the end of that hall." The blue-haired lady pointed with her needle. "Wonderful man. You'll like him."

"When was the last time you checked you hearing aid batteries?" Patricia muttered sarcastically. Now flustered she checked her watch. *This is just great!* she thought. Patricia slapped the counter, spun on her heels, and made an intuitive guess as to where the office might be. The wing to the left of the information desk looked like it held the most promise. She spied a custodian working the hallway.

"Could you direct me to Dr. Keith Murdock's office?" Patricia pleaded.

The custodian was on his hands and knees cleaning a sticky spot on the floor. He struggled to his feet.

"Anything for a pretty lady. Just go straight to the end of the hall, turn left. Most of the offices are in that wing. Murdock is about halfway down the corridor. It'll be on your right."

"Thank you very much," Patricia said and hurried down the hall. The janitor watched her walk away.

"Mm-mm, I wish I had fries to go with that shake," he said quietly.

—

Patricia was ushered into Dr. Murdock's office by his secretary.

Murdock came around his desk and extended his hand.

"Come in, come in, Mrs. Duncan. Please, have a seat. I was just reviewing your file." Murdock went back to his chair. Patricia settled into a chair in front of his desk.

"Your application indicates you are fresh out of nursing school. Looks like you have good grades. Your recommendations are very good. What prompted you to apply to our facility? With your academic record, you could choose from several different hospitals. Why did you choose us?"

Patricia had already carefully thought out her response.

"Well, I certainly looked at other places, but I live relatively close, and I am familiar with the excellent reputation of this hospital. This is my first choice, and I feel I could have a long career here."

"Well, we could certainly use more people with that attitude," he replied. "It's hard to keep the same staff at a hospital these days. We try to offer an excellent working environment. But there are some areas where we just cannot compete with some of the larger surrounding hospitals. The pool of good nurses is a shallow one right now." He flipped back a page in her file. "I notice you listed no job experience. That seems to be about the only problem with your application. Have you ever held any type of job, even if it was just flipping burgers in the summer during your high school years?"

"No. I always concentrated on my studying, and I married at a young age."

Murdock was puzzled. "But according to this application, you are single."

"Yes, that is true. I lost my baby son and my husband in a car accident when we were on vacation in Missouri recently."

Murdock's face filled with sympathy.

"I'm so sorry."

"That's okay. I am just trying to rebuild my life. Starting over is not easy. It's been tough. But I realize it's just something I have to do."

Murdock dropped her folder back on his desk. He leaned back, looked out the window, and took a deep breath. After a pause he continued. "Well, we could really use the help." He slid a folder across the desk. "Look over this salary scale and list of benefits. Would you consider accepting the base salary and agree to a six month probationary period because of your lack of work experience?"

Patricia didn't even look at the folder of information. Her heart raced with excitement. "Sounds reasonable to me."

"But you didn't look at the salary scale."

"I'm not that concerned about the salary. I know it's fair. I just really want this job." As an after thought she added, "If I do get the job, I do have one small request."

"Let's hear it," said Murdock.

"I would like to return to using my maiden name, Jones. I know that sounds strange, but I'm trying to completely start my life over. I think it's kind of my way of finding closure with all that's happened recently."

"I think we can handle that…Miss Jones. If you are hired, we would have to use Duncan on your payroll information, social security card, and W-2s. We can't do much about that. But everything else can reflect Patricia Jones."

"That's wonderful. I know that sounds odd, but—"

"Not at all. I understand. I had a secretary a few years back who did a similar thing. She just wanted to start over, like you."

"Well, when will I know something about the job?"

"Let me complete a little paperwork. I'd say the job is yours. I'd say call the office next week, and I'll give you the details."

"I'll do it," Patricia said. She stood, shook hands with Murdock, and left the office. She had a big smile on her face as she exited the automatic doors at the hospital entrance. The interview had gone well, and she walked away at a happy, leisurely pace, this time enjoying the unseasonably cool and breezy morning. Once again she pulled the collar of her jacket up around her neck, still getting used to her newly cropped hair cut.

After walking a few blocks, she found herself turning up Washington Street. The oak trees were huge and evenly spaced down either side of the road. Acorns crackled under her feet with each step she made. Occasionally a green and yellow leaf spiraled to the ground. Patricia watched one leaf as it floated over the ornate wrought iron fence and landed momentarily on a tombstone then fell to the ground. The old graveyard, Little Oak Cemetery, was the focal point of her journey.

Patricia had found the letter from Ken on the living room floor a few days ago that described the burial site of their child. Despite her anger with Ken, she was grateful that the envelope included a rough hand-drawn map of the location. She entered through the main gate and pulled the letter from her purse as she walked. A well maintained gravel road connected various sections of the cemetery. Patricia consulted the map and determined that she should take the leftmost fork. The graveyard was a lonely, quiet place. She studied the area, feeling like she was on some sort of morbid treasure hunt. She was close to her quarry.

Differing emotions swirled within her heart. Her hands began to tremble. Then she saw some freshly disturbed sod. "That must be it!" She dropped the letter and ran to the marker. "It's beautiful." She gently placed her fingers over her lips and repeated the name that they had given to the child. "Anthony, oh little Anthony." She sank to her knees at the foot of the tiny gravesite. Picking up a handful of the freshly turned earth, she let the soil trickle out between her fingers. Patricia crawled forward and caressed the tombstone, tenderly cuddling the cold object as if it were her little child. But it could never be a substitute for the little soul buried there. Her bitter pain crushed in on her. Tears rolled down her face and dripped onto the cold stone.

Twenty minutes passed before Patricia regained her composure. She was still angry, indignant. The rage would not go away. Patricia forced herself to stand up and bid farewell.

"I love you, Anthony. I always will. I won't let them get away with this." She turned and walked away. After a few steps she stopped and looked back one last time from the entrance. Even from a distance, the small statue was touching. An angel with drooping wings and a bowed head. The inscription read, "Anthony Patrick Duncan - loved for an instant on earth - loved forever in heaven."

Patricia's feet ached by the time she returned home. It had been several weeks since she had done that much walking, and those last few strides seemed to be the most tiring. She unlocked her front door and announced her arrival as she stepped inside. Patricia went to the kitchen and pulled a can of beef stew from the cabinet. She shoved the family-sized can into the electric can opener. It spun around lazily, and the top popped open. Her nose wrinkled up.

"Oh man, smells like dog food," she griped. "Well, I guess it's better than nothing."

Patricia sank into the sofa. She got halfway through the bowl of stew, chased it with a beer, and eased back into the cushion. She placed the back of one hand on her head. Soon she grabbed a couch pillow and clutched it tightly. Too tired to get up, she stretched out on the couch and closed her eyes. Sleep did not come easily. Three hours passed, and she was still wide awake.

"This is ridiculous."

She forced herself up and went into the bathroom where she looked through the medicine cabinet.

"Woe, I haven't been in here in a while." She tossed the out-dated prescriptions into the trashcan. Anything labeled for Ken was automatically thrown away until she came to a bottle labeled carisoprodol. "A muscle relaxer from Ken's bricklaying accident. Wow, 350 milligrams. That will work. Thanks for leaving these, Ken, ol' buddy." She popped the cap and shook out three tablets. "I just want to sleep all night, not all week." She put two back in the bottle.

Stepping back into the living room, she spotted the bookshelf and thought, *Hey, maybe a good book would help, too.* She blindly pulled an old hardback book from the shelf, tucked it under her arm, and walked back down the hall to the bedroom. The old book's binding was almost torn away. Patricia tossed the book up near the headboard. It bounced to the floor unnoticed. She gathered the covers and folded them back, fluffed the pillow, and fell into bed. She tracked down the wayward book, retrieved it, flipped it right-side up, and opened it to the title page.

"Oh great, where did this old thing come from?" she asked herself sarcastically. "Of all the books in that shelf, I grab a Bible. Well, it doesn't get much more boring than this." Even though she opened the Bible, she never read a line. It tumbled again to the floor. Her drug-induced sleep came quickly. Even under the influence of the beer and medication, her sleep didn't last long. The neighborhood dogs barked continuously. The racing thoughts about her new nursing career then kicked in, and it was just too much for sleep to overcome.

The next morning, feeling ragged and nearly hungover, Patricia got out of bed and trudged to the kitchen. The first thing she did was grab the last beer from the refrigerator.

"A toast to life as it could be," she said to no one. She went to the table and plopped down in the chair. "Well now, what's a gal like me going to do this weekend?" She went through a checklist. "Let's see, I've got no friends, no husband, no baby, no nothing. Life is just grand!"

Just then the phone rang. Startled by the noise, Patricia jumped out of the chair and headed for the white wall phone.

"Hello."

"Miss Jones?"

"Yes."

"This is Dr. Keith Murdock from Hall Park General." Patricia's heart raced. "Yes, sir, Dr. Murdock. How are you?"

"Fine. Listen, after careful consideration I think you would be a great fit for the nursing position we talked about. I would like to offer you employment with us if you're still interested."

"Yes, sir. I'm still interested. Yes, sir." Patricia tried to sound calm, but it wasn't working.

"Good. Well, when would you be able to start?"

"Today or whenever you need me."

Murdock thought for a moment. "Okay, what about today? We need the help, and the sooner you get into the system the better. Today we could handle all the paperwork then talk about policies and procedures. Then we can start getting you familiar with your co-workers and work area."

"Great. I will get there as soon as I can. Would eleven o'clock be satisfactory?"

"That would be fine. See you then."

"Yes, see you then. Thank you so much. Goodbye."

Patricia gently put the receiver back in its cradle, leaned her head back, and closed her eyes.

"Yes!" she exclaimed. She waltzed away from the kitchen toward her bedroom. She selected a classy looking blue dress and put it on. Unsure of her duties on the first day, she grabbed her nicest nurse's scrubs and packed them in a bag in case they would be needed. She stood in front of the mirror, taking extra time to blow dry and style her hair. She went to great pains to highlight her beauty mark. Patricia hadn't spent this much time primping since her high-school prom. She raced the clock, constantly checking the time. She needed to be out the door by 9:30 at the latest in order to make that great first impression.

Suddenly she panicked. "Where is my purse?" She frantically looked for it. "Not on the counter. What did I do with it?" She walked from room to room, retracing her steps and then remembered hanging it on her bathroom door knob.

She lifted it off the knob and quickly pulled out the smaller wallet. The change compartment was empty. Panic nearly set in, but then she remembered her change jar on the dresser and ran into the bedroom. *I'm so glad Ken didn't take this,* she thought. She dumped the contents out on the dresser top and picked out all the quarters. *Super! This ought to help on bus fair for my first week.* She reassembled her purse, finished getting ready, and left her house ahead of schedule.

—

Patricia arrived at the hospital about forty-five minutes early. She bought a soft drink at the cafeteria and sipped on it, occasionally crunching pieces of the small crushed ice between her teeth. To kill time she read the hospital newsletter posted on a long bulletin board in the hall. A few feet away, somebody yelled a name over and over. It was about to drive her crazy.

"Elizabeth, Elizabeth." The person called out one more time. "Elizabeth." This time she felt a tap on her shoulder. Patricia pivoted on both feet and turned completely around. "Oh, I am sorry. I mistook you for a doctor that works here. I wondered why you weren't in uniform. You're not related to Dr. Elizabeth Shircliff, are you? Your hair color, your features. You could pass for her sister." The stranger cocked his head sideways and with a bewildered look on his face, said, "Say, have I seen you here before? You look familiar."

"I really doubt it," replied Patricia.

"Well, maybe it is just the resemblance. Are you sure we haven't met before?"

"I doubt it. Today is my first day," she quickly replied

"So, you mean you'll be working here?" the doctor asked.

She nodded affirmatively.

"Then I'm glad I am here for your inauguration."

"Is that a pickup line?" she asked, smiling.

"I don't know. Is it?"

Neither knew what to say next.

The man extended his hand and introduced himself. "I'm Dr. Vanhouse. Robert Vanhouse, emergency medicine, at your service."

Switching her drink to her left hand, she returned the handshake. "My name is … Patricia Jones," she said, using her new identity successfully for the first time.

"Where are you assigned?"

"Well, I am not sure. There are two openings. I have an appointment with Dr. Murdock at eleven o'clock to discuss my choices."

"I could use an assistant!"

"Is that another pickup line?"

"Oh, I hope so."

Then his beeper sang its annoying tune, icing the red-hot start of the relationship. Vanhouse turned and trotted to the stairwell. He looked over his shoulder and said, "Very pleased to meet you." Patricia returned a smile and a childish five-finger wave.

Hey, the disguise worked! He didn't even recognize me. Kind of a handsome guy. Patricia looked at her watch and decided it was time to go to her appointment. She walked down the hall in the opposite direction, toward the elevators.

—

Murdock walked from his desk and stood in front of his secretary.

"I am going down to the cafeteria. I'm having a chocolate attack. Would you like me to get you something? My treat."

"Well, you must be having a really wonderful day if you are buying! I guess I could use some orange juice."

"Consider it so. Hold down the fort." Murdock paused just as he was about to step into the hall. "Oh, I almost forgot. I have an appointment at eleven. If I am a little late, just make her feel at home and explain that your boss is a chocoholic."

She smiled. "Sure."

He walked to the elevator and caught a ride down to the basement. The doors parted, and Patricia stood there waiting for the elevator to take her to the main floor. Even though they had only met once, the two recognized each other.

"Miss Dunc…Jones! What a coincidence. Say, I might be a little late for our appointment. Would you like to reschedule our meeting in the cafeteria?"

"How nice of you to remember the name thing. Well, you're the boss," she said, smiling as they walked back to the cafeteria. On the way Keith introduced her to all the items she had just recently discovered for herself like the bulletin board, vending machines, and restrooms. Patricia pretended like it was all new to her. The two sat at a booth, and Keith talked of specifics about the different jobs.

"I don't know where your career interests lie," said Murdock. "But like I said we have a couple of openings, and they are in two different areas. The first is in our oncology department. Dr. Lin Hoi is currently in charge over there. He is extremely talented and really keeps abreast of the current advances in treatments and pain management, which is no easy task. The only problem working under him is that you have to listen very closely when he speaks. His English is not that good. However, if you can work through the linguistics, he is an excellent teacher. The second job, the one I would recommend, is up in OB/GYN. Women are so much more comfortable being cared for by women. That is one of the reasons we appointed Dr. Elizabeth Shircliff to head that department. She has made several changes that I believe have really benefited the patients and their families. I think you would enjoy working under her. She'll bring out the best in you. She is an excellent supervisor and a wonderful teacher. But don't let my opinions sway your thinking. Once you decide which position you prefer, we can get you started."

"It's an easy decision. I focused my studies in prenatal and neonatal care. I would love to work with moms and newborns. In fact, I'm familiar with Dr. Shircliff."

"Where do you know her from?"

"I don't know her personally. I've just watched her work. We've never been formally introduced."

"Well, I'll see that changes. Tomorrow I'll take you up on the floor. You'll meet Dr. Shircliff, and we'll get you settled in. You and the nursing supervisor can work out your hours and training schedule. Right now, let's take you over to personnel and get your paperwork filled out. Then we'll get the employee handbook and protocol manuals."

"Sounds real good to me!" said Patricia, anxious to get started. Excitement rushed through Patricia's body. She was fearful and excited at the same time. *Okay, here we go! If Shircliff doesn't recognize me, I'll be home free.*

—

The first couple of days at Hall Park General passed quickly. Since Patricia was the rookie nurse, she found herself subjected to very unusual scheduling. She was assigned to work on each shift at some point during the week. At least for this day she drew a decent time slot from five till midnight. She reported to work earlier than necessary.

"You must be the new gal," remarked the nurse at the desk.

"Hi. I'm Patricia Jones," she said, interjecting her new name once again.

"Hi. They call me Tank. I reckon it might have a little to do with my size. You can call me that, too. It doesn't bother me. I like to eat! In fact, if you ever bring doughnuts to work, I'll be your friend for life."

Patricia didn't know how to respond to this oversized co-worker, so she just smiled politely.

"How long you going to stand there with that silly grin on your face." Tank handed her a few folders. "While you're waiting, file these in that rack over there. The head nurse will be back in just a few minutes. She won't waste any time in giving you an assignment. You can count on that. She is retired army."

"Thanks for the warning. I'll keep sharp." Patricia stowed the files and then tried to look busy.

"You catch on real quick, soldier." Tank laughed aloud. "Oh hey, you're off the hook for a while. Here comes Dr. Shircliff. Have you met her?"

"No, not yet. Somehow our schedules haven't jived."

Tank stood up. "Dr. Shircliff, I'd like to introduce you to … uh … " The resemblance between Elizabeth Shircliff and Patricia stopped him cold.

"Patricia Jones." Patricia's stomach churned with anger. She fought the urge to slap Dr. Shircliff. Instead she extended her hand. *Smile, Patricia, smile.*

"Glad to have you with us," Shircliff said as she and Patricia shook hands. "Do I know you from somewhere? You look awfully familiar."

Patricia's anxiety level and blood pressure spiked. "No, I don't think so."

"Man, you two could be sisters," Tank said.

Shircliff dismissed the observation, staying focused on the business at hand. "Oh well, anyway, we've got your file. And I hope that I'll be able to spend a few moments with you very soon. I like to do a short initial training period and then periodic reviews with all my staff at least once a year. But none of that will happen today. Glad you're here." Shircliff selected a patient file and walked away. Relief flooded over Patricia. It was all she could do to keep her knees from buckling under her, but she kept her composure. Revenge would come. She would celebrate later.

"She's really nice. Once you get to know her, you'll like her," reassured Tank.

Patricia nodded, burning inside.

9

Rebecca had slept well. The first noises she was cognizant of came early in the morning. A nurse appeared at the doorway with the breakfast cart.

"Mrs. Wells, I have your breakfast. Ready or not, here it comes." She sat the covered dish on the rolling bed tray. "How's it feel to have somebody else cook the meal for a change?"

"Oh, I guess I should count it as a blessing. I usually cook for seven."

"My lands! Five children are enough to put anybody in the hospital."

"Six if you count my husband."

"And you're fixing to add one more to the count."

The nurse positioned the table so Rebecca could reach her tray comfortably and eat. She was about to continue the conversation when she noticed Rebecca praying over her morning meal. Instead she said nothing else and quietly left.

Thirty minutes after breakfast another nurse tapped on her door.

"Hello, Mrs. Wells, my name is Patricia. I came in and turned off your television last night. I didn't want to wake you, so I saved the introduction for now. She checked

Rebecca's wrist bracelet to confirm her identity. "I'm sure we will be seeing a lot of each other. In fact, you'll probably get tired of me." She checked Rebecca's pulse rate and blood pressure then pulled out Rebecca's arm and wrapped a rubber tube around it just above the elbow. "I need some blood samples from you. All I can do is promise that it won't hurt me a bit," joked Patricia.

Rebecca stared at the young nurse. "They're taking more blood?" Patricia brushed the hair out of her eyes and then Rebecca inquired. "Have we met before?"

"Don't think so, unless maybe you babysat me sometime," she said, making the obvious connection between their ages.

"Give me a break. I am not that old. You really do look familiar. I remember faces. Tell me about yourself," requested Rebecca.

"Here is my personal profile. There is really not much exciting going on in my life. I am an Oklahoma girl. I'm pretty much a homebody. I eat, sleep, work, and then repeat the process."

Patricia stuck the needle in Rebecca's arm, and the test tubes filled quickly with blood.

Rebecca looked away but still kept the conversation going. "Where do you go to church?"

"Oh, I went to a pancake supper at a church once. Does that count?" Patricia grew uncomfortable with all the questions and chose to remain distant as she tidied up the table and small dresser in the room.

"Do you have any brothers or sisters?" asked Rebecca.

"Do you need any ice?" asked Patricia as she passed over Rebecca's question.

Rebecca feared she had somehow offended the young nurse and asked nothing more.

There was a tap at the door.

"Come in," said Rebecca.

Patricia used the opportunity to exit. But as she pulled open the door, there stood Dr. Vanhouse. Patricia blushed.

"I assume you're here to see the patient?" Patricia winked and brushed past the doctor as she left the room.

Dr. Vanhouse was caught off guard by the flirtatious comment. He couldn't come up with a line before she was out of sight. He stepped inside.

"Mrs. Wells?" he asked.

"Yes?"

"Hi, you may remember me from the ER. I am Dr. Vanhouse."

"Oh, yes. How are you?"

"Fine. I talked to Dr. Crawford, and he said he would probably admit you. Anyway, I just stopped to say hi and to see how you were doing." Vanhouse pulled her chart and was reviewing it while they talked.

"I always check up on my patients. If I see you in the ER, I'll always see you later if you end up being admitted here."

"Well, that is so kind of you to take the time," Rebecca said. "You don't have to."

"That's just part of small town hospital care. I wouldn't be able to do this at a larger metropolitan hospital. Besides, I really enjoy this."

"I just wish all doctors were as cordial as you."

"Thank you, ma'am. How are you feeling today?"

"I'm exhausted from boredom," Rebecca said.

"Oh, I know. And you've got a long haul ahead of you."

"I hope it is only a few days. I'd love to be home before too long."

Vanhouse continued reading her chart as they talked. "I bet everything will be just fine, and you'll be home barbequing hamburgers and baking pies with plenty of summer left."

Vanhouse didn't write anything on the chart, but he did jot a few notes concerning the information on a smaller pad of paper that he pulled from his pocket. "Your chart looks good, and so do you," Vanhouse proclaimed. He closed the book and placed the note in his right jacket pocket.

"Thanks for stopping by," Rebecca said.

"You're welcome. I'm sure I'll see you again," Vanhouse said as he turned

and walked out. He had only been gone a few minutes when Elizabeth Shircliff came by on her rounds to check up on Rebecca.

"Mrs. Wells, how are you feeling?"

"That is the same question Dr. Vanhouse just asked me."

"Vanhouse?" Shircliff questioned.

"Yes, he just stopped by to say hi and see how I was doing. He seems like such a nice guy."

"Robert is a great person and a good surgeon. He has been on staff for several years and, you're right, he is a likable guy."

Shircliff retrieved the chart and added her update.

"Mrs. Wells, your test results are almost complete. We want to compare the blood work this morning to some of the previous tests. We will watch you closely. I don't like to give expectant mothers medication, but in your case it will be necessary. The medication will be given three times daily, and it should keep you stable. The bad news is that we can't let you go home until after that baby gets here, but I think you probably already suspected that."

"I guess you might say that." Rebecca sighed as she leaned back on her pillow.

—

George Mason had been a concern for Vanhouse. The power line worker had been seriously injured from a twenty-five foot fall. Robert had knitted him back together as best he could, but his injuries were extensive with a lacerated spleen, broken ribs, and cracked vertebrae being among the most serious. Mason was expected to recover but only after surgeries and a long period of recovery. The morphine drip he was attached to only took the edge off the pain.

Robert knocked lightly and entered the room.

"Mr. Mason?" he asked in a quiet voice in case he was asleep. The curtain was drawn around Mason's bed. Robert walked around the bed and pulled back the curtain.

Jimmy Wyatt jerked around. He jumped out of the chair and faced Vanhouse.

"You! What do you think you're doing?" Robert exclaimed. Then he noticed the tourniquet around Wyatt's left bicep and the syringe in his right hand. A small stream of blood trickled from the needle puncture site. His empty gaze and glazed eyes told the story. Wyatt had been siphoning the morphine from Mason's automatic pump line and injecting himself.

Wyatt grabbed a handful of tubing. "Okay, Doc, what's it gonna be? Save the patient or mess with me?" He yanked the tubing from Mason's IV bags and critical oxygen supply. Wyatt darted toward the door. Robert lunged at him, planting his head into Wyatt's chest and wrapping his arms around him. The two men flew into the corner of the room, crashing over the bedside table. The flowers and pitcher of water that had been there were thrown against the wall.

"Help!" Robert attempted to get the attention of anyone out in the hall. The clinched bodies wrestled on. Wyatt tried to free himself from his captor with a burst of strength. Vanhouse's grip would not loosen, and the two men fell together. Wyatt struck his head on the bed. The sharp corner dug deep into his head, flinging blood onto Vanhouse's white coat. When they tumbled to the floor, Wyatt's head cracked as it hit the tile. It sounded like a pumpkin splatting on concrete. His body went limp. Blood began pooling under his body from the head wound.

Two nurses rushed into the room, having heard the battle. Robert was bent over Wyatt's body, checking for signs of life. "He's still breathing. Get a gurney in here!" One of the nurses immediately exited.

The remaining nurse put her hand on Vanhouse's shoulder. "Oh my God! Doctor, are you okay?"

"I'm fine. Check on Mr. Mason," Vanhouse said, pointing up to the patient. He looked over at Wyatt. Robert placed his fingers at the side of his throat. There was a faint pulse.

Security personnel arrived and took over the scene. People had crowded into the room and overflowed into the hallway. Everyone was eager to find out what had happened.

"All right, folks, let's clear the area," ordered one of the uniforms.

Vanhouse gave orders also. "Move the patient out of here. He doesn't need this stress."

"Okay, but everything else stays as it is. This room is now a crime scene."

Vanhouse slumped back against the wall, exhausted.

—

Keith Murdock, Lieutenant Steele, and Robert Vanhouse were all seated in Murdock's office. Wyatt's return was the topic of conversation.

"Well, I've certainly spent more than a little time here lately," Steele began.

"No offense, Lieutenant, but I would just as soon not see you," Murdock responded. "Robert, how are you? Are you doing okay?"

"I'm fine. I still can't believe he tried that in the middle of the day."

"Hey, drug addicts need their fix all the time," the lieutenant explained. "It doesn't surprise me in the least. I've had guys shooting up on street corners during the day. Wyatt just worked here and knew the layout. He thought he would be safe."

Murdock looked over at Vanhouse. "What about Dr. Vanhouse here. Will you need him any further? I thought I would send him home for the day."

Steele shook his head. "No. We've gotten his statement. He's in the clear. We're sure what happened. Wyatt was stealing morphine, and Dr. Vanhouse here walked in on him. We'll have to file it with the DA, but I don't expect anything further to happen."

"Hmm, I wonder if he could have had anything to do with Bonnie Rowden's death?" Murdock said.

"I guess it's going to be hard to get any more information from Wyatt without offering him drugs," quipped Lieutenant Steele. Vanhouse chuckled. He had not said very much during the meeting.

Murdock turned to Vanhouse. "Robert, I'm sending you home. Take this afternoon off, and tomorrow, too."

"I'm really okay," Vanhouse responded. "I've seen a lot of combat, but I've never been that closely involved before. I'd like to keep working if that's all right. It will be good to keep busy."

Murdock leaned back in his chair, placing his hands behind his head.

"Robert, it was clearly an accident. Besides, you didn't kill him. He just cracked his skull, and that was it." Murdock paused and then continued. "Well, there is really no policy for this type of case. I'm going to insist you go home today. But I'll let you be the judge about any further time off."

Robert rose from his chair, shook hands, and left the office.

"Awfully calm, isn't he?" Murdock observed.

"People respond differently, I guess," Steele said. "Keep an eye on him for a while just to be sure he's okay. I'm sure he will be fine."

—

The arena was full, standing room only. Wyatt was sprawled across the canvass mat. Robert stood over him with one foot planted triumphantly in the middle of Wyatt's chest. The referee raised Robert's gloved hand in the air, signifying that he was the champion. The crowd went wild.

Patricia ran into the center of the ring and threw her arms around Robert's neck. He scooped her up and began to carry her out of the ring. The crowd roared. Robert looked over his shoulder as some army medics were taking Wyatt's limp body away on a canvas stretcher. One of the medics waved at Robert.

"I'll take care of him! Don't worry!" the medic yelled above the clamor of the audience.

"David!" Robert exclaimed.

"Don't worry!" repeated David.

Robert watched as the medics dumped Wyatt's body over the ropes. The body plopped on top of a pile of dead soldiers. Robert turned back around and continued his triumphant walk out of the ring. He glanced down at Patricia, but instead of seeing her pretty face, he saw the face of a soldier.

"Sergeant Branch!"

Robert bolted upright, his heart exploding out of his chest. His breathing was almost uncontrollable. He rolled out of bed and stumbled to the bathroom. He washed his face in cold water. A glance at the clock... 5:00 a.m. He decided to report to work early to try and forget.

—

The morning had zipped by uneventfully. Robert was thankful for that. After yesterday's excitement, he needed a quiet day. Now he needed lunch.

The cafeteria was crowded as usual at lunch time. He pushed the tray down the line while he scanned the room for Patricia and tried to make his food selections at the same time.

"Dr. Vanhouse, would you like a salad today?" asked the waiting cafeteria worker.

"Huh? Oh sure, and the chicken fried steak if you've got it."

"Coming right up." The old woman served his request. "Here you go. Looking for anybody in particular?"

Vanhouse looked at her and smiled. "Caroline, as a matter of fact, I was looking for a new nurse who just started a few days ago. She looks a little bit like Dr. Shircliff. Short, red hair."

"Look behind you. I think she just walked in."

"Thanks!" Vanhouse picked up his tray and went back to the beginning of the line where Patricia had just started ordering her meal. He stepped in line behind her.

"Hey there. I saw you come in, and I just thought I would see how you were doing."

She smiled at him. "Hi. I still have lots to learn, but I think I'm off to a pretty good start." They moved down the line to the register.

"Hey, if you need a tutor, I'm available. I'll tell you what, I will buy you lunch, and we can sit down and talk."

"Can't refuse a deal like that," replied Patricia.

Vanhouse paid for both meals, and then the couple sat at a table for two.

After exchanging conversation on the usual first date, get acquainted topics, Vanhouse suddenly asked, "Hey, you'll have to forgive me if I seem a bit forward, but what would you think about spending the day with me? Murdock has wanted me to take a day off anyway," he elaborated. "I thought it would be fun to goof off. Go to some antique shops. Go out to eat. What do you say to that? I'm not saying skip work. I mean as soon as you have some free time."

"I heard about what happened. Are you okay?" she asked.

"Yep, I'm doing fine. So what do you say?" he asked again.

He waited for the response. She smiled. "Would it bother you too much if I said ... Okay?"

"Great. Oh, there is one problem. I don't know where you live."

Patricia smoothed out her napkin, drew a simple map, and wrote her phone number across the top. "This should help."

Vanhouse grabbed up the napkin, folded it, and stuffed it in his shirt pocket.

"I'll keep this close to my heart."

———

"Code blue! Code blue! Room 268!"

Elizabeth Shircliff tossed her clipboard on the counter as she sprinted down the hall. *That's Mrs. Crane. How could that be?* Elizabeth thought. *I checked on her only an hour ago.*

Myrna Crane had required surgery to repair an abdominal aneurysm.

Elizabeth bounced off the door jamb as she entered the room.

"No pulse or respirations!" exclaimed a nurse. She continued trying to find a radial pulse with her stethoscope. Another nurse was doing chest compressions. "She's not responding at all! Crash cart is on the way!"

The two women automatically prepared the patient for defibrillation. The crash cart entered the room, along with two more nurses. Electrodes were attached to the patient's chest. Someone else covered her face with a mask and helped her with respirations.

"Clear!" ordered Shircliff. She placed the pads and pushed the button. The patient's body jerked off the bed. No signs of life came back.

"Up the voltage. Clear!" Shircliff yelled again. Again, the body jerked from the jolt of electricity. And again, no response.

"One more time. Come on, three's a charm!" The body jerked for a third time with no results. The patient was gone.

The room was quiet. The nurses began removing leads and putting equipment back on the crash cart. Shircliff leaned on the bed railing. It is never easy to lose a patient, but it is worse when the death is a surprise.

Patricia had raced down the hall to room 268 from the elevator. Lunch with Vanhouse was interrupted by the code. "What do you think happened, Doctor?" she asked Shircliff.

"I don't know. I was sure I repaired the aneurysm. I guess she might have thrown a clot or had internal bleeding. Who knows?" Shircliff said.

Or maybe you messed up another one, Shircliff, Patricia thought secretly. She stood in the doorway breathing heavily.

—

Jeff Hibbitts was standing and gazing at the spring day outside. Robert Vanhouse was seated on the sofa on the other side of the office.

"Thanks for meeting with me again, Jeff," Robert said.

"It's no problem at all, Robert. I want to help. These dreams must really eat at you." Jeff turned to look at Robert's face to gauge his response.

"I'm not going to lie to you," Robert said. "These dreams are bothersome, no question about it. Sometimes they are battle scenes, and then there will be a dream with a nurse, a babe, and I'll be taken in by her beauty."

"I've seen a lot of guys with issues related to the war in Vietnam," Dr. Hibbitts said.

That was encouraging to Robert. He didn't feel quite so alone. "So, what can you tell me about dreams?" he asked.

Jeff walked over and sat in one of the office chairs near the sofa.

"Wow, that's a big question. I'll see if I can give you the Cliffs Notes version. It seems like maybe your fears or war experience may be a trigger for the nightmares. There are many different theories about dreams. It seems to me that the only thing that the experts agree upon is that they can't agree."

"Great," Robert said. "So we don't know a whole lot about this, do we?"

Hibbitts continued. "The fascination with dreams dates back thousands of years. In Bible times they were looked upon as predictors of future events. Even today some people believe this still happens. Then there is déjà vu. A person may have a dream and after a period of time, live through that same dream experience. I'm under the impression that these dreams might be a way of your unconscious state trying to get you to address or confront a problem area in your life. The continued recurrence of these nightmares may have something to do with your inability to cope with something in your past. I'm guessing that it's your battle experience in Vietnam. Is there something in Vietnam that sticks out as a particularly significant event?"

"No. It was all pretty bad," Robert responded.

Hibbitts looked at his watch. "Oh man, I've got a patient coming in about five minutes. I'm sorry, Robert. Why don't we set up a formal appointment, and we can talk longer."

"Maybe I will sometime. In the meantime, I'll try to remember anything of importance from Nam. If I think of something, I'll come talk to you about it." Robert stood up and made his way to the door. "Thanks again, Jeff. This has been a big help."

"You bet. Keep me updated on what's going on with these dreams of yours. We'll try to get to the bottom of it."

The two doctors parted company, one thinking about his next patient, the other thinking about his dreams and about a woman.

Robert pondered his meeting with Hibbits. A talk with his brother might provide a way to sort things out. Even though Robert had trouble talking to his brother, it was time. He felt compelled to visit, especially in light of the conversation with his friend, Dr. Hibbits. And besides, he had more tapes for his brother to transcribe.

Robert pulled into the circle drive, slammed on his brakes, and skidded to a stop. If the outside of his mother's house was any indicator of David fulfilling his responsibilities, then David was failing with his duties. He tapped the horn a couple of times, grabbed a box full of tapes, and walked to the porch. Normally the front door was locked. Robert twisted the knob and found that not to be the case today.

"Hello," he yelled as he stepped into the small entry. "Mom … David? Hey, it's Robert."

Odd, no reply. Surely they heard me. Robert made his way into the den and sat in a wingback chair. He opened the box and considered any special instructions to give David. After perusing his notes, he found no additional information required. He scanned the room. *House keeping's not too shabby.*

He picked up a beer can off the maple coffee table beside him, lifted it up, and hollered, "Okay, David, I know you're here. You left your evidence lying around. Come on into the den. We need to talk." Robert heard creaking on the floor above.

"Look, David, I don't care if you come down. I want you to know something. I'm going to keep talking." The talk was more of a lecture than anything else. "I realize your burden and I'm sorry. But you have got to make this deal work. Mom needs round the clock care. No sense calling in hospice since we are both doctors. I'm sorry you have to see her waste away. Just keep her comfortable, and if you need anything, let me know. I assume things are going well since you haven't called me. I brought another set of notes on cassette that I need transcribed. You're a little behind, so I'll try to come mow the yard soon." David still did not comment. Only the creaking floor upstairs betrayed the silence.

"Okay. I know you're not real happy with this set up, but I don't know any alternative. I think this is the best I could do for you. Look, I'm sorry, we will talk later." Robert left in a hurry, before David could react.

10

CHAPTER

Vanhouse turned up the volume on his radio and tapped the steering wheel to the beat of an old Beach Boys tune. He pulled his 1957 fire engine red Corvette into Patricia's driveway and honked the horn. He got out and walked up the sidewalk. On the way to her front door, he tucked in his blue denim shirt, tightened his belt one extra notch, and pulled up on the waist of his blue jeans.

Patricia heard the honk and met him on the porch. She was wearing a nice black skirt and an apricot sleeveless sweater twin set.

"Hey, pretty lady. You look great! I forgot to tell you there was no need to dress up."

"I can change," she replied and even stepped back toward the door.

He grabbed her arm. "No, that's fine as long as you're comfortable."

"Well, okay, but I do need to go get my purse anyway."

"No need for a purse. This date is all on me."

"Oh, I must take my purse. I feel naked without it. Besides, it has all my worldly possessions, like my house key and lipstick."

"How could I refuse you those luxuries?" He chuckled.

Vanhouse waited, and when Patricia returned he escorted her to the Corvette and opened the car door for her.

"Oh my, so much a gentleman!" Patricia exclaimed.

"You bring out the best in me," he replied.

"Do you have a line for everything?"

"I really mean it. I have never met anyone like you. I've never been so comfortable around a woman. I knew the first second we met that you were special. Pardon me, but I really find you to be an intriguing individual, and your good looks are just a bonus."

Patricia smiled. "You do have a line for everything."

"Let's get rolling." Robert started the Corvette, and the radio played. "Hope you like oldies."

"Anything but country and western."

"Look at that, we already have at least one thing in common," he replied. "I can't stand country either."

He continued to make small talk while they traveled. "You're really going to love the cafe I've selected. I just know you will."

His look was directed toward her more than the road. Occasionally Patricia would gasp or jerk, and he took that as a hint to pay attention to the driving, but she never verbally complained about his recklessness because she drank in the attention. With every gaze she felt drawn closer, intimately closer.

"So where are we going?"

"Antique Alley. Ever been there?"

"Nope. Sounds great though."

The section of town known as Antique Alley had been one of the first residential areas built in the city. The old restored two story wood frame homes with large maple and sprawling elm trees in the front yards had been transformed into a dozen antique shops, a couple of law offices, two bed and breakfast inns, and, in the center of it all, Gail's Tea Cup, a coffee shop known for its huge cups of cappuccino, excellent lasagnas, and unique quiche recipes. The off-white paint, the green-shuttered windows, and perfectly manicured lawn drew customers in the door, and then the excellent food kept them there.

Gail's was the first stopping place for the couple. They entered the establishment. A tiny brass bell dangled above the door, announcing their arrival. Gail herself smiled and greeted the new arrivals.

"Table for two?" she inquired.

"Yes. Something quiet, please," Robert replied.

She led them to a little round ice cream parlor style table in the corner, which was small enough to provide a romantic dining atmosphere. Gail removed an extra chair, passed out the single page menu, and lit a small lavender candle on the table.

"I will let you two look over the menu while I wait on some other people."

"This is much nicer than our first meal together," remarked Patricia as she looked around, marveling at the unusual decor.

"This is a neat place, and there is no contest when comparing the food here with the hospital cafeteria. I enjoy looking at all the antiques they decorate this place with. In the back room they have a booth that has upholstered commodes for seating at one of the tables."

"You're kidding." Patricia laughed. "I have got to see that before we leave."

"I will give you the grand tour of this whole area. There are some really neat gadgets in some of these shops. Every now and then I find some really crazy stuff. One of these places had a harmonica that worked like a player piano. You blow in the mouthpiece and turn a crank that rolls a paper that was perforated to play a tune."

"I could tell you liked old stuff when you pulled up in that 'vette."

As the evening progressed, Patricia and Robert really enjoyed each other's companionship. They talked about their likes and dislikes as they walked through all but two of the shops.

The sun moved closer to the horizon. "It'll be getting dark soon. Are you ready to call it an evening?" asked Vanhouse.

"We don't really have to." After a pause Patricia added hopefully, "How about you take me back to my house, and I'll fix supper?"

"I don't know, that depends. I have a couple of questions. What are we going to prepare? And are you a good cook?" Vanhouse smiled so that Patricia would know he was just joking.

She picked up on his teasing. "I make a great ham sandwich. But seriously, I think I have a couple of steaks. How about a steak and baked potato?"

"Now you're talking to my taste buds. Can't go wrong with a menu like that."

The two left the antique district, walking hand in

hand back to his car, acting more like a teenage couple on their first big date. As they approached the passenger side, he twirled her around, and they ended up in an intimate embrace. She licked her lips, moistening them, waiting for a kiss. Her body tingled with excitement.

Robert opened the car door. The kiss didn't come. Disappointed, Patricia slipped slowly from his grip into the leather bucket seat, yet she knew Robert was to be the new man in her life.

—

The next day Robert whistled, "Hey, sexy! Where are you going?"

Patricia blushed. She recognized the voice, stopped, and waited.

"Hurry up, Robert."

Robert jogged a few steps and wasted no time. "You think you could fit a wonderful, romantic dinner into your busy social calendar this evening?"

"Well, that depends. What did you have in mind?"

"I thought we might venture out to Lake Thunderbird and grab a bite at the Clear Bay Café. It's right on the water with a nice deck. I guarantee you'll love it."

"Let me check my schedule." Patricia put her hands together and opened them like a daily planner. "Let me see here," she said as she scanned the imaginary book. "Okay, it just so happens that I have no appointments for the next thirty years."

"Maybe I'll need to do something about that. For starters I'll pick you up at six. We have to be out there early. We don't want to miss the sunset."

Patricia glanced at her watch. "Wow, I'll barely have time to get ready. See ya soon."

Robert grabbed her hand. "Hey, you almost forgot my goodbye kiss."

They kissed passionately. Patricia tenderly pushed away.

"Whew, if that was a goodbye kiss, I can hardly wait for the hello."

—

Robert was quick to pick up his date. The trip to the café was beautiful. Scrub oaks intertwined with one another as they battled with the tall pine and cedar trees for turf. A deer darted across the road, narrowly missing Robert's front bumper.

"That was a close one," Robert said. He pointed ahead. "Look up there." A couple of red-tailed hawks circled lazily above.

The asphalt road wound back and forth, rising and falling over gentle hills. Robert revved the powerful Corvette engine and depressed the clutch as he pulled into the lot. It was a flashy show to the patrons seated outside on the tiered deck.

"Here it is. Clear Bay Café. What do you think?" Robert walked around the car and opened Patricia's door.

"Perfect. You were right. It's really nice," Patricia said as she stepped out of the car.

"It's better than perfect. The food's good, and you can't beat the view. I like to watch the boats come and go. And the sunsets are awesome."

"You left out one of the most important things."

"What's that?"

"Me," quipped Patricia.

"Oh yeah, you're right. I almost forgot. And then of course there's … me."

Patricia elbowed him. "Okay, Dr. Vainhouse, come down off your pedestal. Let's go eat."

The couple sat on the lower deck. A gentle vapor of water fogged over them from sprayers lining the upper deck framing.

"Robert, this has been everything you said it would be."

"Well, I really like it here."

"I suppose you've brought other women out here before."

"Believe it or not, the only other woman I've brought here is my mother."

Patricia was astonished. "You're mother? I'd like to meet her sometime."

"Oh, she's not doing well. In fact, my brother takes care of her."

"You're brother? How many more secrets are you keeping from me?"

The conversation turned serious. "Well, it really is a sort of a secret, and I'd like you to keep it that way."

"I don't understand," Patricia said expectantly.

Robert grabbed her hand and looked into her eyes. "Look, I'll make a long story short. My mother is an invalid. I have a twin brother who is also a doctor. We served in the army together. He went AWOL. I arranged for him to come to the States a few months ago. It was about that time mom became totally bedridden and dependent on us.

I made a deal with my brother. If he would stay confined to her house, then I would take care of him. You can't tell anybody, or he will be in Leavenworth for a long time. I don't mean to be so mysterious. I know we haven't known each other very long, but I feel like our relationship is going somewhere, and I thought you deserved the truth. I don't want anything to stand between us. I know I can trust you. Kind of strange, huh?"

Look at her. She thinks I'm nuts. Why did I tell her all of that? I must be crazy about this girl, or just crazy.

Patricia paused for a moment and sighed. Robert's story was intense. Possibly too intense. Part of her wondered whether she should get caught up in all he was saying. But more than that she figured she should just chill. She didn't want to blow this. Not now. She liked him too much.

"No, not at all," she finally responded. "I understand. That's got to be a difficult situation."

"I'm not proud of it," Robert continued. "I could probably get in trouble. My brother would be court-martialed, and I guess I would be fined or jailed or something for harboring my criminal brother."

"I'd still like to meet them sometime."

"Maybe. I don't see them that often." A few seconds went by, then Robert said, "Let's just keep it you and me for now."

Robert put his arm around her shoulders and drew her close. The light breeze blew through her hair. She leaned her head next to his, and they drank in the view. "You know we should come out here again. We should check out Calypso Cove some time."

"What's that?"

"It's a boat dock, but I know the owner. I thought we might rent a boat and cruise the lake."

"Are you serious?"

"Yep, I think we would have a great time. Actually, I was just thinking how good you would look in a swimsuit."

Robert and Patricia continued to talk long after finishing their meal. In fact, they stayed until the workers began putting chairs on the tables and emptying the trash.

"Guess that's our queue to vamonos."

—

Vanhouse pulled into her driveway. Patricia leaned over and gave him a kiss on his cheek.

"This has been a great evening. You are too good to me."

"It's easy to be good to somebody like you." They stood toe to toe and stared at each other. Patricia melted on the inside. She wanted to kiss him but patiently waited for him to make the first move. It drove her crazy to hold back, so she broke the awkward stillness by taking off her glasses and turning slightly to one side.

"I am going to change into some more comfortable clothes. Why don't you put on some music? The system is over there."

Patricia walked down the hall to her bedroom. Deep down she hoped Robert would forget about the music and follow her. She looked over her shoulder just to see if her dream would come true. No luck.

Once in her room, Patricia straightened a few things. She picked up some dirty clothes and tossed them into the hamper. She shoved in a couple of dresser drawers that protruded then tried to decide what to change into. She really had nothing in mind. Patricia went to her closet and started going through her clothes.

"Well, I don't want to drive him away. I just want to drive him crazy."

As she ran her fingers up and down the clothes rack, she decided on a cream-colored blouse with a plunging neckline that buttoned up the front. And then she pulled out a pair of tight fitting blue jeans that molded to her curvatures like a pair of surgeon's gloves.

Patricia was still changing, so Robert decided to familiarize himself with her house. He was looking at the assortment of trinkets in a small curio cabinet when Patricia meandered back into the living room.

The photographs on her living room wall had Robert's attention. "Who is this woman in this picture?" he asked. "Do you have a sister?"

Patricia was not prepared for that question.

"Uh, yes, my sister. I have one sister. She is a year older. Rachel is her name. That's her husband." Patricia pointed out the man. "They live in California, so I hardly ever see them."

"You know ... that guy looks so familiar. I think I have seen him before someplace. Rachel's husband. What's his name?"

"Ken," she replied, unable to come up with a bogus name at that intense moment. She wished she had taken the pictures down.

"You know when you are without your glasses the

resemblance between you and Rachel is remarkable. You could pass for identical twins if your hair were longer and the same color."

Robert was being too inquisitive for Patricia. He moved a few steps, studying, and asked more questions about the pictures on display. Patricia became very nervous and tried to change topics. Now she was angry at herself for not hiding the pictures.

Robert's attention was being soaked up by the gallery displayed on the wall. He looked at her nursing diploma. He looked at the framed wedding announcement. She was afraid of the questions he was about to ask. Robert again looked at the photograph of the man. "I know I have seen that guy before. I remember faces. What was his name again?"

"Ken."

The names Ken Duncan and Patricia Jones jumped off the framed wedding invitation. He directed a question to Patricia.

"I thought you said your sister's name was Rachel."

Patricia felt ill. "I did say that."

"Okay, I am totally confused. If Rachel is your sister, and your name is Patricia, then who is this Patricia shown on the wedding announcement? And why would you have somebody else's wedding announcement stuck on your wall?" he asked.

"A sorority sister from college," replied an exasperated Patricia.

Robert interrupted. "What's that diploma from nursing school that's hanging above your bookshelf? The degree was given to Patricia Duncan. Who is that? Isn't your name Patricia Jones? Something is very odd here."

He looked at Patricia, seeking a simple explanation, but before he could say anything else, tears rolled down her cheeks. In a broken voice she said, "Robert, I did not want anybody to know the truth."

Patricia threw herself at Robert, hugging him tightly around his waist. She wept like a child. She tried to talk. Her sentences were broken by deep gasps and unintelligible groans. She blubbered a few words. Silky streams of tears flowed over her cheeks. She slobbered. Her nose drained. She was out of control.

"Hey there, let's sit down," suggested Robert. He tugged on her hands and led her slowly to the couch. They sat side by side, and Robert rocked her gently back and forth. Occasionally he wiped strands of tear-soaked hair away from her eyes and placed them tenderly behind her ears.

"Ssshh, it will be okay. We are friends. We can talk. Tell me what happened. I care about you." He gave her a butterfly kiss on her tear-slicked cheek.

Patricia put both hands over her face. "Oh my, I must look awful! I'm so sorry for losing it that way. This story is so complicated. But I guess it's my turn to be truthful. You were right. We should not have any barriers in our relationship. I don't know if I can explain it so that you will understand."

"I'll try to listen. I want to understand." He pulled her hands away from her face and tenderly placed them in her lap. He gently stroked the backs of her hands.

"I don't know where to start." She looked at Robert.

"Go ahead. Try from the beginning. We've got plenty of time."

"I don't have a sister. I was married to Ken, that guy in the picture, until about a month ago. My married name is Patricia Duncan. My maiden name was Jones. Besides just being married, I was also seven months pregnant. My baby died at the hospital, at our hospital. It was not that long ago. I wish I could blot it out of my mind, but I will never be able to forget." She could not continue talking and now wept once again.

Robert began to put some of the puzzle pieces together. "Now I remember where I have seen Ken. I knew he looked familiar. It was me that told him of your baby's death and advised him as to what he should do. It was tough on him, so I tried to console him as best I could."

Patricia brightened. "You mean you were there?"

"Yes, actually, I entered the room immediately after the delivery. I took the baby from the nurse because they were busy with you. I ran him up the elevator to NICU. He was beginning to look cyanotic even in the elevator. I just couldn't get there fast enough. I'm so sorry."

Patricia looked directly into his eyes and saw the pain. "Oh, Robert, I know you did everything you could for him. Had Shircliff not bungled the delivery, Anthony would not have been in trouble. I don't blame you. You were like the cavalry coming to the rescue."

Robert just sat still and listened.

"My real reason for accepting the nursing position was so I could observe that bungling witch, Elizabeth Shircliff."

"What do you mean?" Robert asked.

"I think she is incompetent, and she was entirely responsible for the death of my baby."

Robert held up his hand. "Hold on. Those are some strong accusations. Do you really believe what you're saying?"

"Yes, I took that job so that maybe I could prevent anything like that from happening ever again. The whole experience ruined my life. Ken left me, my baby died, and I was devastated. I felt like I had to restart my life. So I started fresh. I changed my hair color and started wearing glasses. Then I decided to use my maiden name. My married name became a thing of the past."

"A new start, a new face, a new name," Robert paraphrased.

"Exactly!" she exclaimed. "And then I meet you, and I felt like I had more reasons for living.

"Well, I am flattered. Look, I know you don't know me very well, but I really hate to leave you in this situation. You are way too upset. Why don't you come over and spend the night at my place. I'm worried about you. If you need somebody, I'll be there. We can talk more if you want. And if not, that's okay. I've got a comfortable guest bedroom."

"Well, I don't know," Patricia said.

Robert pressed her. "Why don't you grab some clothes and come on over. I've got running water and everything."

Patricia paced as she thought. Though she hesitated on the outside, on the inside she was thrilled.

"I guess it would be all right."

"Great! You grab your things, and I'll be in the car."

—

Murdock paced the floor while reading Wyatt's chart. Wyatt was stable, but his condition was not improving. The monitors beeped out a steady rhythm. Wyatt lay still. He had experienced a few waking moments but was still being fed intravenously.

Murdock closed the chart and moved closer to the bed.

"I have big problems around here. Unexplainable deaths. After your little escapades as of late I'm beginning to think that you might have something to do with all this. Honestly…ripping life support from the patient. What kind of an animal are you?"

Murdock assumed Wyatt was sound asleep. He bent closer to his ex-employee and whispered, "How many patients have you killed? Was it for fun? Or was it just to steal their drugs?"

With his eyes still closed, Wyatt weakly grasped for Murdock's collar. He pulled Murdock down until they were face to face and whispered obscenities. He kept Murdock there for a few seconds.

Murdock easily pushed him away and stepped back. "You're a worthless piece of trash. I'm going to have Lieutenant Steele investigate you so thoroughly that you'll regret ever having worked for me or even being born."

Wyatt replied with a simple smirk of a smile.

—

Brent swung by the hospital that same evening on his way home from work. He walked past the nursery. The shades were drawn back, and four bassinets were just on the other side of the glass. Each tiny bed sported a recent addition to the community. A young married couple, the wife in a terry cloth robe, the husband in his work uniform, stood gazing at their baby. Brent stopped to take a peek also.

The man standing next to Brent looked at him and asked, "Which one is yours? That little guy is our first." He pointed to one of the beds.

The question bothered Brent because Rebecca's pregnancy was not going as smoothly as the first five.

"Oh...none. My wife isn't due for another three weeks."

The stranger didn't know how to respond. "Well, I hope everything turns out well for you."

Brent didn't reply but pushed away from the window and walked quickly to his wife's room.

Rebecca's door was open. When he entered he found her nibbling away at a turkey and dressing dinner.

"Hi honey," she said with her mouth full. She took a drink of ice tea so she could clear her throat and talk to her husband.

"Hi, beautiful. How are you doing?" He stooped, kissed her on the cheek, and patted her hand. A small latch hook rug lay across her feet at the end of the bed. The hook and a few strands of dark blue wool were lying out loose on the bedspread. "I see Gloria must have paid you a visit already. So, I see you have started working on the rug!"

"No. Gloria did that little bit. She was just showing me how it was done." Rebecca reached for a paper. "Here's what the finished project should look like. Don't you think that would look wonderful in front of my grandmother's wooden rocker?"

"Perfect."

Brent pulled a chair up close to the bed and sat down, slouching low in the seat.

"You look tired," observed Rebecca.

"Yes, I'm exhausted, and you've only been in the hospital a couple of days.

—

The medical compound was a sea of military green structures and people. Jeeps and ambulances rushed down the lanes between the tents. The MASH unit was full of activity as Robert pulled back the tent flap and emerged into the warm rays of sunlight. He placed his hand against his forehead to shield his sensitive eyes from the glare.

"Morning, sir." A young corporal saluted as he walked by.

"Morning," Robert replied. He began walking around the camp. There were white coated doctors, young nurses, and dust everywhere. He passed the mess tent. The smell of coffee made him breathe deeply to take in as much of that wonderful aroma as possible. He turned toward the door when his attention turned to a female doctor entering a nearby tent. *Hey, I know her!* he thought. He only saw her for an instant before she disappeared into the tent. *I swear I know her, but I can't remember where!* His curiosity overcame the lure of coffee. He began making his way over to the tent where he saw the mysterious lady doctor.

He opened the door and paused to allow his eyes to adjust to the dark interior. The white-coated figure was startled. She had been bent over a patient and jerked upright. Robert could see the fear in her eyes. He also saw her place a syringe in her coat pocket.

"Elizabeth Shircliff?" he questioned. "What are you doing here?"

"Robert, I ... I was just checking on this young man. He's a patient of mine."

"What did you give him? What was in that syringe?"

"What syringe?"

"The syringe you just put in your pocket."

There was pause in the conversation as Elizabeth considered her answer. "Oh, Robert, I had to do it. I had to. He was suffering so."

"I thought so. I knew you must be the one."

"What do you mean?"

"You are the reason for the deaths at the hospital. I have to tell Murdock."

"What are you talking about? There's no Murdock in this unit. Besides, it's just your word against mine. I'll deny everything you say."

"We'll see." Robert turned to go.

The ambulance sped through the camp on the way back to the front. The driver saw Robert coming out of the tent but could never have anticipated what happened next. The driver did not see the pair of hands that shoved Robert into the path of the ambulance.

"No!" screamed Robert.

———

Patricia didn't remember falling asleep. In fact, she didn't remember much at all when she awoke. She and Robert had stayed up late talking and drinking, enough drinking to help dilute Patricia's problems, at least for a while. She looked around and pushed herself up quickly.

"This is not my house," she gasped. The sofa was not familiar to her. For some reason she picked up the pillow and noticed she had drooled.

"What have I done?" The night before was a blur. Patricia stood up and made her way down the hall.

"Robert!" she yelled. There was no answer. Her clothes were disheveled. Her sweater was held together by one button. She noticed the cool wood floor and wondered, *When did I take off my shoes and socks?* Patricia pushed open wide the bathroom door and was really bothered by her image in the mirror. Her cheeks were red. She felt her face. It was chapped. Her lips were dry and chapped. "I remember kissing him a few times," she said. She combed her fingers through her hair. "I must have done more than I thought."

The phone rang.

"Where is it?" The phone continued to ring, and Patricia followed the sound to the kitchen counter. She picked up the receiver on the fourth ring.

"Hello?"

"Hi, sexy," said the familiar voice.

Those were welcome words. "It takes one to know one," replied Patricia. "I am so glad to hear from you. I just woke up, and for a moment I could not remember where I was, who I was, or—"

"I didn't want to wake you this morning. In fact, my right arm is sore from your sleeping on it last night. I had to wriggle it out from under your head this morning. How are you feeling?"

"Okay, I think. Did I do anything stupid?"

"Nope. We just talked, kissed a little, and fell asleep on the couch. You were a lady as usual."

"Well, thanks. I had a good time. How did you do? Did you sleep all right? I mean, besides your arm being cramped?"

"Yes, I did. I did have a weird dream though. I'll tell you about it later."

"Hmm. Okay."

"I was also calling to ask you to lock my house when you leave."

"Sure. But I was hoping you were calling to find out when you could you see me again."

"That will happen soon enough."

"That's it. I'm officially naming you Robert Vainhouse," teased Patricia.

Robert chuckled. "Well, I've been called worse. And speaking of names, your new one is safe with me. It will be our secret."

"Thanks, Robert. That's great."

"Okay. Say, I'm at work. Look me up when you get here. See ya." Robert hung up.

—

Rebecca Wells was all but well. She was a woman of faith with inward strength but outwardly the delicate form of a flower. Her condition upon admittance was not serious, but physically she was not improving, and her health was becoming a concern for her personal physician, Dr. Charles Crawford.

Crawford spent some time with Elizabeth Shircliff discussing the prognosis after his rounds that day.

"I just want you to know that I am very concerned with my patient Rebecca Wells."

"So am I," Shircliff replied. "We have been watching her closely. Her blood chemistries and urine protein are not all within normal limits. I have made my nurses aware of things to watch for. Her urine output has been extremely low. She's swelling, retaining fluids."

Crawford added his diagnosis. "My main concern comes from … I guess you might say doctor's intuition, if there is such a thing. I have known Rebecca for many years. She almost seems like family. This pregnancy is just not like her previous ones. I think there is something wrong, but I just can't place my finger on it. Perhaps toxemia, preeclampsia, I just don't know. And her health seems to be deteriorating each day."

The two doctors finished exchanging their concerns when Robert Vanhouse approached.

"Whoa, why such serious faces?" He spoke in a low voice so as not to alarm any patients.

"Rebecca Wells," Shircliff began. "She is not responding to our treatments like she should. We would welcome any suggestions. Do you think you could look in on her? Maybe you could look over the chart. Maybe there's something we're missing. A third set of eyes might pick it up."

"Well, I will be glad to help if I can. I've just been stepping in to say hi occasionally. I haven't really paid much attention to her because she didn't actually require my services in E.R.," stated Robert.

"Of course, Robert, but any advice you can give us is always helpful," suggested Shircliff.

Crawford added his approval. "We are open for suggestions."

"I will start checking her charts, and if I come up with any ideas, I'll let you know. Right now I have three patients to see, and it is quiet in ER. If I don't get busy, I might actually get an uninterrupted lunch today." Robert took a few steps down the hall and tapped on Rebecca's door.

"Come in."

"Mrs. Wells, how are you feeling? Where is that smile of yours?"

"Laughter is good for the soul, but sometimes the soul just doesn't feel like laughing," Rebecca muttered.

"If you won't go for a laugh then how about a little smile? You look a bit peaked. I'll ask again. How are you feeling?" persisted Robert.

"Let's just say I've been better," Rebecca replied.

"Well, I just saw Doc Crawford and Doctor Shircliff in the hall. They are on the case and will have you feeling better in no time."

"Promise?" Rebecca asked.

"Promise."

—

Patricia searched Robert's house for her purse. When she found it, she dumped the contents on the couch and picked out some lipstick and face powder.

"I hope this is enough to restore my face. This will have to do."

Patricia went into the restroom and hurriedly camouflaged her bright red chapped cheeks.

"My outfit is wrinkled … looks like I slept in my clothes." There was not enough time to go home and change.

Patricia scurried into the kitchen, combing her snarled hair as she walked through the house. She picked up the phone and dialed the hospital.

"Hello, this is Patricia Jones. I am so sorry. My power must have gone out last night. I just woke up, and when I turned on the television, I realized I had overslept."

"Save your story for Shircliff," came the reply from her co-worker. "And you better rethink your line on the way in. Shircliff tried to call you this morning. If I were you, girl, I would just get here as quick as you can and hope Shircliff doesn't ask questions."

"Thanks for the warning. I'll be there soon."

Patricia hung up the phone, and a note next to the sink caught her attention. She read:

> *Hope you are feeling much better. I let you sleep in. Feel free to drive my Thunderbird that is in the garage. (The keys are in it.) I had a wonderful time last night. I had to go to work early. They were short on staff.*
>
> *Love Robert*

He said "Love Robert." Patricia clutched the letter to her heart just like a grade-school girl might have done at the first hint of being loved. She waltzed into the garage, punched the door opener, and was soon on her way to work.

———

Robert finished his rounds and hurried downstairs to the

cafeteria. He took a table by himself at the back of the lunchroom. Most of his co-workers had already returned to their shifts, so he hadn't even bothered looking for familiar faces. He was content to sit alone. Robert tore open the plastic silverware package, set his napkin to the side, and started to saw through his chicken fried steak. *Snap!* The plastic knife broke in half. He sat there frustrated.

"How are you going to complete the operation," Patricia teased as she stepped up to the table.

"Hey there! I was hoping maybe you would assist. Could I borrow your knife and finish the procedure?" Robert smiled and motioned for her to have a seat.

"I've got to report to my station in fifteen minutes. I was late to work, and I'm giving back most of my lunch break to make up for it."

"Then we need to make this quality time."

Patricia sat down across the table from Robert.

"I felt like such a fool, such a baby last night," she confessed.

"Don't apologize. I understood your actions and your motivations. As a matter of fact, I … " His pager went off and he checked it.

Patricia waited patiently for him to continue, but she had to reignite his thought. "As a matter of fact … "

"Oh yes. I wanted to tell you last night, and I don't have time to tell you the whole story now. But I can give you the short version. You will have to meet me tonight if you want the unabridged edition." Patricia scooted to the edge of her seat and leaned forward. Robert leaned in and spoke in a much softer voice, a scale above a whisper. "You need to know that I have been investigating Dr. Shircliff."

"You're kidding—for what?"

"It should come as no surprise to you. Negligence, malpractice, incompetence … I am not sure exactly what the problem is, but there is a real crisis developing under her watch."

Patricia slammed her palm down on the table.

"I knew she was incompetent!" she quietly exclaimed. Her grudge now carried a genuine backing.

"The reason I'm sharing this with you in confidence is because this whole investigation swung into high gear with the death of your child."

"What do you mean?"

"The mortality rate in OB/GYN started to slowly increase almost immediately after Shircliff took the head position on that floor. The board suspected that perhaps there was a problem with following proper procedures or something like that. But the death of your son intensified the whole matter. The death of your child was recorded as failure to thrive. Even though there were complications with the baby after your delivery, he was never considered to be that critical. It was unacceptable."

Patricia clenched her jaw. She wanted to scream. The anger bubbled inside her. "So tell me exactly what is going to happen. How is the investigation going?" asked an anxious Patricia. "And how can I help?"

Robert looked at his watch. "Afraid our time is up. I need to go, and you need to get to your floor, Miss Banker's Hours."

"Leave me alone. I'm still trying to get used to this work thing. And it's your fault anyway," Patricia retorted.

He backed away from the table, picked up his tray, and walked over to discard the leftovers. He looked over his shoulder and motioned with his head. "Come on. Walk with me. We can talk as we walk."

Patricia got up and eagerly followed him. Just like a little puppy wanting his total attention and affection. She spoke softly as they walked from the cafeteria into the hallway.

"You can't leave me hanging. I want to know more about this investigation."

"I know that! Give me a call tonight, and maybe we can meet some place. I would be more comfortable discussing this matter outside these hospital walls. How about I come pick you up?"

Patricia nodded in agreement.

11

CHAPTER

"Room 227, please."

The phone rang, echoing in an empty room. Finally the hospital switchboard operator came back. "I'm sorry, sir, there is no answer."

Brent panicked. "That can't be! Try the room again!"

"But sir … "

"Try again," snapped Brent.

"Yes, sir," the operator fired back with unmistakable sarcasm.

The results were the same. Brent was at a breaking point. He hung up the phone, pushed it to one side, and then planted his elbows on the desktop. He leaned over his work and let his head rest gently in his palms. But it was not about work. His eyes watered. Brent's cubicle was his territory, a private place. To a hall wanderer, it looked like he was studying. But his thoughts were of life and of his wife.

"God, this doesn't make sense," he whimpered. "Something is wrong. I sense it."

Brent got up and left his space. He walked quickly to the end of the hall, keeping his head bowed as he passed each cubicle. When he passed the break room, he looked away. He avoided eye contact with everyone, especially his lunch buddy, Andrew Chain.

Brent walked into his boss's office unannounced. He sat down directly across from the man. By this time tears were running down his face.

"What's the matter, Brent? Is it your wife?"

"Yes, sir. I don't expect you to understand. I just sense something is terribly wrong. I can't concentrate on my work. I'm afraid she's dying."

His boss could tell the feelings were genuine. "What happened? Has there been a significant change?"

Brent looked at his boss. "I just called her room, and there was no answer."

The boss gave a reassuring smile. "You know you've been through an awful lot. Sometimes when we get pushed to our limits, things seem worse than they really are. I'm sure it's nothing. Maybe they are running tests on her. Maybe she is napping. Don't jump to conclusions. I want you to take the rest of the day off. You're not focused on work, understandably so."

Brent stood and gratefully accepted the offer.

"But, Brent, you've got to understand that we have work here to be done. I'll try to work with you, but certain schedules have to be met. I can only stretch so far."

"Yes, sir. I'll make my deadlines. Thank you, sir." Brent left.

Relieved, he went immediately to see his wife. His journey to the hospital was an emotional one. The closer he got to the hospital, the harder it became to remain stable. He walked through the lobby and boarded the elevator. Brent did fine until the elevator doors opened to Rebecca's floor. Those sliding metal doors acted like the gate that held his emotions. Tears streamed down his checks, and only seeing Rebecca could slow the flow.

Just outside Rebecca's room, Brent wiped his eyes on his shirt sleeve, took a deep breath, and entered. Rebecca was asleep. Her latch hook rug lay across her lap, and her hand was still cupped around the hooking tool. Brent lifted the small half finished accent rug. Rebecca roused and smiled.

"How's my favorite man?" she said as she stretched her arms and legs.

His voice quivered when he answered, "Fine."

Rebecca looked at him through drowsy eyes

"Do you always cry when you're doing so well? And what are you doing here this time of day?"

"Uh, well, ah, shoot, I can't hide anything from you. I'm worried about you."

Rebecca was worried too but remained strong in spirit. "Honey, they are watching me like a hawk. Every time I doze, a nurse comes in and pokes, prods, or has me swallowing something."

"What does Dr. Crawford say about the baby?"

"The worst scenario is they may have to do a C-section. He says that will be more for my benefit than the baby's. Although I don't see how cutting into me is a benefit. It will mean no more bikini's for me," Rebecca teased.

"I'm glad you can still joke about all this. I'm bothered by everything. And now I guess I'll have to take your Father's Day present back. I bought you a two-piece swimming suit."

Rebecca smiled. "Now that's a scary thought. A mother of five in a two piece." The more they talked the better they each felt. But Rebecca tired quickly, so Brent left the hospital. He felt better prepared to face the challenges on the home front.

—

Robert pulled up into Patricia's driveway and honked. Patricia came bounding out of the house dressed in tight jeans and an even a tighter blouse. She opened the door and scooted into the bucket seat.

"You might need a sweater," said Robert. "It's a little cool this evening."

"I was counting on you to keep me warm." She scooted close, leaned over, and kissed him on the cheek. He revved the engine.

"Just that little kiss made you do that?"

They both laughed.

"Where do you want to go?" asked Robert. "We set a date time, but we never chose a place."

"Well, we mainly need to talk, so I'm open for suggestions," Patricia said while she opened a compact and touched up her face.

"How about Calypso Cove at the lake?" Robert asked. "We could toodle around the lake and talk."

"Sounds great. Let's go."

The trip to the lake was a short one. Robert laid on the gas pedal, and they were there in ten minutes. Robert almost leaped out of the car. Patricia tried to keep up. They bounded down the concrete stairs to the boat dock lined with sailboats and yachts. A man in a baseball cap, worn jeans, and a sleeveless T-shirt came out of the screen door.

"Hey, Jonathon." They shook hands and hugged. "I need a boat."

"We got 'em."

Robert rented a fifteen-foot boat with a fifty-horse motor.

"You know how to operate this thing?" Patricia inquired.

"Sure. I used to go fishing with my dad all the time."

Robert cranked the motor and puttered out of the "No Wake" zone into the main body of the lake. "We could tour the lake, or I know this little cove that would be great for sitting and talking," Robert said.

"The cove sounds good to me. Just go slow so I can drag my hand in the water."

It was a short journey to the cove. They talked and laughed their way across the lake. Robert pulled the boat around to face the lake, killed the motor, and threw the anchor overboard. Patricia splashed Robert as he sat back down.

"Oops, sorry."

"Oh, come on. I need a better apology than that." He reached for her, and they kissed passionately.

After several minutes, Patricia broke the embrace.

"Wow, apology accepted," Robert said. He leaned back in his seat. "So, beautiful, how was your day?"

"Not bad. How about you? Any interesting cases? Anything new with the Shircliff business?"

"I know something's not right. But, hey, we'll talk later. Now is our time. Try to focus on my good looks and charm."

"Oh, excuse me, your highness," she quipped. "I forgot I was in the presence of Prince Vainhouse." She elbowed him in the ribs. They laughed.

The remainder of the evening was relaxing for both of them. The hour they spent in the cove at Lake Thunderbird was just what they both needed. When they brought the boat back to the dock, they were greeted by Robert's friend.

"Hey. How'd it go?" Jonathon asked as he tied up the bow line.

"It was fantastic," Patricia answered.

"Thanks, Jonathon. The cruise was great."

"You bet. See you next time." Robert gave him a couple of bucks for the gas. He and Patricia made their way back to the car. Robert opened the car door, expecting Patricia to get in. Instead she wrapped her arms around his neck and they kissed.

"Thanks for a great time," Patricia said softly. She slid into the car.

"You're welcome," Robert said as he closed the door.

"Well, what do we do now?" Patricia was not ready to split up and go home.

"We could go to my place." Robert paused. "You didn't take too kindly to that suggestion last time."

Patricia looked away from the mirror and shyly stared at him.

"That was before I knew you."

"And you think you know me now?"

"Yeah, I think I've got you figured out. At first I thought you were a real tiger. Just chasing the women and taking them to your den."

"How do you know those aren't my intentions?"

"Well, even if I'm wrong, it might be fun finding out."

"Then I say, away to my lair!"

The drive zipped by. Robert drove straight to his house, pulled into his garage, and closed the door behind them.

Patricia followed Robert into his bachelor pad, commenting, "You know, I was very impressed when I was here the other night. I was expecting to see dirty laundry hung over chairs and half eaten TV dinners on the counter tops. But it was almost like being at the hospital. Everything is squeaky clean and in its place. And then you have such an interesting house. I feel like I'm in a museum or something with all those antiques and collectibles of yours."

"Well, I guess I do pretty well for a guy. I don't have a housekeeper. I do it all myself. Of course, with just one person there is never much of a mess."

"I can relate to that," replied Patricia as she walked into the living room and investigated her surroundings. *Maybe we should set up housekeeping together.*

"Have a seat on the couch. I'll get you something to drink. Do you like beer?"

"I have more of a champagne taste," she claimed.

"I figured that. I mean … you're like me! See, champagne is classy. I'm classy."

"I don't know about classy, but for sure you are vain."

"Speaking of veins, I think I have one drink you'd like to get into your circulatory system. It's a little something I created in college. It was a big hit at all the frat parties."

"I guess I'll give it a try. I trust your judgment."

While Robert worked at fixing the drink, Patricia prowled about the room. She scanned the bookshelf.

"You have quite an assortment of old books."

"I pride myself on many of my collections."

A variety of old doctor's instruments hung on the walls. Some she could identify. Others she could not. "What is this?" she asked.

Robert looked over his shoulder. Patricia eyed a very old three quarter inch round dowel rod hinged to another. The two wooden sticks formed a *T.* Robert chuckled.

"You wouldn't be able to guess what that was in a million years."

"Tell me," Patricia said.

"It's a sand trap rake. After a golfer hits out of a trap, he uses a rake to repair the sand."

"Interesting."

"If you think that's interesting, perhaps you'll like the other wall. See my antiquated people repair tools? How would you like to be operated on with some of those gizmos?"

"No thanks. I guess surgery has come a long way."

"The changes come faster and faster. It's hard to keep up," said Robert as he walked in with the drinks. "Here you go." Robert handed her a goblet.

Patricia held the drink in front of her. "Robert, I need to ask you something."

He sat down. "Sure."

"Well, about the other night ... It's a bit embarrassing."

"Relax. We don't need any secrets between us."

"You're right," she said, but she still fidgeted. "I don't

remember how I got to your place. In fact, I don't remember much of anything about that night."

Robert gave her a sincere stare. "Babe, I would never do anything to hurt you. We drank. We probably drank way too much. But I had to calm you down. I didn't know of any other way."

"Did we … you know … " she asked.

Robert reached for her hand, took her drink away, and pulled her onto his lap.

"If I said the thought never crossed my mind, I'd be lying. But we did nothing more than kiss."

Patricia sighed, relieved.

"Now I must add that it was a pretty intensive kissing session."

"How intense?" She smiled and embraced him. "Thank you for being the gentleman. Maybe tonight we could do a little more than kiss."

"Oh, babe, I'd love to make that a reality, but I need to fill you in on Shircliff." He kissed her lips and down her neck and pulled away. "This situation with Shircliff is serious. We can have our time later."

"Promise?"

"I promise. I'm a man of my word." Robert motioned for her to sit opposite him. "Are you ready to hear this stuff?"

"More than you could ever imagine," she replied.

"Man, this situation has weighed heavily on my mind. I even had a dream about the woman the other night on the couch."

"Great, you're with me and dreaming about her."

"No, it's not like that. It was a dream about walking in on her just after she'd put down a patient."

"You mean she killed a patient?"

"Yes, and even admitted it. She said something about ending his suffering. Maybe it's a premonition of things to come."

"It's probably just that you're stressed about all this. You know, people dream about things they are going through."

"Well, maybe. Okay, here is what I know. There have been several questionable deaths under Shircliff's watch. We don't know if she is directly or indirectly responsible. Our investigation was kicked into high gear when your baby died. There was no apparent reason for your son's death. As you well know, even though you had some difficulty and the baby struggled, there was still no reason to believe it was life threatening."

Robert paused. The thought of that awful night replayed in Patricia's mind, and Robert waited for a reaction. As soon as he realized she was okay, he continued. "Only a few days later, a severely injured mother-to-be expired under our care. A few other patients have become mysteriously ill or suffered unforeseen complications. We are talking about a half dozen recent instances that bring about concerns and possibly lawsuits."

Patricia sat fully attentive to his explanation of events. "Have you ever known another time like this?"

"Not in the time I've been here. My current concern is over a woman I know you're familiar with."

"Who would that be?"

"A Mrs. Wells. I believe her first name is Rebecca."

"Yes, I know her. She has been there several days now."

"My point exactly. She should be getting better with hospital rest, but she is not improving. I have been watching her."

"I've notice she seems to be tired, sleeping more than she should."

"I was thinking the same," said Robert.

"She is a sweet woman. I would hate to see anything happen to her baby."

"I was hoping that would be how you would feel." Robert's voice took on a more serious tone. "I'm going to share something that you must keep in strictest confidence," he said, looking deep into Patricia's eyes. His gaze pierced her heart.

"You can trust me." She sealed her promise with a kiss to his cheek.

"I am hoping that you can even help us uncover the problem."

"How? I'll do anything, especially if it would take away Shircliff's right to practice medicine."

"Well, it could end with some heavy discipline if this matter is as extremely bad as it appears."

"What can—"

"What can you do?" Robert completed her question and then answered, "I told you that this must remain between us. I noticed Rebecca's decline myself. She is not my patient, so it is difficult for me to intervene. But I have done something totally against hospital policy. I started Rebecca on a special drug regimen. I don't know if it will pull her through, but it can't hurt. It's hydralazine, a drug for improving blood pressure.

"Hydralazine? For blood pressure?" Patricia was puzzled.

"Yep. I read a recent article about it recently in one of the journals. Should keep her stable, bring her blood pressure in line. They may have to perform a cesarean if she continues her decline. But this new stuff should improve things."

Patricia eagerly asked, "So what can I do to help?"

"I need you to continue the dose. In fact, I would like to make sure she regularly receives the dose twice a day. "

"But Shircliff can read the chart," Patricia pointed out.

"I will write something fictitious and illegible on the record. You don't worry about that!"

"Couldn't we get in trouble?"

"No! I have informed Murdock of my plan, and it meets with his approval. The rules of the game have been changed. Again … this is extremely confidential. As our investigation continues, I will keep you informed of any changes. You must report only to me, and I'll report to Murdock. I might be stretching my neck out by letting you help in the investigation, but I know how important this is to you."

"Thanks for letting me in on this."

—

That next day Patricia peeked into the room and cheerfully greeted Rebecca. "Good morning, Mrs. Wells. How's things this morning?" chimed Patricia.

"Well … not too … " began Rebecca sleepily. She muffed up her hair.

"Beautiful morning, isn't it?" Patricia interrupted. She drew back the curtains, letting in the morning sun. "How's that? I wonder if it will rain any today."

Rebecca didn't answer. She still looked groggy. Patricia began working around the bed, straightening the blanket and fluffing up the pillows. She grabbed the blood pressure cuff and wrapped it around Rebecca's arm, placed her stethoscope just below the cuff, and listened to the pulse sounds. "Let's see how you're doing today."

Rebecca looked up. "How many days have I been here?"

"This is the beginning of your tenth day … I believe," Patricia answered as the air released from the cuff. She repositioned the cuff on Rebecca's arm. "I think I'll take another reading … if that is okay with you?"

"I'm not going anywhere today."

She repeated the steps. " Hmm … still a little high. She replaced the cuff in the holder and recorded the reading on the chart. "Let me see your arm." Patricia held her finger on Rebecca's wrist and counted her pulse silently. "Eighty-one." She logged in that information also.

Rebecca winced as she pulled herself to a sitting position. "This hospital bed leaves something to be desired when it comes to comfort. I've got a backache. Say, can you tell me how I'm doing?"

"Well, for the most part you and the baby are doing pretty good. Most of your body seems to be functioning normally, and your blood work is looking okay."

"I think I heard you use the word most. What part of my body is not working so good?"

"I'm sorry, that's about all I can share with you. And I probably wasn't supposed to say that much. Your doctor will need to give you all the specifics. I know they are concerned with your blood pressure, and you still have swelling around your ankles." Patricia refilled the pitcher with water and set it on the night stand. "You're not going to be headed home for a while, that's for sure."

"Pardon my lack of enthusiasm, but I'm ready to be back home. I miss my children. I miss my husband. I miss the noise, the messes, the hugs, the kisses, the laughing, and the screaming. I miss it all."

"Screaming? I just can't picture you raising your voice at anyone," replied Patricia.

"Well, they have to push me really far, but when I do lose my temper and raise my voice, I guarantee they remember it for months. But you know it's hard for me to get upset with anybody, especially the ones I really love. I wish I were at my home in my bed cuddled next to my husband with the children trying to butt in for their hugs."

"Sounds wonderful. I guess I understand how you must feel." Patricia checked the catheter in Rebecca's hand, which had been placed there to assist in administering medications. "How is this line feeling? Any pain or discomfort?"

"Not really, I'm just not used to being held on a leash." Rebecca ran the fingers of her left hand through her hair, afraid to move the right hand too much for fear of bumping the tube. "I must look like a truck ran over me."

Patricia grinned. "Maybe we can get you cleaned up and refreshed a bit. But first I need to put some medication through the catheter."

"What medication is it?" asked Rebecca.

"Ah, just a little something to help with that blood pressure issue you've got going on. Patricia took the syringe of clear fluid and inserted the needle through the rubber septum of the line and then pressed down slowly and evenly on the plunger. "There, all in. Eventually this should bring your blood pressure in line."

Patricia noticed a book on the table. "What are you reading?"

"Oh, that's a Bible," Rebecca replied.

Patricia didn't look up as she discarded the syringe in the red plastic sharpies box on the medication tray.

"I never could stand to read that stuff. Just doesn't make much sense." Patricia stopped and picked up the book. She looked at the cover. "Didn't understand what it was supposed to do for me. Those stories...like the one about Moses in the boat saving the animals. You don't believe that, do you?"

"Noah."

"I'm confused," said Patricia. "If you don't believe it, then why read it?"

Rebecca giggled. "You misunderstood. I didn't say no. I said Noah. It was Noah who built the ark, not Moses. But that is off the subject. To answer your question, I do believe the Bible. The Bible is not just a history book, but it teaches us how to live. And not only does it teach us how to live on this earth, but it promises eternal life." Rebecca enjoyed these kinds of conversations.

"Slow down," warned Patricia. "I'm not ready to hear a sermon this early in the morning."

Rebecca apologized. "I didn't mean to sound that way. But really, you should read it sometime."

"No thanks. I'll wait for the movie." Patricia returned to the nurse's station. She enjoyed being in the room with Rebecca, talking about her family. It gave her a warm feeling inside to think of love and happiness. *On the other hand, that God talk gives me the creeps, makes me sick.*

—

Dr. Charles Crawford was seated at his desk at his office, flipping pages in a file marked *Rebecca Wells.* As happened quite frequently, his bifocals had managed to slide to the end of his nose. He didn't notice. He was shuffling papers all over his desk, searching for a particular report.

"Betty!" he called out. "Have we received the latest lab report on Rebecca Wells?"

"What!" came the reply. And a few seconds later his nurse, Betty, appeared in the doorway.

"I asked have we received the latest lab report on Rebecca Wells?"

Betty entered his office. "I haven't seen it if we did. Would you like me to check with the hospital?"

"Go ahead," replied Crawford. "Order the report, and have the hospital send us over a copy. Tell them it's urgent." Within an hour the hospital courier delivered the report.

"These should be the most recent results," Betty said confidently. She laid the report on Crawford's desk.

"Thanks. I think you have come through once again." Dr. Crawford studied the information carefully while Betty waited to see if more data were required. Crawford rubbed his fingertips across his forehead.

"What is bothering you?" she asked.

"Oh, I am really not sure. Rebecca Wells is just not improving at the rate I would like to see. Maybe it's just her frame of mind. She has that big family, and I know how desperately she would like to be home for the summer. Sometimes depression can slow recovery."

Betty stood up. "I don't know if you're arguing with yourself or if you are asking for my opinion. But for whatever it is worth, I would really be depressed if I were in her position."

"So would I. It looks like I should change her treatment, but I guess I need to give Rebecca another couple of days before I make any decisions."

—

Brent was unable to visit his wife every day. As it was, he was barely able to juggle all his responsibilities. He was almost pulling a double shift at his office so that he could keep pace with his assignments. The children were really stretching him. It was one of those weeks where each child had a different activity going on daily. Thankfully his daughter Sara could take up some of the slack now that she had her driver's license. She often shuttled her brothers and sisters all over town in a little compact car a friend had loaned them. Two out of the past four days, their neighbor Mrs. Marsh had done the grandmotherly task of tucking the children in bed. Brent only saw Rebecca when there was enough time in the day. Today he would have to settle for a simple phone call to his wife.

"Honey, how are you feeling today?"

"I'm tired. My back hurts. Guess this lying around is getting the best of me."

"I'm not going to get to see you today. I don't like that, so I'm thinking about taking a longer lunch break from now on and spending my meal time at the hospital. Being able to see you gives me the most comfort."

"Me, too," replied Rebecca.

—

Elizabeth Shircliff was exhausted and ready for a good rest. Before she could leave, she had to check up on Rebecca. She tapped on the door as a courtesy but entered immediately before Rebecca could respond. She walked over to the side of the bed.

"I heard you weren't feeling so good today," she said as she reviewed Rebecca's chart.

"I have felt better before." Rebecca pushed the mute button on the remote control unit, and the television hushed. "It's hard for me to decide if I'm sick because I'm pregnant, or if it is all this other blood pressure stuff that is putting me in a tizzy."

"It has been years since I have heard somebody say 'tizzy.' Let's check you out here." Shircliff took Rebecca's pulse. "Open your eyes wide for me. You look a bit yellow, but maybe it is just your complexion. Your eyes are okay. My nurses tell me you have a little backache. Is that true?"

"It's nothing. It's probably from being so still," she answered. "Is there any chance I'll get to go home before Father's Day?" pleaded Rebecca.

"I sure hope so." Shircliff flipped quickly through the chart, scanning it for anything unusual. She closed it and slid it back in the holder. "We'll do our best to get you home."

Dr. Shircliff patted Rebecca's shoulder. "This entire matter is up to you and your baby. That baby, of course, could help by making an early appearance. And you are going to have to start responding to these treatments. You need to start thinking low blood pressure."

Shircliff seemed to be satisfied that nothing unusual was taking place. "I think a little more rest and some more time for the treatment are the order for you. I'll see you tomorrow."

Shircliff turned away. "I'll check on you again soon. Work on getting that blood pressure down."

——

Brent ushered the children into the hospital room that evening. They were visibly awed by the entire situation and not acting like the children Rebecca knew so well.

"Come here," ordered Rebecca as she stretched out her arms. The children all focused in on the tube stuck in the back of their mother's hand. "Don't worry. I'm fine. I haven't been quarantined either. So, who is going to be the first to come over and hug me?"

Sara stepped forward and was quickly followed by the others. They landed on all sides of her. And Kara plopped right on her mother's chest.

"Oh my goodness, what wonderful hugs!" The children drank the affection just as much as Rebecca did. "Okay. Be careful now. I've got to watch this tube. You kids go from one extreme to the other."

She settled them down, and then they all shared as

much as they could. Sara told of her driving experiences. Ryan showed off all the signatures on his cast. Kara handed her mother a homemade get-well card. Sara promptly tried to outdo the gift by presenting some homemade cookies. Then a soothing bell sounded three times, signaling the end of hospital visiting hours. After some quick kisses, the family went back home, leaving Rebecca calm and with a glowing smile on her face.

—

The next morning Patricia was making the rounds. Hello, Rebecca, I'm here again." She came in, toting the medication tray. "Time for your mid-morning drug fest."

"I sure hope this stuff works soon. Have you looked at my chart? Am I doing okay?"

"Hasn't a doctor been in to see you today?" asked Patricia.

"Last night Dr. Shircliff saw me and said my blood pressure needed to stabilize. Then earlier this morning Dr. Vanhouse peeked in on me for a moment."

"Well, Rebecca, you just need to relax and quit worrying. I can guarantee that you are being watched closely. We want to get that baby into this world without a hitch. You have three good doctors watching your progress. I know that Shircliff, Vanhouse, and Crawford are comparing notes. And you're also the main topic in the nurse's break room."

"I guess it is nice to be noticed."

The women were both silent while Patricia took all the vitals. "Rebecca," said Patricia seriously, "I just want you to know that I'm going to be here for you. I lost my son at birth not so long ago, so I know what you're going through.

I know some of the emotions you're experiencing and some of the thoughts that must be churning in the back of your mind. That's why I've been giving you as much information about your condition as I can. It is really against hospital policy to do some of the things I am doing. They don't want us to get too involved with the patients, but I just can't help it because your condition is so close to my heart."

Rebecca smiled. "That makes me feel good. I know I can put extra trust and confidence into what you say." Rebecca looked at the nurse and then asked, "I hope you don't mind this question, but was your baby stillborn?"

"Oh, I wish." Patricia responded, chuckling grimly. "It would have made the death easier to cope with. I gave birth to a beautiful baby boy." Patricia gathered her thoughts. She still had trouble talking about it. "Anthony, he struggled for his first breaths but never made it on his own. At least that is what I was told. He died within a few hours."

"I'm so sorry."

"Thanks. Well, that's all in the past. It helps some to be working here. But it's you and your baby we need to be concerned about now. Let me get this dose into your line, and I'll leave you alone for a while"

Rebecca just watched the young nurse work. She didn't say a word until Patricia started for the door. "Wait," whispered Rebecca. "Thanks for sharing your baby's story with me. I know you must have experienced some deep, deep pain."

"I'm sorry to have bothered you with my problems. You're almost a complete stranger. I just ... oh, never mind." Patricia turned and left abruptly.

—

Brent left for work early that morning so he could begin those extended lunch hours and spend the time with his wife. Arriving unannounced at Rebecca's room, he quietly pushed open the door and tiptoed inside. The television was on and turned down low. Rebecca was sleeping soundly.

Brent cautiously placed, atop the dresser, a small potted flower he had purchased at the hospital gift shop. The tiny velvet textured violets were dwarfed by the size of the décor-less room. They looked cheap and unimpressive sitting all alone on the far side of the room. So Brent moved the tiny bouquet closer to Rebecca, placing it on her bedside table. In the process he knocked over a yellow plastic pitcher of water. It tumbled over the edge and bounced on the floor.

The clatter wakened Rebecca. "What?" she mumbled. She squinted from the noon sunlight shining through the open blinds.

"Oops ... sorry, hon," Brent said sheepishly. "You go on back to sleep. I'll clean up this mess," he said, grabbing a towel and mopping up the spill.

"You got me flowers," Rebecca said and smiled. "I need to come to the hospital more often. Thanks for the flowers, honey. They're beautiful. Violets are my favorites."

Brent caressed her forehead, swiping her hair back out of her face and tucking the strands behind her ear.

"Do you feel okay? You don't look so good."

"Thanks, dear, for the flowers. I love you too. I'm just so very tired." She closed her eyes and sighed deeply.

"Maybe I should get a nurse."

"They were here not to long ago. It's probably because

I haven't eaten anything for lunch. I'll be okay. Don't worry. You always accuse me of worrying too much."

"Hey, I should be allowed to worry a little every now and then," protested Brent. Rebecca kept her eyes closed and lay very quietly on the bed.

"I'll be right back." He walked quickly down the hall to the nurse's station. Patricia was sitting at the desk, adding notes to a patient's chart. She laid down her pen, slightly annoyed her work had been interrupted, and asked, "Is there something I may help you with, sir?"

"Yes. Could you come and take a look at my wife? She doesn't look so good to me."

"Maybe you've been married too long." Patricia replied sarcastically.

"What?"

"Oh, never mind. Give me a few minutes. I need to finish these notes."

"Please hurry," he said impatiently while he paced back and forth in three-step increments in front of the nurse's station. Patricia stopped writing.

"All right, sir, let's go have a look at your wife. Lead the way."

Brent took off down the hall with Patricia a half step behind.

"Thank you," he said. "I know it is probably nothing, but she just looked so pale and tired." Patricia did not recognize Brent and was surprised when he turned into Rebecca's room.

"All right, let's see what is going on here," said Patricia as she grabbed the cuff to check Rebecca's blood pressure.

Rebecca was very still. As soon as she placed the stethoscope onto Rebecca's arm, Patricia could hear trouble.

"Hmm," said Patricia. "I'm glad you asked me to come check her. Your wife's blood pressure is going through the roof. Her pulse is racing, and her respirations are rapid and shallow."

Patricia hit the call button and bent close to the microphone.

"Yes," came a voice over the intercom.

"Get the on-call doctor down here now! Call Dr. Shircliff in immediately, and then you get down here yourself. We've got a problem!" Next she turned to Brent. "Sir, I'm going to have to ask you to step down to the waiting room, please. I think she's okay, but your wife has taken a dramatic turn. If I'm reading this right, she may have to go to surgery to get the baby out now because she's toxic. We are going to have to move fast."

Brent was more or less pushed out of the room before he had a chance to ask any questions. A young doctor came sprinting down the hall, and Brent quickly jumped out of his way, hugging the wall. When another nurse headed toward him, he sought her attention.

"Ma'am, I'm Rebecca's husband."

She slowed down to speak to him.

"Oh, yes sir. I'll be sure you're notified as soon as we know something."

Brent leaned on the wall, waiting.

12
CHAPTER

"Good evening, Crawford residence."

"Charles?"

"Speaking."

"Elizabeth Shircliff here. I'm calling from my car on the way to the hospital. I'm very sorry to bother you at home, but I thought you would want to know that Rebecca Wells has taken a downturn."

"Uh-oh, that's disturbing. I just reviewed her records at my office. Do you have any idea what happened?" Charles asked with a tone of concern.

"I know I haven't seen as many of these as you, but I think the preeclampsia is moving into eclampsia. She is lethargic, and the edema is still a problem. She is still having the proteinuria. Her blood pressure is sky high. Her electrolytes and creatinine are wacky."

"Renal failure?" Crawford was getting excited. "That doesn't sound good. I think you are right. Sounds like classic early eclampsia."

"Any trouble with the baby?"

"Don't know yet. Yesterday it looked like everything was fine, although Rebecca complained of feeling weak and fatigued. If it is eclampsia, I've never seen a pre-eclamptic case go bad so fast. I'm almost to the hospital. Do you want to join me?"

"I'll meet you there as soon as I can. Thanks for the heads up."

"Let's hope we're in time. See you there!"

Crawford hurriedly finished the remaining bites left in his bowl of chocolate ice cream. He flipped down the footrest on his recliner and released a frustrated sigh as he walked to his front door then turned back to yell to his wife.

"Honey, I've got to go to the hospital. It's an emergency. I'm not sure what it will involve, so don't wait up for me." His wife waved to him from the far side of the living room and blew him a kiss.

"Be careful driving home," she shouted. "If it goes too late into the evening, will you please just sleep in the doctor's lounge?"

"Yes, dear. Don't worry." He left, jiggling the doorknob to make sure the huge entry door had locked securely behind him.

———

Patricia stood by Rebecca's bed, realizing that this could develop into a critical situation for both Rebecca and the baby if something wasn't done in short order. She had called the resident working the floor, and the young doctor responded immediately. "What's up?" he asked as he burst into the room. He quickly reviewed the patient's chart as Patricia recited the most recent vitals. Even though it was cool in the room, tiny beads of perspiration appeared on his forehead as he thought. He hesitated briefly and then barked out instructions.

"We need another chem-seven, hematocrit, and blood gases stat. Let's also get the fetal monitor running to check the baby."

"Right," said Patricia, anticipating the orders. She was already filling lavender top test tubes with Rebecca's blood for the lab. She had enough knowledge to understand what was coming. When the tubes were filled, Patricia moved the fetal monitor in place, carefully adjusting the holding straps around Rebecca's plump stomach. Attaching the leads, she began the strip, paying close attention to the baby's heart rate. Rebecca was unresponsive and oblivious to the chaos around her. Patricia listened with her stethoscope.

Lub-dub, lub-dub, lub-dub. The heart sounded strong, and the rate was good.

"The baby seems okay right now," Patricia said to the resident. She looked up to see the doctor's response.

"Who is the attending? Has anyone called the attending? We are going to need some help."

"Dr. Shircliff … and yes, I have called her. She should be on her way." Patricia finished checking the monitor and grabbed the blood samples. As she headed out the door to get them to the laboratory, she took one more look at Rebecca. She was quiet, almost too quiet. Her face was white, her eyes sunken and closed.

"Not good. Not good at all," Patricia whispered angrily. "Another Shircliff screw-up."

———

Brent was sitting in the waiting room, his elbows planted on his knees and his hands cradling his forehead. "Lord, take care of my girl, please," he prayed. The ashen look on

Rebecca's face spooked him so that his mind was racing. Too troubled to sit still, he finally got up and wandered back and forth between Rebecca's hospital room door and the waiting room.

Brent needed to talk to somebody, anybody. He went to the payphone in the waiting room and dialed his home phone. It was the most familiar number and the only one he could call to memory at the moment.

Mrs. Marsh picked up the phone on the second ring.

"Hello, Wells' residence."

"Mrs. Marsh," Brent's voice crackled. He took a deep breath. "I probably won't be home anytime soon. Rebecca is…"

Mrs. Marsh broke in at the pause. "Brent, dear, are you okay? Is it Rebecca?" She had noticed the anxiety in his voice.

He couldn't pretend. "I'm scared. I think something might be seriously wrong. I'm worried about Becky and the baby."

"Are you crying?"

"No, ma'am, but I wouldn't admit it if I was."

"Brent, don't worry about the children. I'll stay here all week if need be. You need to relax as best you can. I'll make some phone calls and get somebody to come stay with you. Where exactly are you right now?"

"I'm in the family waiting room on second floor. But the way the nurse was talking, I may be headed to the surgery waiting room. You don't have to call anyone. I'll be all right. I feel better just talking to you."

"Nonsense. Now you go get a little something to eat

and sit down. I'll call pastor, and I guarantee I'll get some-body from church to come stay with you."

"Thanks, Mrs. Marsh. God bless you. You're like a member of our family."

"You can adopt me as a grandma anytime." She chuckled.

———

Robert Vanhouse was leaning on the nurse's station coun-ter, glancing at the chart of a recent arrival to the ER when he noticed Elizabeth Shircliff running through the department.

"Beth! What's up?" he shouted at her across the ER desk. She didn't slow down and continued heading for the elevator doors.

"It's Rebecca Wells. She's crashing big time! Trouble, eclampsia! I think she must be in renal failure," hollered back Elizabeth as she fidgeted in front of the elevator after pushing the up button. She thought about taking the stairs, but she heard the elevator begin its downward journey, and she watched the floor display lights above the door slowly change. 4 … 3 … 2 … 1 …

"It's about time," she griped as the doors parted. She stepped inside then poked her head back out the door and yelled again at Robert.

"Hey, keep an eye out for Doc Crawford, and send him up as soon as he gets here, would you? Second floor!"

"You bet," said Vanhouse, but as soon as Shircliff dis-appeared, he shook his head. *You've got big problems, lady, and everybody is watching, especially me.* He leaned his right elbow on the countertop and stared in the direction of the elevator. "Wait till Murdock hears about this one." Vanhouse started for the administrator's office then paused, deciding to withhold the information until he knew the status of the patient.

He returned to the counter. "Ladies, I guess you heard Doctor Shircliff asking for assistance from Doctor Crawford. When he gets here, will you send him up to the second floor? I am headed home."

"Yes, sir."

—

The nurses in the second floor nursery had been overwhelmed with work the past few hours. They were exhausted. Two emergency C-sections among the other routine deliveries of the day had filled the cribs in the small ward with precious pink and blue bundled infants. In addition to all the business, the staff was now shorthanded. Only two nurses out of a compliment of four had shown up to work the late shift. The two nurses on duty were having a very difficult time keeping up with routine duties. They had put off entering some chart data and were scurrying around the nursery like bees in a hive. They were simply trying to keep up with the demands from the newborns.

"At least there aren't tiny special need babies with us right now," commented one of the nurses.

"Thank goodness for that. We would be thrown from our mild chaos into a total panic," replied the other nurse as she picked up one of the screaming infants. The two nurses continued with their duties. They paid little attention to the white coated figure that entered through the secured nursery door. The person went directly to the crib of a little girl. She was awake and wiggling. The figure read the identification bracelet.

"Rachel Hutchison, mother Jamie, Dr. Elizabeth Shircliff."

A small 3cc syringe with the needle removed was brought out of the white coat. The individual placed the syringe barrel in the baby's mouth, and she eagerly sucked on the syringe tip. A large thumb gently pushed the plunger, delivering the contents slowly enough for the baby to swallow it all. The syringe was replaced back into the coat pocket, and the white clad figure slipped silently out of the room.

Both nurses were aware somebody else was present in the room, but neither one said anything till they heard the click of the nursery door when the individual left.

"Who was that?" questioned the senior nurse.

"I'm sorry. I wasn't paying attention. I was changing a diaper," replied the other. "Must have just been a doctor checking information or something. Wasn't around long enough to offer us any help."

"What a snob. If I'd been thinking, I'd have drafted whoever that was to help us for a while."

"Oh well."

—

Dr. Shircliff, clad in her white coat, came barreling through the doorway into Rebecca's room.

"What's the story?" she asked. The floor resident updated the doctor, giving her the most recent information.

"Blood pressure, 180 over 110. Respiration's nine and deep. The baby still sounds okay. I've ordered more blood chemistries. I'm thinking maybe mom is in renal failure, probably eclamptic."

"I think you're right," Shircliff said as she examined Rebecca. She gently lifted Rebecca's hand just as any mother would have done with her own daughter. "Any seizure activity?"

"One slight episode. I gave mag sulfate," the resident responded.

"Good. That should help us with pressure and seizures. Nice going." Shircliff continued dictating her own set of instructions. "Alert the OR team. I want them on standby. And dialysis too. Let's get some hydralazine ready, just in case the magnesium sulfate won't keep the pressure down. And if this seizure activity returns, we might need to fall back on diazepam."

"Got it!" the resident replied.

Elizabeth bent close to Rebecca and spoke inches from her ear.

"Rebecca! Rebecca, can you hear me? Do you understand what I'm saying?"

"Um," the sedated patient could only groan.

"Rebecca, we are going to wait a little while and then get that baby out of there so we can get you well!"

Once again she replied, the response indiscernible.

Shircliff asked, "Hey, where the devil is that blood work?"

"Right here, doctor," interrupted Patricia as she returned to the room. "I have the current lab report right here."

"Great! Let me see it."

Patricia handed over the information. The room was

quiet, except for the steady rhythm of the monitor. Finally Shircliff turned to her staff.

"I want to wait awhile before we attempt to take the baby. We need to make sure the patient is stable. I expect her renal function to improve. It's six o'clock now. Let's hold off to nine o'clock to make sure the seizures are controlled and the urine output has improved. Let's get prepared for inducing labor. Have a room ready and order an oxytocin drip. It's better if we can do this naturally."

"Right," Patricia replied. The resident nodded in agreement.

"Do either of you know if any of her family members are present?"

"Yes. Her husband is here," said Patricia. "We asked him to go to the waiting room when all this started. I assume he is still there."

"Good move. He didn't need to see all this, but I'll need to go talk to him while she is stabilizing." Dr. Shircliff moved toward the door then turned and said, "Be prepared for a long night. I may need more assistance. We will just have to see how this plays out." She left the room and walked quickly to the waiting area. Her mind was racing. It didn't make sense. Rebecca's status was going in exactly the direction they were so vigorously trying to avoid. *What am I going to tell her husband?*

She turned the corner and stepped into the waiting room. A man stood alone, staring out the second floor window, his back facing Shircliff. She stepped closer to him.

"Mr. Wells?"

"Yes," he said, turning quickly to face her.

"Are you okay?"

"How's my wife? Will she be okay?" Brent asked anxiously.

"Let's go out in the hall where we can talk." Elizabeth led him into the corridor. The waiting room sounds faded. He slowed, stopped, and just leaned heavily against the wall, his face pointed toward the floor.

"Mr. Wells," Elizabeth began, "your wife is a pretty sick lady right now. The preeclampsia, the condition we brought her in here for in the first place, has gotten suddenly worse, moving into eclampsia. This is a much more serious condition in which the patient's kidney function decreases, and the blood pressure goes up. Rebecca has had the classic array of symptoms, including even a small seizure."

"A seizure?" he gasped. Brent's face paled. Tears welled up in his eyes. "Oh, dear Lord." He crossed his arms then raised his right hand to his chin. He shifted his feet and ran his fingers through his hair. "What is happening now?"

"Mr. Wells, I think—"

"Brent," interrupted a voice. It was Dr. Crawford. "Hello, Elizabeth. I just got here. What's going on?"

"I was just starting to explain his wife's condition. I believe the preeclampsia is progressing and is forcing us to consider inducing labor. It could be tricky, but I think it is necessary for the good of both mom and baby."

"What do you mean tricky?" Brent asked. His voice cracked as he struggled with his emotions.

Dr. Crawford put his arm around Brent's shoulder.

"Brent, I know you are worried. We are going to monitor Rebecca very closely. The primary problem is her blood pressure, but now add in the minor seizure, and of course her pregnancy, and you've got multiple issues. It's just not a good combination. The labor and delivery will not be exactly as we planned it."

"What do you mean, not exactly as we planned?" questioned Brent.

Shircliff explained. "We are going to see if Rebecca will continue to remain stable. Right now things look good. If the situation stays constant, then around nine o'clock we will begin to induce labor. I believe that it is always better to have a natural delivery whenever possible. We like to stay away from C-sections, but we will do what is best for Rebecca and the baby."

"I guess I just have to trust your judgment," Brent said. "Can I see her now?" "Sure. Let's go."

Elizabeth, Crawford, and Brent walked quietly down the hall toward the room, Dr. Crawford's arm still around Brent's shoulder.

"She'll be okay. I think we've got a good plan," he whispered.

—

Elizabeth Shircliff was stumped.

"Charles, I don't get it. I just don't get it. I thought Rebecca had stabilized. I thought we would be inducing labor, and the baby would be born. I thought she would be home for Father's Day and I could go onto another case. Instead, here we are scrubbing for surgery. What do you make of it?"

Dr. Crawford shook his head in bewilderment. "I'm as shocked as you are. I guess it can happen. Preeclampsia is pretty unpredictable. We've both seen patients fine one day and horrible the next. Rebecca has been a roller coaster from the beginning. The whole thing has been so frustrating; I can't recall anything this extreme."

"It's definitely different," replied Shircliff. Then she turned to one of the nurses in pre-op. "Did anybody let the husband know we were headed to surgery? I had already told him it was a possibility."

"Yes. He was pretty shaken. We requested the chaplain escort him to the surgery waiting room. No one else is here for him right now."

"Thanks." Shircliff returned to her discussion about Rebecca. "I have some bad feelings about this case."

"Don't worry, Elizabeth, I think we have a window of opportunity here, and we need to take it. She hasn't had any further seizure activity, and her blood pressure has been level for the past thirty minutes. I think we have a good shot at saving everybody without any further crisis. By the way, thanks for letting me assist."

"You bet. Glad to have you around, Charles. It is reassuring to have an old pro like you at my side."

"Well, it's been awhile since I've participated in a tricky one like this."

"You're right, Charles. We'll get it under control. It's like going on vacation. You're always a little anxious at the start, but once you get moving everything seems to settle down."

Dr. Crawford chuckled. "You obviously have never been on vacation with me." The two physicians finished scrubbing, and the nurses helped them into their surgical gowns.

Rebecca had already been given a small dose of valium and was being further sedated by the anesthesiologist in the operating suite. The surgery team took their positions. They prepared, removing the gleaming surgical instruments from the sterile wrappings and laying them out in proper order on the tray, while others prepped the patient.

Elizabeth leaned over the patient.

"Rebecca … Rebecca, can you hear me?" she asked loudly. There was no response. "Rebecca, we are going to get that little gal out of there so both of you can get well, okay?" Again, not a muscle twitched.

Elizabeth stood and addressed the team. "Gang, let's go get this kiddo." She looked to the family physician. "Charles, stay ready, my friend."

"I'm ready."

"All right, let's see what we've got. Scalpel," she commanded. The nurse beside her promptly produced the instrument requested and slapped it into Shircliff's waiting hand. The doctor made a slow precise incision just below the bikini line on the left side.

"Nicely done," complimented Dr. Crawford.

"Plenty of practice," came the reply. "Let's see what we can do. "Suction please." The surgical nurse immediately met the request and cleared the area.

"Looking good. Things seem to be progressing well, don't you think?" asked Crawford.

"How are our vitals?"

"Stable but elevated. She is 190 over 110," the anesthesiologist replied immediately. "I would feel much better if we had the baby in hand."

"Well, once the baby is born, that should bring her back down to normal."

"Let's hope so. It should," said Shircliff. She made another incision. This cut was made in the wall of the uterus, near the apex.

"Feel free to jump in anytime here, Charles."

"Don't mind if I do. I've delivered all her other children. I might as well keep the string going." He stepped into position. "All right, little one. Let's introduce you to the rest of the team here." A small hand could be seen, then a leg. Dr. Crawford maneuvered his hands gently under the legs, very carefully cradled the head, and then lifted it slowly, straight up. "Well, we don't know your name yet, young lady, but let me welcome you into a bigger, pretty confusing world."

The infant girl squirmed as she was brought out into the cold environment of the delivery room. The baby screamed her opinion to all who would listen.

Crawford studied the unhappy newborn for a moment. "Amazing. It is always amazing, isn't it?"

"That it is," agreed Shircliff. She cut the life supporting umbilical cord and clamped it shut. Then Crawford turned and handed the baby to a nurse. "Here you go. Pretty her up for mom to see when she wakes. Another girl. That will keep the sides uneven at the Wells home."

"They always look so ugly at first, all covered in bloody fluid and so scrunched up."

"Yeah, but I still say it is some kind of miracle," boasted Crawford.

"You're just turning into a real softy these days," teased Shircliff.

Crawford pleaded guilty. "You are right on target. I know, I know. I'm a real softy. But I really am amazed at the miracle of birth. Always have been, always will be. Guess that is why I do what I do." He looked at Shircliff and asked her, "What is your reason? How did you wind up as a specialist?"

"Do you want a noble answer or the truth?"

"Just the facts, ma'am," joked Crawford.

"To be honest, I enjoy what I do. But I figured a woman doctor treating women could pretty much write her own ticket as to her success. So, I guess the money was a big motivator. Life is good when you have the money to enjoy it."

—

Brent Wells sat quietly in the waiting room. The television was playing. Other families were present, but Brent was oblivious to it all. He picked up the current copy of *Sports Illustrated,* tried to read the latest college football news, but he couldn't concentrate on the words. He kept thinking of Rebecca's pale face. He couldn't chase the image of her sunken eyes from his mind.

"Lord, you gotta take care of Becky and the baby," he mumbled to himself. The expression of despair on Brent's face did not go unnoticed.

"Tough time, is it?" a stranger asked from the couch next to the window. Brent looked in the direction of the voice and saw the calm face of an elderly gentleman. He was dressed in tan plaid slacks, a white shirt with an undershirt showing over the top buttons, and a brown sport coat. He spun his fedora hat between his wrinkled hands.

"Yes sir, it is a tough time. My wife is having an emergency delivery. She had a blood pressure problem and got into trouble."

"So you're having to worry for two. First child?"

"No, sixth. But none of the others gave us … her … this much trouble."

The old man smiled. "Six children, what a blessing. I hope you will train them well. I'm sure you will. You seem like a man of integrity. Oh, by the way, I thought I heard you mumble the name of a friend of mine."

Brent looked puzzled. "I'm sorry, sir, but I don't believe we have met. Who's this person that we both know?"

"I've probably known Him longer than you. I'm saying that because I'm much older than you." The old man paused. Brent just stared at him with a dumbfounded look. The old man continued as the silence grew uncomfortable. "I just want you to know that through all my many years, that one friend was the only one I have ever been able to count on completely. He never abandoned me. He shared in my joy and sorrows and cared for me when I was hurt or troubled."

Brent nodded. "Sounds like he's much more than a friend."

"He is. Come here and sit next to me, and I'll tell you more."

Brent sat down next to him. "Okay, so tell me the rest of the story."

The old man had a gleam in his eye. "My friend was everything I said, but what is truly amazing is that I have ignored Him so many times in my life. Yet He is still there for me. In fact, when I was watching you, it reminded me I should give Him a call. I figured since we both know Him, you might want to talk also. What do you think about that idea?"

"Sure, I'll talk to this friend of yours. It may help the time pass a bit faster. There's a phone in the corner."

The old man reached out for Brent's hand. He smiled. "No need for a phone. Just bow your head. I'll do the talking, but if you have anything to add, feel free to jump right in. He listens."

"Thank you, sir," Brent said humbly, nearly in tears from his own lack of faith. The two men prayed.

—

Shircliff turned her attention back to Rebecca. "Blood pressure still high?"

"Yes, doctor," replied the nurse.

"It should start coming down pretty quick here. Keep me posted. We'll get things finished." She had removed the placenta and now closed the wounds. She moved very cautiously, taking longer than the average, avoiding any mistakes. She pulled the thread and knotted the final stitch. "I'm not the world's best seamstress, but this looks pretty good." She double checked and admired her work. "All right, let's get Mrs. Wells to recovery and watch her closely. Her troubles should be over."

Dr. Shircliff stepped back, sighed, and turned to Crawford. "Charles, would you want to go talk to her husband? I would sure appreciate it."

"No problem. You did most of the work. I guess that is the least I can do."

"How's the blood pressure now?" Shircliff asked the nurse.

"No change yet."

"We've got to have improvement!" Shircliff frowned.

—

Brent looked up from a magazine to see Dr. Crawford walking down the hall toward him. Brent knew his anxious look asked all the questions.

"I think we are going to be just fine," said Dr. Crawford, smiling. "And congratulations again. You have a new daughter to add to your family. Rebecca tolerated the procedure well and is in the recovery room. Her blood pressure was still up there when we left the room, but that should resolve shortly."

"When can I see her?"

"Let's give her some time in recovery. She has been through a lot and really needs some good rest. I will instruct a nurse to come get you when she's ready. Everything went fine, and we expect to see remarkable improvement in her condition. It just requires a little time, a little patience."

"What about my daughter?"

"She's doing fine. Eight pounds, two ounces, twenty inches long. She's got dancer written all over her. You can see her down at the nursery in just a few minutes. She'll be in there as soon as they clean her up a bit."

Brent's shoulders slumped with relief. "Thanks, Dr. Crawford. It looks pretty good then?"

"Yes. I think we're gonna be all right."

Both men were smiling. The old gentleman in the corner smiled, too.

—

After Rebecca Wells and her new daughter seemed to be stable, Dr. Shircliff had one more stop to make before going home. Weeks ago, when Murdock first talked to her about the mortality rate at the hospital, Shircliff was of course concerned, but with the passing of time, the situation had changed. More patients had died on her watch. She couldn't believe all of the things that had happened at once. Coincidence? Did it make her look bad? Many of the victims were on her floor. And what about Wyatt? Was he involved in the deaths? *He may be the answer,* she thought. *What if he dies?*

"Good morning, ladies," said Shircliff to the nurses at the desk in the intensive care unit. "How's our trouble maker, Mr. Wyatt?"

"Good morning, doctor. And to answer your question … he's hanging on."

"What room is he in?" asked Elizabeth.

"Room four."

Elizabeth walked to his room and paused briefly outside. A glass window separated them. *Maybe I should just stand out here. I don't know what I would do if Wyatt grabbed hold of me like he did Murdock. Surely he wouldn't treat a lady like that.*

She took a deep breath and pushed open the wide metal door. Wyatt turned his head.

"You're awake."

"Yes," he whispered. "Can you help me?"

"I'm sorry, I didn't hear your question." Elizabeth stepped closer cautiously, staying just beyond arm's reach.

"Help me," Wyatt pleaded. "I'm cold. I don't' want to die."

She was alarmed. During her career she had experienced a few times when that had been the patient's final words. Her first instinct was to step out and get help from the station. *Maybe death is not such a bad thing for you. You can take the blame for everything that has happened. I'll be in the clear. Nobody will care if you live or die.*

Elizabeth grabbed Wyatt's hand. "Okay, I'll help you."

"I'm so cold."

"I know. It will pass very soon. Trust me."

Her promise came true. Wyatt flat lined. The monitor alarm went off. Shircliff stepped back. Nurses poured in.

13

"David!"

Robert sat up in bed. He rubbed his eyes and scanned the room to make sure he was in his own bedroom. "Why are you here? You shouldn't be here. You're supposed to stay with mom. That was our deal."

The dresser creaked as David leaned against it, his back reflecting in the bedroom mirror. "We have to talk, Brother. You got me out of a spot in Nam. You got me back to the States. Now I'm gonna repay the favor. You are in trouble."

"What are you talking about?"

"I'm talking about that girl."

"What girl? Patricia?"

David continued. "Look, you bonehead, Dr. Shircliff is not responsible for those deaths at the hospital. She had nothing to do with them. You've been investigating the wrong person."

"How in the world do you know?" Robert asked.

"It's right in front of your nose. You are just too involved with her to see it."

"See what?"

"I think you know. In the back of your mind I think you know she's the one. I told you she was trouble."

"Whoa, hold on. What do you mean she's the one? She's

been … wait a minute." Robert began to comprehend what David was saying. "You think she's involved in the deaths at the hospital?"

"I know she is. Just think about it. When you come to mom's house, you talk about her being involved in almost every case that you are involved in. Then I found her initials in the nurse's notes on multiple patients." David continued to present his case as he paced around the bed. Robert crossed his arms and leaned back against the headboard.

"She was far too willing to assist with Rebecca's treatment, wasn't she? Remember how angry she was with Shircliff? She wanted the good doctor to lose her license. Patricia would do anything in her power to make it happen. Think, Robert. That woman of yours was admitted to the hospital after her kid's death about the same time all this began to happen. I say she roamed the halls like the angel of death even before she was hired on."

"That's crazy!" responded Robert.

"No, it's not. And I'm warning you. If you don't do something soon, she will turn the tables, and you'll be the fall guy."

Robert gazed down at the bed covers. "I love her."

"Listen, you idiot. She only cares about revenge. She couldn't care less about you."

"I don't believe that."

"Look, I saved your life on that hill in Nam, and I'm ready to do it again. You can prove it to yourself. I've got an idea, but I can't do it for you. You'll have to be a man of action."

"What's your idea?"

"Well, I took the liberty of scripting it out for you, and I mean literally. On your kitchen counter you will find a short list of questions and a tape recorder. Ask Patricia on a date and get a few drinks down her. Turn on the recorder and ask the questions. Her answers will implicate her. She won't have a way out, and you'll have the confession on tape to convict her. I guarantee it."

"Guarantee it? Great, you guarantee that I'm going to hang my girl."

"Have I ever misled you before?"

Robert did not answer.

"Fine, ignore me. You're a fool!" David slammed his fist against the wall.

—

Robert's eyes sprung open. He was under the covers with his head buried in the pillow. He tried to focus on the alarm clock on the bedside table. Was that a dream, or was that a real conversation? *One way to find out, I guess.*

Robert hesitated at the side of the bed then reluctantly walked to the kitchen. There on the Formica countertop next to the telephone was a pocket tape recorder and a legal pad with handwritten notes. It was just where David said it would be.

Puzzled, Robert sat down at the breakfast table and began reading the questions. He committed the words to memory. His brother had never misled him.

—

Patricia worked beyond the end of her shift until the decision was made to perform an emergency cesarean section on Rebecca Wells. It angered Patricia, knowing another patient, particularly this patient, was suffering under the care of Dr. Shircliff. There was a burning in the pit of her stomach. *This shouldn't be happening,* she thought. *I've got to do something.*

Even though her eyelids felt the weight of fatigue, her feet throbbed, and her back ached, she decided she had to talk to Robert, and talk to him immediately. She was so deeply shaken, she felt like there was no other choice but to stop at his house on the way home and inform him of this latest disaster.

Patricia's mind kept churning as she drove. *I can't believe that Shircliff is doing it again. This time she is unnecessarily butchering my patient. Rebecca could easily die in that surgery, and so could the baby. They don't deserve this. I should have stayed to assist with the delivery.* She zipped straight through a red light without noticing her mistake.

Suddenly her furrowed brow gave way to a nasty smile.

"Wait a minute," she told herself, "What am I thinking? Why am I so angry?" She happily slapped the steering wheel. "This is great! I think we caught you on this one, Shircliff. You've obviously misdiagnosed a case, caused an unnecessary surgery, and brought hardship on the patient, which should all be documented. Shircliff, you're going down this time."

Patricia turned on the radio, celebrating her revenge. But the fate of Rebecca and her baby was still a concern. Patricia's eyes teared up. Then she did something she only remembered doing once or twice as a young girl. She prayed, from her heart, a genuine and sincere prayer.

"God, please don't let anything happen to Rebecca or the baby. No mother should ever have to suffer such a loss as I did. Rebecca believes in you. Give me a reason to believe, too."

Minutes later she whipped into the driveway and parked just outside the three-car garage at the home of Dr. Robert Vanhouse. She got out quickly, rushed to the porch, and knocked sharply on the huge mahogany entry door. She impatiently rang the doorbell several times and banged on the glass window with her car keys.

"Come on, Robert!"

This matter was just too important to put off. Something must be done. "Come on, Robert, wake up. You're supposed to be here!"

She heard Robert shuffle to the foyer and fumble with the lock. He poked his head around the edge of the door wearing a tee shirt, flannel pajama bottoms, and possibly a bit drunk.

Finally!

"Patricia! What's going on?"

"Oh, Robert, I'm sure glad you're home."

"Come on in, babe. I've always got time for you." She recognized the tone of his voice.

"Is that all you think about?"

He grabbed her arm and pulled her close. "It seemed like a pretty good thought right now," he said and smiled.

Patricia pushed his arm away, entered hurriedly, then looked at him with a grim expression. "Well, now's not a time to play. We've got some serious talking to do. It is that Rebecca Wells case at the hospital. She crashed big time this afternoon. I was there. As we speak she is in surgery, a C-section. It shouldn't have happened. We were watching her so closely. I was giving her the extra injections daily, just like you told me. How could this happen?"

"Yeah, I know … so?" replied Robert as he walked across the living room.

Patricia was shocked by the indifference in his voice.

"What do you mean *so?*" Patricia lashed back. "This woman is another victim of Shircliff's incompetence. I thought we were working up a case to bring her down. Doesn't this give us enough evidence to go to Murdock? Surely you have some ideas as to what we can do?"

"Patricia, will you calm down!"

"No, I won't! She's gonna die if I calm down! Don't tell me to calm down!" Patricia stomped around the room, arms crossed. Robert walked after her and grabbed her shoulder.

"Babe, calm down. Let me fix you a drink. I'll mix up my specialty, we'll both relax, and we can talk this out." He gently walked her over to his wet bar and sat her on a stool. He pulled two oversized champagne glasses from the overhead rack. He slid back the lid to the ice machine, scooped up some crushed ice, and divided it evenly between the two glasses. Patricia heard the ice chink against the sides of each glass. Robert had his back toward her. He gently stirred each drink without speaking a word.

"You're acting rather odd. Don't you care? I thought you were just as eager as I was to pin this whole fiasco on Shircliff. Was I mistaken?" she quizzed.

"I'm sorry I came off like that. I have a little more evidence to collect. Once I've got everything I need, you'll be the first to know. This case needs to be rock solid. There will certainly be severe discipline handed out, so the evidence must be beyond debate. A few items still need to fall in place so that there will be no way out for any of the parties involved."

Patricia gasped. "You mean there is more than one person responsible?"

"Oh yes. I'm very certain of that."

"Who else do you suspect? Do I know them?" Her curiosity was piqued.

Robert looked straight at Patricia. "Possibly. This is a delicate situation. I've got to be cautious with how I address the problem. It can be handled internally, but I just haven't decided what to do with all the information I have. I've just come across some recent information that changes things dramatically."

He handed her the drink. Patricia took the goblet and held it with both hands, pacing nervously.

"Let's go sit in the living room," Robert calmly suggested. "I just installed a new stereo sound system, and it is just like taking a seat at the concert hall. It is one of the best investments I've ever made. I'll put on some music. It'll help you unwind."

Patricia followed him into the spacious living room. The two relaxed and listened to some golden oldies. Robert sat on the couch. Patricia, remembering what happened the last time they started out together on the couch, sat in the leather recliner opposite him. She was about half finished with her drink.

"Yum. Did you work your way through medical school as a bartender? This drink is delicious."

"It's my own recipe. I call it the steam roller. You don't see it coming till it runs right over you."

Patricia chuckled. After thirty minutes and a few more sips, she began to feel lightheaded.

"Wow, you're right about the drink." She sank further into the recliner.

David's words came into Robert's head. *Now's your chance, Robert. Go get the tape recorder and get this done. She's nothing but trouble.* Vanhouse walked into the kitchen. He opened the utility drawer and took out the recorder and glanced at the list of questions David had written out.

Robert hesitated. He leaned on the counter and stared at the recorder. He couldn't do it, at least not right now. He closed his eyes, slowly placed the recorder back in the drawer, and walked back to the wet bar. *She's the best thing that's ever happened to me.*

Patricia had slumped a bit sideways in her chair, and Robert approached her.

"A little dizzy, are you?" He bent over to raise the foot rest of her recliner. "Lie back till you feel better."

"I'm really dizzy," she replied. Patricia tried to sit up but couldn't. "How come you're still vertical?"

"My drink was a little different."

Patricia looked up at Robert. "I don't feel so good. I think I'm gonna—"

"Pass out?" suggested Robert.

"Yeah…" She lifted her head and then dropped back into the recliner.

"I better get you home quickly. Can you hear me?" Patricia nodded weakly. Robert lifted up her arm and then dropped it. It fell limply across her chest.

"Well, the concoction worked well," he whispered. "A little alprazolam and a little alcohol make an excellent sleep aid. You'll be asleep for a good long while." Robert bent at his knees and thrust his arms underneath her. "Here we go." He plucked her out of the recliner. Patricia's head bent sharply backwards, her right arm dangled loosely, almost knocking over the table lamp as he lifted her. He took a deep breath and carried her out to one of his cars in the garage.

—

Robert pulled into Patricia's driveway. After he cut the engine, he reached over and grabbed her purse, sifting through its contents until he produced her house key. He hurried to the front door, quickly unlocked it, and felt the wall for the living room light switch. The one light was enough to brighten his path. He walked through the living room into the kitchen and disappeared into the garage. He twisted the release and yanked up on the metal garage door. It was lightweight and loudly raced down the rails, rebounding a bit when it reached the end and almost returned down the tracks from its own momentum. Robert scanned the doorways and windows of the closest neighbors then stepped outside confidently, positive that nobody was watching him.

At least I got you home okay, he thought. Robert slid into the driver's seat and had the car inside the garage within seconds. He shut the garage door, went around to the passenger side, and opened the door. Patricia's body slipped sideways, almost falling out onto the pavement. She was nearly impossible to gather up, but after making several clumsy attempts, he finally grabbed her underneath the armpits and pulled. Her feet clunked on each stair step, and one of her shoes fell off when the heel caught on the door frame. He breathed heavily as he continued to pull the dead weight. He worked his way through the kitchen, the living room, down the hall; one final effort he ran backwards, lifting as high as he could manage just before reaching her bed. The final surge landed them both on the mattress. Patricia ended up on top of him. He shoved her off to one side. Patricia's legs dangled over the edge of the bed. He lifted her legs, giving one last heave to get her entirely situated. Then he collapsed beside her, breathing like he'd just run a sprint. Sweat beaded on his forehead.

"Man, what a work out," he grunted.

He took labored breaths and tried to relax as he lay next to the unconscious body. As soon as his breathing returned to normal, he turned and kissed her on the cheek.

"Better get you comfortable," he mumbled. Robert rolled her limp figure onto her side. He pushed a pillow under her head and placed another between her knees. He slid off her remaining shoe, and then he tossed an afghan over her, tucking it tenderly under her arm. He stood at the edge of the bed, admiring her figure and her beauty. He looked at his watch.

"Wish I could stay, babe, but I need to go." Robert turned off the light and closed the bedroom door behind him as he left. Looking at his watch again, he calculated that she would start to wake around lunch time. "Maybe I should leave her a note." He returned to the kitchen and scribbled a few lines on a brown paper grocery bag. He tore off the note and hung it near the phone so it could be readily seen. He left for the hospital, dreading the next meeting with his brother. David would not be happy.

—

Dr. Shircliff managed to grab a few hours of sleep in the doctor's lounge. The Rebecca Wells case haunted her. She replayed it over and over in her mind, analyzing and reviewing every little detail of her past treatment all the way up to her current condition. It didn't make sense, and deep in her gut she felt that Rebecca was not going to snap back like she should.

"I guess it's time to tackle the day." Shircliff sat up on the couch and stretched her arms high above her head and wiggled her shoulders. As the stiffness waned away, she pulled her arms down and looked at her watch. It was 6:00 a.m., and the first shift was gearing up for a new day. She walked over to the mirror above the sink and grimaced at her unkempt image.

"Look at my hair. Yuck!"

Shircliff went over to the lounge refrigerator. Her breakfast selection was limited. She shuffled around a few items, tossed a spoiled milk carton, and eventually settled on an orange juice and a chocolate bar for her morning meal. Another doctor entered the room.

"Healthy diet," he said sarcastically.

"Yeah, I never eat like this. I've been here all night," she said with her mouth full. "But I have a lot on my mind this morning and not enough time to run down to the cafeteria." Shircliff left the lounge, gulping down the food on the way to the nurse's station. "What is the latest on Rebecca Wells," she blurted, still several feet away from the counter.

"They brought her back to her room just a few hours ago," answered the nurse. She handed her the chart. The doctor sat her bottle and candy wrapper down, tucked the chart under her arm, and turned down the hall. Shircliff studied the records carefully, flipping pages to make sure she hadn't missed any new information as she stood outside Rebecca's room. Now feeling up-to-date, she tapped lightly on the door and hearing no response, entered. She didn't bother to wake the patient but just lifted the sheet and peeked at her ankles. Rebecca didn't respond to the slight movements of the sheets.

"Dang," whispered Elizabeth, disappointed to see those still-swollen ankles. She flipped open Rebecca's chart and rechecked the most recent information. Shircliff shook her head in disapproval.

"Looks like I'm going to have to start you on dialysis. Your kidney function is approaching critical." She walked back to the nurse's station to give the order and get the process started in the event that the procedure would be necessary.

—

Keith Murdock started his day off with the alarming news of the Rebecca Wells case. He sat at his desk, rubbing his forehead as he reviewed the recent update. To make matters worse, his secretary walked in bearing even more discomforting news.

"Sir, I know you won't want to hear this, but there was an incident in the nursery that you need to be aware of."

Murdock looked up from his work. "Go ahead. Might as well get all the bad news at once. Can't get much worse!"

"This is a bad one. Soon after the shift change in the nursery, one of the infants was found dead in its crib."

"Was it Sudden Infant Death Syndrome (SIDS)? Who was attending? Where's the baby now? What are they saying was the cause of death?"

"This is all I have on the case at the moment," she replied. She plopped the report on his desk. Then she stood there waiting for his reaction.

"Great, just great." Keith moaned, shaking his head. "We're going to need an autopsy on this one. Who was the attending?"

"Shircliff," came the reply.

"Is Shircliff aware of this? Has she seen the family?"

"I don't know, sir. She spent most of the night involved with the Wells case."

"I suppose that was a stupid question. That's what I've been reading for the past thirty minutes. Page Shircliff," he snapped angrily. "And have her report to me."

"Consider it done."

—

Patricia woke. Her head ached, her throat was dry, and it felt like she had a hairy log for a tongue. She raised her head and then just dropped back on the pillow. As she drifted back and forth from her sleep state, she tried to remember coming home.

"Robert!" yelled Patricia. There was no reply. "Robert!"

she called out again. Her cries went unanswered. Struggling to her feet, she stumbled toward the living room.

"I've got to get ready for work," she muttered. Patricia wobbled into the kitchen holding her pulsating head, which seemed to explode with each step she took.

Man, I can't work feeling like this, she thought. She massaged her forehead, pressing down hard in an effort to ease the pain. *I better call the hospital.*

The red light on her answering machine flashed three messages. She pressed the play button.

"Patricia, we need you to come in early today if possible. It's almost 0400. Give us a call."

The second message was a little more desperate. "Patricia, we are really shorthanded and could use your help early. Call us immediately. It's 0600."

The third was also the hospital. "Patricia you're scheduled to start work at noon today. Would you be able to work a double? We've got several bases to cover today. See you soon."

"Great, that's just great! I'm feeling horrible, and they want me to work twice as much." Patricia reached to pick up the phone. *I need to call in.* Strategically stuck next to the receiver was the brown bag note from Robert.

Patricia,

> I'll stop by after my shift. Don't worry about calling in.
> I knew you wouldn't be up to working today, so I'll cover
> for you. When I report to work, I'll tell them that you are
> sick. Just rest up! We'll talk later tonight, and we'll get that

*whole thing about Shircliff resolved. Don't worry about it!
Just trust me. I've got things under control.*

Patricia smiled. "Thank you, Robert. You're such a sweetie." She placed the receiver back on the phone and smiled. *Robert takes such good care of me.* She sauntered back to her bed, plopped down, pulled up the covers, and thought about Robert. Turning on her side, she wrapped her arms around her king size pillow, pretending it was Robert. She felt warm and comfortable in her fantasy and soon fell back asleep.

—

Elizabeth Shircliff reported promptly to Murdock's office. *How am I going to explain the Wells case?* As she stepped into the room, Murdock rose and studied her face.

"Elizabeth, you look exhausted."

"I've been up most of the night on the Wells case."

"How's it going?"

"She never responded to our treatments. Dr. Crawford and I performed a C-section. I wish I had better news." She plopped down in a chair.

"Wish I had better news, too," Murdock shot back. "The Hutchison's baby died."

Elizabeth fell back against the seat crushed by the news. "How? I hadn't been informed. When did that happen?"

"Here is the report I was given." He handed it to Elizabeth and added, "I want you to talk to the family. We need to do an autopsy on this case. Tell them why. Answer their questions as best you can."

"This is terrible," she said, glancing at the report, obviously upset. "Is the baby down in pathology?"

"Yes," Murdock replied grimly.

—

Steve and Jamie Hutchinson were overwhelmed with a mixture of shock and anger when told that their apparently healthy seven pound ten ounce baby girl had died. They dreaded talking to Shircliff, but at least they thought they might have a better understanding of what happened.

Steve sat beside his wife on the edge of the bed, squeezing her hand and wiping tears from his eyes with the other. Looking up at Dr. Shircliff he said bitterly, "I don't understand how this could happen. Why didn't a nurse notice something? You people are trained specialists."

Shircliff replied in a quiet, direct tone. "At this point we do not know exactly what happened. Your baby at birth was breathing fine. Her heart rate was good. No signs of jaundice. Everything seemed to be okay. About four o'clock this morning when the nurse taking care of your baby went into the nursery to do the routine checks, she found Rachel dead.

The mother, Jamie, sobbed. "She was my first…my precious…There's got to be a reason." Her husband tried to calm her.

Elizabeth felt the pain. Tears came into her eyes, and she hung her head. "I'm so sorry, so very sorry. I wish I had answers for you." She paused as the mother wailed.

"With your permission I would like to have an autopsy performed. There could be some genetic problem. This is your first child, so if there is something, we need to discover it now in the event you decide to get pregnant again."

"Of course, go ahead," the husband said quietly.

"I'll have a nurse bring in some papers for you to sign. Both of you need some rest." Elizabeth pulled open the door and stepped into the hall. The chaplain on duty happened to be making his rounds. Elizabeth leaned against the wall, looked toward the ceiling, and a tear rolled down her cheek.

"I came to see the couple. But are you okay?" asked the chaplain.

"No, but I'm better off than they are."

"Come by my office, and we can talk."

"When I get some time," said Elizabeth.

"Make some time!"

The chaplain entered the Hutchinson room. Elizabeth trudged down the hall, oblivious to her surroundings. She was angry, profoundly sad, very confused, and possibly for the first time in her career, her confidence was shaken. *What went wrong? It was a normal delivery. What did I miss? The child was hours old, technically too young for SIDS. Had to be genetic.*

—

Patricia awoke in the early afternoon. Her headache was tolerable now as long as she moved slowly. She began to tidy up the house in anticipation of Robert's visit. She tied up the loose ends of living. She put away the newspaper, filed and sorted her mail, picked up dirty dishes, and even reshaped the couch pillows.

Once the house was presentable, she took a hot shower.

She stood with her back to the spray head and just let the water cascade from her head to her toes. It refreshed her, and she stood almost motionless, just enjoying the massaging touch of the water flow. Steam filled the small room. By the time she finished, water was condensing and running down in long squiggly lines all across the bathroom mirror.

—

At the hospital, near the end of her afternoon rounds, a weary Dr. Shircliff confronted Rebecca with the disheartening news.

"I'm sorry we have to do this, but there are no alternatives. We are going to have to start you on dialysis. This treatment is going to be a little rough on you since you're also recovering from the surgery. I'm sorry. I don't know why your kidneys failed. I just have no idea."

Rebecca listened attentively.

"We have placed you on the organ donor list," Shircliff continued. "I'll be honest with you. A transplant looks inevitable. We received back some old X-rays from Dr. Crawford and discovered that you actually have one kidney. It is what we call a horseshoe kidney, which is a fairly rare condition. But what really complicates things is your rare blood type. It may be difficult to find a match for you." Shircliff paused. "On the bright side, you are in good health otherwise and should do well with the treatments. If a compatible kidney does become available, there will not be as much competition for the organ because of your rare blood."

"So this dialysis, is it a daily routine?" asked Rebecca.

"No. We will probably schedule you three times a week," replied the doctor. "Does it hurt?"

"Only a few people have real problems. Nausea is a common side effect until your body gets accustomed to the routine. It is mainly just a time consuming procedure. You'll have to spend about three hours with each treatment." Shircliff reached out and took Rebecca's hand. "I'll tell you what. I'll be sure to have a nurse assigned who can answer all your questions when we hook you up to the machine the first time. The reason we have to do this, of course, is because your kidney has quit functioning. You are therefore retaining fluids and toxins. The dialysis machine acts as an artificial filter to remove those toxins from your body."

"Will I have to do this for the rest of my life?" Rebecca asked.

"Not if we can find a good donor match," Shircliff said, trying to sound upbeat.

"But if not?" Rebecca pressed.

"If not, well, you will be getting the treatments."

Rebecca smiled. "I'm having a little trouble getting excited about this whole idea. But my God is a big God, and I can rest in the fact that he will work mightily in this whole situation. This illness is not easy for me, but while something like this would be a nightmare for many, I'm positive some good will come out of this whole ordeal."

Shircliff just sighed. She was at a loss for words. She felt responsible. She backed away from the patient momentarily then decided just to share her heartfelt thoughts.

"Rebecca, there are so many things I see in my day-to-day routines. I am sure there is a God. But I struggle when babies die, when people get sick for no apparent reason, when women are abused. I don't understand. Why does

God allow such things to take place? Life doesn't make sense in times like this."

"I couldn't agree with you more. But don't let that shake your faith. There is only one God. The Bible tells us He is all powerful, all knowing. There are many things we are not meant to understand. God reveals His plan in His time, and both of those are always perfect. We are not to worry."

"Thanks. But since when did the patient start helping the doctor feel better?" Shircliff strolled out of the room in awe of Rebecca's strength.

—

"Doctor Shircliff. I need to see you in my office immediately," requested Murdock as he walked past her in the hall.

"I'll be there in just a few minutes," she replied.

"Good," he countered, looking back over his shoulder.

That was pretty abrupt. He almost seems mad at me. Elizabeth jotted down a few final notes to herself, closed her notebook, and slid it into a slot on a counter organizer. She made the journey downstairs to his office. *What in the world could be so urgent?* She tapped on the door frame.

"Come in, Elizabeth, and have a seat."

She plopped down in a chair directly in front of his desk. "Doctor Murdock, forgive me if I'm mistaken, but have I done something wrong? You act perturbed."

"Frankly, I thought you might tell me. I just found out about Mrs. Wells needing dialysis due to kidney failure. Things do not look good. Not only do we have this situation, you have been involved in two recent incidents in which you are the only individual in a room with a dying patient. What complicates the situation is that there have been several other questionable deaths since your appointment. They have happened under your watch, and I don't have any logical explanation. I have the board breathing down my neck asking why?"

"Sir, if you are referring to Wyatt, I can only say that when I stepped into the room, he asked me to help him. He had this blank stare. I grabbed his hand. He said he was cold. Before I could do really anything, he had flat lined. The team rushed in. There was nothing that could be done. I'm just a victim of being in the wrong place at the wrong time."

"And alone," Murdock added.

Elizabeth placed both hands on the arms of the chair as if to rise. Her tone of voice revealed her indignation. "What are you saying, Dr. Murdock? Are you questioning my medical competency? Because if you are, you're dead wrong."

"Elizabeth, I know you are a good doctor. But you must see how this looks. You were alone in both death cases. Taken with the Wells situation, these events cast doubt on your abilities. All I can do right now is give you a fair warning. If there are any more episodes in the near future, I will be forced to take some sort of disciplinary action."

Elizabeth fumed but thought better about storming out of Murdock's office. "Look, I'm sorry. I won't let anything else happen. I'll not leave myself or the hospital open to any potential compromise. Believe me, I don't want my record tarnished, and I know the hospital deserves my best."

"Thanks. Now go back to your duties," ordered Murdock.

Shircliff left without further discussion. She rounded a corner in the hallway and leaned on the wall. She had not expected this. She thought with the passing of Wyatt the problems were solved. *Guess they need a scapegoat,* she thought. Shircliff pushed off the wall and walked toward her next patient's room. *Well, they're chasing the wrong goat.*

—

Patricia still felt a little nauseated that afternoon, but out of guilt she decided to go in and work, at least for a few hours. Besides, she wanted to see how Rebecca had fared through the surgery, as well as check on the status of the new baby. As soon as she clocked in, Patricia darted straight for Rebecca's room.

Patricia immediately noticed the pale complexion and sunken eyes. "Hey, girl. How you doing today?"

Rebecca looked up from her reading. She placed a bookmark on the page, shut the book, and held it in her lap. Rebecca reached for the control to raise her bed. Patricia grabbed it instead.

"Here … let me do it. Do you want to sit up?"

"Sure, just about halfway," whispered Rebecca.

"You're not wearing your normal smiling face," commented Patricia while she looked at the many flower arrangements filling the window ledge and scattered about the room. "Surely all these beautiful flowers have brightened your spirits." Patricia bent to smell a bouquet of daisies.

"Things could be better. Dr. Shircliff just told me I must start dialysis treatments," replied Rebecca.

Patricia frowned. "I'm sorry to hear that, but it's probably all for the best." Then she quickly changed topics. "Say, I haven't seen your baby yet. Is she gorgeous, healthy, and all that?"

"Yes, of course. There's no such thing as an ugly baby. They say she is as healthy as can be. Eight pounds, ten ounces and twenty inches long."

Patricia smiled. "That's good to hear." She tried to keep the conversation rolling.

"Where did all the flower arrangements come from? There must be a dozen or more."

"Family, friends, several are from people at my church."

"I must say, I've never seen a rose in a vase like that."

"That is an interesting use for a specimen cup," agreed Rebecca. "My husband brought me the rose after surgery. He cut the stem off. And just in case you're wondering, that is water in the cup."

"It's a beautiful rose." She bent over to smell that dark red flower. "You must have a very thoughtful husband."

"He is a wonderful man. I love him dearly. How about you? Do you think you will get back with your husband?"

Patricia grimaced at the thought. "No. He wouldn't consider it. I don't know that I want him back. Besides, there is another man that I've grown rather close to."

"You sure you're just not on the rebound? You know, the Bible tells us that marriage should be a lifelong partnership."

"Why are you always preaching to me?" Patricia huffed. "It's like everything we talk about always ends up ... God said ... or the Bible says. What about what I say or what I feel?"

Rebecca calmly answered, "Let me just ask you this. If a manufacturer makes a lawnmower, wouldn't it be a good idea for him to throw in an instruction book on how to operate and care for the machine? I mean, don't you think it would run a lot better and last much longer if you knew exactly what to do? What kind of action to take when the thing is broken or not running as smooth as it could?"

"You've lost me. First we're doing Sunday school talk, and suddenly we've changed to broken lawn mowers." Patricia was annoyed.

"No. I am simply trying to tell you that God created each and every one of us, and he left behind an instruction manual of sorts, the Bible, to tell us how to get the most out of life. I just like to see people reach their full potential."

Patricia didn't know what to say. Rebecca continued, "I just hate to see you give up on your husband."

"He gave up on me. I don't think you could ever understand," Patricia said in a challenging tone. "Besides, I think Dr. Vanhouse will be the new man in my life."

"Are you serious? He's probably twice your age. Personally I'd be a little suspicious of a guy that old, rich, and unmarried." Rebecca couldn't believe she had just been so blunt.

Patricia defended her decision. "I find him to be very kind and thoughtful. You'll have to agree that he is very dedicated to his work. He's coming over to my place tonight."

"He does seem to be very nice. But I don't want to sound like your mother, but if I were you, I'd proceed with caution. He might be just playing with your broken heart," advised Rebecca as she tried to be a little more understanding.

"No! He cares. You just don't know him like I do."

—

"You blew it! You outright blew it! Unbelievable!" David yelled.

"I love her. I can't hurt her that way!" Robert meekly replied.

"Did you hear that another baby died?

"Yes, I heard about it. Another one of Shircliff's patients."

"Curious, isn't it?" David's question cut deeply.

Robert knew what he was saying. Patricia may have killed another patient.

"Look, David, I just can't do this. I didn't anticipate how much I would care for her."

David was unmoved. His anger was unleashed. "Yeah, well because of your supposed love for her, we're goin' down. She's setting you up. That's right, and then both of us are goin' down. What did you think would happen when they discover me and the fact that you've been harboring a fugitive?"

"I hadn't thought about it that way," Robert said.

"Well, you better think of it that way. If we go away, Mom gets left behind with no one to look after her."

Robert considered his brother's words. "All right, all right. I'll do it. We've got a date tonight. I'll do it then."

14

CHAPTER

After working nearly four hours, much longer than she planned to be at work, Patricia faked an illness. She went to her shift supervisor and with a very squeamish expression, pleaded, "Miss Jenkins, I've got to go home. I'm sorry. I probably shouldn't have come in at all. I feel terrible, like I have flu symptoms. I really need to go home and go to bed." Patricia grabbed her stomach convincingly. "I think I'm getting sick."

The charge nurse was quick to respond. "Not here!" She glared at Patricia. "Your timing is not great. We've been short on help all day long. But I guess I'd rather you just miss one day instead of trying to tough it out and end up missing a week. No need spreading whatever you've got to the rest of us. Go on home; take care of yourself."

"Thank you. I'm sorry. I hope I'll be better tomorrow. I promise I'll call in as soon as I wake up in the morning," replied Patricia.

"Just like you did this morning?" snapped her supervisor sarcastically.

"Sorry," Patricia apologized "It won't happen again."

She clocked out and promptly left the ward before there was a major confrontation. She hurried straight home and put on a comfortable pair of blue jeans and her favorite long sleeve blouse with the monogrammed rose on the front. She fixed herself a cup of hot tea, sat on her couch, snuggled up comfortably in a quilt, and listened to music on the radio.

The sun went down, and she finished her tea. She grew tired of the music and paced the room impatiently. *Robert should have been here by now. Maybe he backed out on his promise of a date.* She finally saw headlights reflect off the living room wall, and her heart leaped in delight.

"Robert..." She sighed. She smiled and hurried to the door, greeting him with a passionate hug as soon as he walked through the doorway. Robert returned her affection.

"Hey, beautiful. I heard you went home sick."

"Well, yeah," Patricia said sheepishly. "I really didn't feel that bad. I just wanted to get ready to see you. I couldn't wait."

Robert put his arms around her waist and stared into her eyes. His love for her was real. He felt that. In fact, he had never felt this strongly about anyone before. But he couldn't shake his brother's ranting about how their mother would be left alone. It was tearing him apart. Patricia wrapped her arms around his neck, almost standing on tip-toes. They kissed and held each other for what seemed like an eternity. Still standing in the foyer of Patricia's house, they were oblivious to all that was around them.

Finally, Robert said, "Guess what?"

"What?"

"There's a carnival in town. I drove by it on the way over here. Wanna go?"

"Sounds like fun," Patricia said. It didn't matter where they went as long as he would be with her.

—

The Birdwell Carnival set up twice a year, usually on a Friday and Saturday night. This Friday night was no different. The aromas of the carnival were a mixture of popcorn, hot dogs, candied apples, and hamburgers. The chaos of carnival sounds included ride motors, loud music, and screaming kids. The lights and banners were ageless. They may have changed colors over the years, but the messages were the same.

Like a couple of teenagers, Robert and Patricia clung to each other as they walked. They were jostled by the crowd of people as they made their way past the various booths of food and games. They rode the Spider, laughing and screaming as it swung the cars around, narrowly missing the cars on the opposite arm. They shared a cotton candy while they made revolutions on the ferris wheel. As they got to the top, Patricia said, "Look! There's our hospital."

"We don't own it just yet," replied Robert. "I suppose if we can solve the Shircliff problem, we may each get a wing named after us." They laughed.

"I'd settle for one wing dedicated to Mr. and Mrs. Robert Vanhouse." Patricia gambled with that line.

Robert smiled and put an arm around her shoulders. "That's an interesting idea."

Patricia's heart pounded with excitement. Her body tingled with thoughts of being married to him. She smiled at him and leaned over, placing her head on his shoulder. As they left the ferris wheel, they walked hand in hand back into the crowd of people.

"Before we leave, I want to go into the house of mirrors," pleaded Robert.

"Sure, that would be fun. Lead on!"

The couple found the Hall of Mirrors. There was a loud speaker with a recorded voice. "Come in and be amazed! See multiple images of yourself in three dimensions!"

Robert bought the tickets, and Patricia trotted ahead of him. "Bet you can't find me," she teased as she disappeared into the maze. Robert entered and wandered through the hall of red light and mirrored surfaces. It was strange to see so many images of himself. He stopped and fixed his hair, making sure his clothes were still looking good and then continued through the hall.

"Hey, where are you? This is a little weirder than I thought," he yelled.

He heard a giggle and pivoted to find Patricia just behind him. "How'd you do that?" he asked. He pulled her close and kissed her. Screaming and laughter were approaching from around the corner behind them.

"Oh, I forgot. This is a family ride," Robert said. He released her. Patricia just smiled and grabbed his hand. They walked through the remaining portion of the attraction. They stopped at the end to play in front of the curved mirrors that distorted their looks and shape. Patricia laughed when she saw how fat her body was. Robert's body looked almost fluidic, curving vertically in the reflection. They both laughed as they passed through the last door and went out onto the midway again.

"Well, have we seen and done it all?" Robert asked.

"I guess so," Patricia replied, not wanting the night to

end. "Would you like to come over to my house?" she asked expectantly.

Robert did not disappoint her. "I was hoping you would ask."

—

The drive to Patricia's had been a short one. They talked of the carnival and how much fun they had.

"I hadn't been to a carnival in years, decades," Robert said.

"Me too," she said. "Thanks for taking me."

"It was a lot of fun except for the house of mirrors. There were a bunch of you. That was pretty scary." He smiled at her.

Patricia playfully slapped his arm. "Ha, ha."

At Patricia's home they collapsed on the sofa with their heads leaning back on the cushions.

"Whew, I'm beat," Robert said. "Hey, you got anything to drink around here?"

Patricia turned her head to look at him. "You bet. What would you like, beer, wine ...?"

"How about some wine?" Robert said.

"Coming right up, my dear," Patricia responded, playfully patting him with her hands. She bounded off to the kitchen. Robert followed at a slower pace. He reached into his left jacket pocket. His fingers wrapped around the small tape recorder. He would wait for the right moment.

Patricia hesitated. "Oh man, I told myself I would not drink so much tonight. I had a killer of a headache last night."

Great. This won't be as easy as the last time. "Okay. Just a little then," Robert said. Robert took the glasses from her. "Are there any pretzels?"

"I think so. I'll check." Patricia returned to the kitchen. Robert took that opportunity to open a small vial of powder and slip it in her glass before filling it with wine.

Patricia returned with a bowl of pretzels. "Here we go."

"I poured you a glass. Is that okay?"

"Sure. I didn't say I wouldn't drink at all." Patricia took a sip. "Hmm, this is good."

"I like it. It really helps me unwind. Here, have a little more."

Robert and Patricia passed the evening quietly, drinking wine and relaxing on the sofa. The wine was having its effect on Patricia.

Robert had made sure that he would not be under the influence of the alcohol by drinking slowly, sipping his glass occasionally. He also made sure Patricia's glass was never empty. Robert eventually turned the conversation to the affair at the hospital.

Robert began the leading questions. "Our strategy for getting Shircliff is working well. I want to make sure we're still on the same page. Tell me everything you have done so far." He coughed to mask the sound of the record button being pushed on the tape recorder.

"You remember," Patricia replied groggily. "I changed my appearance and my name and then applied for the nursing position."

"So do you think your plan to get Shircliff is working?"

"I think it is."

"Have you been doing anything about Rebecca Wells?" Robert asked, continuing to try and lead her into answers.

Patricia's eyes were closed as the alcohol and alprazolam moved through her body. "Yes, I've been giving her the injections to help her."

"You didn't record those anywhere, did you?"

"No, I didn't put them in the notes because Shircliff or her nurse would see them."

Click. The sound of the recorder button was almost silent. Certainly it was not heard by the now sleeping Patricia. The tape had been made and would be incriminating for Patricia with a no editing.

Robert put her to bed and cleaned up. He left feeling guilty and angry. He was angry at his brother for making him do this to someone he cared so deeply for. But it had to be done. The trap was set. Robert silently left the house and drove home.

—

The carnival lights and sounds flooded the dream. Robert was standing at the ticket counter, buying two tickets for the Hall of Mirrors. There was one difference, however. This time he was with David instead of Patricia.

"David, what are you doing here? Hey, I did it. I taped Patricia's so-called confession."

David didn't say a word. He just grabbed a ticket and ran into the maze.

"David, wait up! I said I did it!"

But David had already advanced deep into the hall and was yelling back to his brother. "I trouble you, don't I?"

"Most of the time. But I don't mind taking care of you, protecting you."

David laughed out loud. He stood where multiple mirrors reflected his image. The red glow of the lights mingled mysteriously with the smoky atmosphere.

"You're funny, Robert. I can't believe you said that."

"What? You know I brought you back from Nam, got you out of that hell hole, and kept you from being court-martialed. I have given you a life here."

"Some life!" David shouted.

"You get to live in a nice place. All you have to do is take care of mom and type a few reports for me." Robert turned his back on David as he spoke. "I've protected you and provided for you for nearly all of your adult life. What more could you want?"

David chuckled as he spoke. "You've got it backwards, brother."

Robert spun around ready to respond. David was gone. Robert looked around the room of mirrors. He searched frantically for his twin. "David?" The only image in the mirrors was his.

"David, would you come here so I don't have to yell? I want to talk to you face to face, man to man, brother to brother. Come on, man, you're making me mad."

Robert felt a tap on his shoulder. He spun around and gasped. David was standing nose to nose with him.

"How about soul to soul?" David said in a low monotone. "Let's have a soul-to-soul talk about all this." David pierced Robert with a fiery gaze. Robert's hands clinched.

His eyes squinted. He saw that David spoke, but his lips did not move yet the words came out strong and clear.

"I've actually been the one to protect *you* and save *you*. I'm the one who has provided *you* a life."

Robert's blood pressure shot up. "What on earth are you talking about? I don't understand."

"Of course you don't understand. You don't want to understand. You've been avoiding the truth for years. But now there's that woman, a woman you love very much. That's changing things."

"But I told you. I got the evidence we need," Robert said. Then he made an odd observation. "Why aren't your lips moving when you talk?"

"This is a dream, you idiot."

"Yes, but dreams can be real," Robert said. "They can be of the past or of things to come. I'm real, you're real."

"Am I?"

The question froze Robert. He stared into David's eyes. Then he reached out to touch David's lips.

"Am I real, Robert?" David asked again.

Robert was agitated now. He thrust his arms out to shove David. His hands struck the hard, cold mirror. Shocked, Robert put his hands against the mirror again. It felt the same. He pulled back and screamed, "Oh my God!"

"Oh my God!" Robert sat up in bed. He was sweating. His heart was racing. The covers were twisted from his squirming. He was beginning to comprehend. Panic was setting in.

"It can't be! It just can't be! David!" Robert leaped out of bed and began running through the house, calling out his brother's name. He had forgotten that David was at his mother's house. He grabbed the back of a living room chair. His fingers dug into the cloth. *I gotta think. I gotta think! I have to protect mother. But how?*

—

The next day Patricia was hung over. *I can't believe I got drunk again.* She reported to work on time but felt like she'd been run over by an eighteen wheeler. Her head pounded like a sledge hammer banging away on her skull. Despite the discomfort she had good memories of the previous night with Robert. She talked about it with a couple of the other nurses at lunch. She was almost giddy about their relationship and the positive direction it seemed to be going. She had no recollection of the tape-recorded incriminating interrogation.

The day passed quickly. There had been three new patients on the ward. That always made for a busy day. Two of the mothers delivered healthy babies. That never failed to hurt Patricia, although the pain seemed to be getting less intense with each passing shift. Three o'clock came, and there was no hesitation. Patricia was out the door and headed home. She needed the rest.

Finally home after the short commute, Patricia threw her keys on the kitchen counter and kicked off her shoes. She plopped down on the sofa and put her feet up on the coffee table. A long nap was just what the doctor ordered after a long day of whiny patients and cocky physicians.

Ding-dong.

"You have got to be kidding me," Patricia said. "Who in the world could this be at nine o'clock in the evening?"

When she opened the door, her surprise at seeing Dr. Vanhouse was evident.

"Robert! Hi!" Patricia flung herself at him, engulfing him in a huge hug.

Robert stood straight, his arms stiff at his side.

Patricia noticed the tension. "Hey, babe, what's wrong?" she asked. "Is everything okay?"

Robert maintained his cold stance and just stared at the wall. Patricia took a step back, confused, then tried to generate some enthusiasm.

"Oh, Robert, I'm so glad to see you. I thought about you all day. I couldn't help thinking how perfect we are for each other. I looked for you at lunch, but I didn't see you."

Robert pushed past her into the living room, raising his hand, signaling her to stop chattering. Patricia was flustered. Something was terribly wrong.

"What is it?" she asked. She reached for his hand, but he deliberately jerked away. "Something is wrong. You're not the same. Have you been drinking?"

Robert stared coldly at her. "You said we were perfect for each other. You're right! We were the perfect pair."

"What do you mean *were?*" Patricia was frightened by his hostile behavior.

"I mean exactly what it sounds like. We were a good pair, past tense. It's history. Our relationship is over."

"Over?" Patricia turned pale. Her spirit was crushed. There was a long uncomfortable silence. "But we have had so much fun together. At least you acted that way. No, I take that back. Everything you said made me believe that I was really special to you." Her eyes watered. Robert just looked at her with a hollow stare, as if there were no living being inside his physical frame. "I thought that maybe even someday we could get married." Her voice crackled with the next words. "I thought you really loved me."

Robert grabbed Patricia's arm and shoved her down on the couch. She bounced off the arm and shot sideways across the cushions, bumping her shin on the trunk that doubled as a coffee table. Patricia quickly scrambled to sit upright. She rubbed her arm and looked at him, not comprehending.

"You're scaring me now. Whatever happened or whatever is bothering you? We can work through it."

Robert stood angrily in front of her, pointing his finger at her like a dagger.

"You shut up and listen!"

He ran his fingers through his hair, and the action left him looking like a madman with his hair wafting wildly in all directions.

"Hear me and hear me good!" he exclaimed. "I know exactly what has happened at the hospital, and I have explained the whole incident to Murdock, the hospital administrator. He was just as shocked as myself to learn the truth and amazed that I have gathered so much physical evidence. In fact, he was talking to board members and was dialing up local authorities as I left his office just a short while ago. That's why I'm here now."

Patricia reached for a pillow and pulled it in front of her defensively. "That's good that you figured it all out. But I still don't understand why you're acting this way. Why are you treating me this way? I didn't do anything."

Robert paced back and forth in front of her, laughing.

"You didn't do anything...I have proof that you did everything."

Patricia cowered behind the small pillow she clutched. "You're talking like a madman."

"I'm not crazy, but people will wonder about you when they hear this sordid story." Robert smiled.

"I don't have a clue as to what you're talking about."

"Let's see, where do I start? Where should I begin?" Robert paced around the room. He held his pointer finger to his lip then slowly lowered his hand into his pocket. "Perhaps I should start with the first night I met you. You were in labor. It was a difficult labor, and your baby only lived a few moments. Now most women would be distraught, but not you. I noticed you were enraged, violent. There is record of you threatening the doctor. You filed a complaint against the hospital, specifically mentioning Dr. Shircliff. And then to top it all off, you were assigned psychiatric care." He paused, facing her. "Wouldn't you say that is all correct so far?"

"Well, of course I would. It is all on hospital records. But what are you driving at?"

He started pacing again. "Now if I'm not mistaken, I believe you applied for a job at the hospital almost immediately after you were released. But before you applied you went to great lengths to change your physical appearance. You even changed your name from Patricia Duncan to Patricia Jones."

"I had to do that," she replied.

"I don't understand why!" he said.

"You do too. I explained that all to you. I wanted to be watching Dr. Shircliff, and I couldn't apply as that same angry brunette who was at the hospital that night. I never would have landed the position looking like my old self. Somebody might have recognized me."

"So, you changed your appearance. You even looked very much like Dr. Shircliff, didn't you?" He said like a prosecuting attorney.

"Yes, but—"

"Then I told you that the hospital was running the internal investigation into the suspicious mortality rate. I told you I was helping with the investigation, and as I remember you were delighted to be able to help."

Patricia scoffed, "Naturally I wanted to be involved. I wanted to at least get Shircliff's license revoked, and if at all possible, I'd even like to see her do some jail time."

"Sort of a revenge thing, wouldn't you say?" asked Robert.

"Exactly!" boasted Patricia.

Robert stood, towering over the confused woman. "You were very eager to help treat Mrs. Wells, weren't you?"

"That's a silly question. Do you think I was going to sit by and wait for that incompetent mercenary to harm somebody else?"

"Is that why you administered the unauthorized doses of medication to Mrs. Wells?"

"Yes."

"You didn't chart that, did you?"

"Of course not. I could get in trouble for giving her that stuff without orders from the attending physician."

Robert reached into his pocket pulled out the recorder that he had used to get the evidence against her.

"This little tape I made will greatly help my case. You said everything the police need to hear. They asked me to tape a conversation with you if I could." *That is a lie, but a useful lie,* he thought. "And you answered all the questions perfectly."

Patricia was stunned.

"You realize that the medication you secretly gave Mrs. Wells could have killed her. It was a little Chinese herbal preparation containing something called aristolochic acid. It is a pretty potent poison that works on kidney function. Fortunately, I decided to expose you and this whole bizarre tale of events before anything more serious happened. I'll get a medal." The corner of Robert's lips turned up in an evil smile.

Patricia felt sick. "Robert, this is not funny. Quit playing games and tell me what really happened."

"Well, babe, I'm not kidding. If this whole thing is coming down just as it appears, you will be prosecuted as the angry young mother who sought revenge. All the motives and the evidence are there. You blamed Shircliff for the death of your child. With revenge as the only thing on your mind, you applied for the nursing job at the hospital. Your application was deceitful. You successfully managed to change your name and physical appearance. I think you purposefully wanted to look like Dr. Shircliff so that you could have access to the same areas she attends and not arouse suspicion."

Patricia sat still, her mouth wide open, unable to speak.

Robert walked to the center of the room. "Ladies and gentleman of the jury, I have evidence that links Patricia Duncan, alias Patricia Jones, to the deaths of several patients. She, of course, killed them, hoping to somehow blame Dr. Elizabeth Shircliff and thus avenge the death of her baby. The most recent victim would be a Mrs. Rebecca Wells. Fortunately, this case did not result in the death of the patient. She will have to undergo a kidney transplant because Mrs. Duncan continually gave her large doses of a very harmful Chinese herbal nephrotoxin."

"Robert," she cried, "quit teasing me like this. It is not funny."

"No teasing here, babe. The way I see it, you will certainly get the death penalty. The most despicable act was when you sneaked into the nursery and killed that newborn. That will really raise the wrath of a jury. To murder a child shows your callousness and illustrates just how calculating and ruthless you are and how determined you are to obtain your revenge. They don't go soft on these serial murder cases, especially in this state. Shircliff will lose her position for poor supervision. And even Murdock could lose his job for being so careless with your job application." He paused and bent down, getting right in her face. "As for me, I'll be somewhat of a celebrity for breaking this case wide open. I'm sure I'll be due a promotion. I might even take Murdock's place."

Patricia slapped him across the face. "You're sick! You're a monster!"

Robert retreated back a step. His face stung, and the outline of Patricia's fingers soon glowed pink on his cheek. He scowled. "You shouldn't have done that! Remember, I've killed people for less than that."

Patricia was terrified, afraid to make a move.

Robert produced a wad of toilet paper from his coat pocket and tossed it to Patricia. It landed in the center of her lap. "But I'll give you a break. Go ahead. Unwrap it," he commanded. Patricia followed his order. It was a single brown bottle of a clear liquid.

"What's this?" Patricia asked.

"It's a bottle of the poison you injected into Rebecca Wells," Robert said.

Patricia immediately dropped the bottle, and it rolled to the floor. Robert picked up the bottle with another wad of toilet paper in his hand. He was careful not to touch the bottle itself and leave his own fingerprints.

"Now that worked well," Robert gloated. "Your fate is now sealed. You have been quite cooperative. Thanks."

"I can't believe this is happening," Patricia whispered.

"Oh, believe it, lady. You are going to jail or worse." Then Robert began to close out his plan. "But look, I have an out for you." From his other pocket Robert produced another paper-wrapped package. He placed it on the table next to Patricia.

"Pick it up!" he roared.

"Pills?" Patricia questioned.

"Not just any old pills. These are the pills you 'stole' from the hospital. They're covered with your own finger-prints. You just saw to that. "I suggest you take the pills, the entire bottle. You really have no choice. You can die peacefully with the pills, or you can die in the electric chair." Patricia looked up sadly. Her eyes were so tear filled she could only see the outline of his face.

Robert savagely continued, "This evening would be a good time to take them. You know, before the police get here to take you into custody. Take the entire bottle. You won't have any bad side effects. You'll basically go to sleep."

He walked to refrigerator and grabbed Patricia a beer. "Here, chase the pills with this. I'm not going to force the pills down you. I figure after you think about everything, you'll choose the pills over the chair."

Robert walked toward the front door, turned, and spoke one final time before he left her house. "You really have no alternative. Think about it. You lost your baby, your husband, you have no alibi for these accusations, plenty of motive." He produced the recorder. "Oh, and now I have this taped confession. You've got no reason to live. Sweet dreams!"

Robert was out the front door immediately, slamming it shut behind him. Patricia stumbled, catching her leg on the trunk as she lunged after him. She came crashing down in the middle of the room. She rose quickly but could not get the door open fast enough. She saw the tail lights of Robert's car as it trailed off down the street and then disappeared around the corner.

Patricia stood on her porch. She was numb, breathing hard, breathing deeply, and still trying to understand everything that had just happened to her. Totally distraught, she turned and walked dejectedly to her bedroom.

She sat crossed legged in the center of her bed, sometimes wailing, sometimes sobbing quietly. She stayed there for hours, swaying back and forth. Slowly the realization of her desperate situation dawned on her with full force.

Robert is right about my appearance of guilt, she thought. *There's not going to be a lawyer in America that will even listen to me. I've got no way out.*

Anger moved her. Patricia stumbled to the bathroom and stared at her reflection in the huge mirror that ran the length of the bathroom counter. Her eyes were dark, mascara blotched her face, and her cheeks were puffy.

Patricia screamed at herself, "There's no way out! Nobody will believe me. That jerk is right. I'll get blamed for Rebecca. I'll get framed for who knows what. Robert, you're too smart, and I'm too blind. God, how can so much happen to one person?"

Patricia picked up her lipstick, pulled off the cap, and touched the creamy red tip to her lip. She started applying the makeup but in another outburst yelled, "You idiot!" She drew an angry red *x* across her reflected image and then leaned heavily on the counter. She cried. Her body shook. Broken, stripped of any hope, she crumpled to the floor and wailed. "How could I have been so stupid?"

When there were no more tears left, she pulled herself up slowly off the floor. For some reason she suddenly thought of the last conversation she had with her husband. She could almost hear his deep voice warning her, "You can't continue to be this angry."

"Ken, I'm sorry. You were right. My anger has destroyed me," confessed Patricia. She then thought about Rebecca

Wells. She has been so good to me. Asking about my life. Trying to cheer me up. And what do I do? Her throat swelled, and she finished her thought out loud in broken words. "Almost … I … almost killed you."

Patricia walked back to the living room and saw the bottle of pills sitting on the table. Picking it up, she said grimly, "I've got no choice. If I run I look guilty. If I turn myself in, I look guilty."

She trudged into the kitchen, picked up a glass on the counter, and filled it with water. She put a handful of pills in her mouth then suddenly bent over the sink and spewed them out.

"No, Robert," she said in a defiant voice, "I'm not going to do it your way." She tossed the container in the trash can. "My miserable life has to count for something. Surely there must be some good that can come out of all this. There has to be some way I can take you down with me!"

Patricia hurried back to her bedroom and got down on her hands and knees at the side of the bed. She pushed back the dust ruffle and looked underneath the bed.

"Ah, it's still there. I'd almost forgotten about it." Patricia reached deep. Her arms were barely long enough. She grabbed the long leather case and carefully pulled it toward her. As soon it was out in full view, she unzipped the case and lifted her father's .270 deer rifle from its resting place. The hunting rifle had not been fired in over ten years, but she was confident it would work. Her dad had taken her shooting when he would sight-in the gun every year. She remembered her dad commenting on what a reliable weapon it had always been, and after all, she only needed one shot.

Patricia cradled the rifle in her arms when she stood up. It was heavy, just like she remembered. She walked into the front bedroom, which served as a study or office. She leaned the rifle in the corner, went over to the desk, and switched on the electric typewriter. She settled into the chair. All the pain she had suffered, all the pain she had caused, and the pain she was about to suffer could not stop her from tapping out this letter. She wrote what she knew to be true.

> *To those who find me:*
>
> *My real name is Patricia Duncan. I am in my right mind and am in control of all my mental faculties. I have been employed at Hall Park General Hospital for about a month under the name of Patricia Jones. When I took this job, I was angry with Dr. Elizabeth Shircliff, the doctor who delivered my little Anthony. I thought that she was fully responsible for the death of my child. It was my intention to expose her negligence and incompetence and destroy her career. I learned that I was wrong, very wrong. Dr. Shircliff is a good physician. It was another member of the medical staff who murdered my son.*
>
> *The guilty party is Dr. Robert Vanhouse. He is responsible for my son's death. I also believe that he is responsible for several recent deaths at the hospital, including an infant that was found dead in its nursery crib (Hutchinson?) just a couple of days ago. I know for a fact that he tried to murder Rebecca Wells, who is currently in Hall Park General. He duped me into thinking he was on an internal investigative*

committee that was to expose Dr. Shircliff for her incompetence. Vanhouse made me think I was protecting Mrs. Wells by giving her a special medication to help control her blood pressure. He instructed me not to record those injections. Actually he gave me a Chinese herbal mixture that was slowly poisoning her, something called aristolochic acid. He is a madman. He knows what he is doing. The only way I can hope to stop him is to validate my confession by taking my own life. I hate that he used me to do some of his work. I regret that I ever became involved with him. Please believe me.

My last wish is that I be buried close to my little Anthony. May God forgive me for my participation in this evil. Please believe me. If you don't, others may die.

Patricia Jones Duncan

Patricia pulled the letter from the typewriter, picked up a pen, and signed it in large legible cursive. She then stood up and took the note and the hunting rifle into the living room. She centered the wooden rocking chair in front of the picture window so that she could see her front yard. She then picked up the telephone and dialed the police department number. Patricia calmly sat down in the rocker and waited for an operator to come on line.

15

CHAPTER

Robert burst through the front door of his mother's home. His feet crunched over a stack of envelopes on the floor. The more he thought about what he had done to Patricia, the angrier he became. He moved quickly passed the foyer and through the living room.

"David!" he yelled. "David, where are you?"

He shoved the swinging kitchen door, and immediately a stale odor slapped him in the face. He paused as he gazed around the room, attempting to locate the source of the foul aroma. It looked like the kitchen had not been visited in months. He remembered sitting at the kitchen table a few months ago. His memory flashed back to that visit. He came over for breakfast and had a short stack of pancakes sitting in front of him at the table. His beeper went off before he could take his first bite. He left immediately for Hall Park General to attend to a patient.

That stack of pancakes was still on the table, along with what was left of a cup of coffee. Instead of golden brown, the pancakes were splotched with velvety green mold, and the syrup had nearly caramelized. The coffee had evaporated, leaving a black sludge at the bottom of the cup. *What is David doing? What's going on?*

Something was wrong. Robert's anger toward David

changed to concern for his well being. "David?" Robert dashed upstairs, taking the steps three at a time.

"David!" he yelled. Still no answer. Robert's anxiety was growing with each passing second. He veered off into David's room. Except for a thin layer of dust atop the dresser, David's room was undisturbed. The bed was untouched. David's baseball bats hung in the gun rack with the picture of his high school championship team still hanging proudly above it.

Robert was perplexed. He walked down the hall to his mother's room. *I don't get it. This just doesn't make sense.* His mind couldn't process the confusing information being sent to it.

He walked into his mother's room. *Gone! She's gone.* His mother's room was immaculate as always. Her beautiful quilts were still hanging in their racks. The bed was perfect with the pink, flowered bedspread and pillow shams in proper order. Her Bible was open on the bedside table with her glasses sitting on top of the pages. Looking over at the dresser, he saw that everything was in order. Nothing appeared out of place. Then he noticed the reflection of the bedroom window in the dresser mirror.

Robert stepped over to the bedroom window and looked through the single-paned glass into the backyard.

"Oh, God," he muttered. He was sick. "It can't be." He placed his hand on the window pane and stared at the plot of dirt. "Surely not."

The longer he looked, the more it resembled a freshly dug grave.

"Oh, God!" he repeated, louder this time. "David is at

it again. First Vietnam, now here. 'Put the suffering down. They'll die anyway.' That's what he said that day on the hill. That's what he believes now."

Robert, nearly in shock, walked back down the hall to the stairs. Slowly, one step at a time, he descended toward the den. Nearly in tears, he frantically thought about what to do. *Police, I've got to call the police. I've got to stop him.* He headed for the phone across the room.

Suddenly Robert heard footsteps. He turned his head to the right, and there stood a figure at the top of the staircase.

"Robert," the figure said in a quiet tone. "You look puzzled. I can explain everything."

Robert recognized the voice, and then he saw the figure more clearly as it descended the stairs.

"David!" Robert turned around to face his twin brother. "Don't you mean to explain your way out of this mess?"

David laughed an eerie, bone chilling laugh. "That's exactly what I had in mind. I want to explain your way out of this."

"*My* way out?" Robert questioned. Did you say *my* way out?"

"Yes. I think you forgot what happened ten years ago on the hill."

"Not so," grumbled Robert. "I'll never forget."

"Or how about the hospital? Bonnie Rowden, the Hutchinson baby, and whoever else there was? Do I need to continue?" David walked down a few more steps.

Robert began to tremble. Beads of sweat appeared on his face like the first raindrops on a sidewalk. "I don't know what you're talking about. What do you know about the hospital deaths?"

David chuckled.

"Give me an answer!" Robert demanded. Robert's attention was fully focused on David. He stared in terror as his brother moved down the steps. He didn't blink. He listened.

David calmly explained. "Robert, the common denominator was that those people I just mentioned were all suffering. You can't handle suffering people. You never could. Yes, the compassionate Doctor Robert Vanhouse found it too easy to put them out of their misery. Just like on the hill in Vietnam."

David reached the bottom of the staircase. He shook his head from side to side. "Robert, Robert, Robert. What am I going to do with you?"

Robert attempted to defend himself. "You can't blame those deaths on me. I've never killed a soul."

"What about Wyatt?" David asked. "You killed him, didn't you?"

"That was an accident, and you know it!" Robert clinched his fists as his emotions exploded. "It's not me that's the problem here. I even gave up the woman I love just to save your hide. Once again I've bailed you out!"

"Wait a minute, Robert," David interrupted. "Think about what you're saying."

"I am thinking about it! I remember exactly what happened on that hill in Nam. I saw you put the soldiers down. Granted it saved my life, but it was murder."

"Then how do you explain those deaths at the hospital?" David asked.

"I can only assume you broke our agreement, snuck out of the house, and continued the killing. It wouldn't be hard to get around the hospital; we are identical twins. You could pass for me without any trouble. No one would give you a second thought.

"Well, what about Mom?" Robert continued. "Is that her grave in the backyard? Did you kill her?"

"Look, this is ridiculous," David said. "I'm not going to argue with you anymore. It's time to set things straight. Look at the mantle."

Robert pivoted and stepped closer to the fireplace. What he saw horrified him. In that split second, his world shattered. Displayed on the fireplace mantle was a triangular, glass case, trimmed in stained oak. Inside was a folded, red, white, and blue flag. Next to the case was a framed certificate. The certificate read in part:

"This is to certify that the President of the United States has awarded the Purple Heart...to Corporal David E. Vanhouse, killed in combat against hostile enemy forces..."

Robert read no further. The tears were streaming down his face.

"No! This can't be!" Robert screamed. He screamed again, "This can't be!" There was nothing but silence in the empty house. He was never so alone.

"David," Robert whimpered as he crumpled to the

floor. "This isn't funny. You are a sick man. I don't understand. I don't understand."

Robert sprawled out across the floor, flipped over on his back, and stared at the yellowed, off-white ceiling. The desperation of the moment had scrambled his thoughts. He turned his head right and left, searching for his brother. But David was gone. Of course, he had never been there on the stairs. Robert scrambled to his feet. *Oh my God. It's true.* He ran his fingers along the glass case. *It's true!* He fiddled with the Purple Heart. He read the accompanying certificate one more time.

It's me! Robert's nightmares had become reality.

—

"Hall Park Police," answered a man's voice. The flashing green computer screen reflected in his glasses.

Patricia spoke slowly and deliberately, "I'd like to report a murder."

He adjusted his headset. "Ma'am, did you say murder?"

"Yes." The calm tone in her voice made the young dispatcher's skin crawl.

"Are you in danger?" he asked.

"The murder is my own."

He sat straight up in his chair and motioned for the other dispatcher to listen along. Both men focused on the call.

"Ma'am, am I to understand that you are about to take your own life?"

"You're brilliant," said Patricia sarcastically. "I'm glad you understand English."

The dispatcher began to perspire heavily. He didn't know whether to joke or plead with this caller. "I'm sorry, ma'am. Please let me help you." He tried to sound calm.

"Oh, I will, I will. I want you to dispatch an ambulance to my house."

"Sure, ma'am. Tell me your name and address, please."

"I'll tell you in a minute. Right now I want to give information to you about a case you are working on. Now I'm leaving a suicide note, and I want you to be sure some police investigators know this. It has some details that will lead them to another man. He has committed multiple murders."

"Multiple murders," he echoed, still wondering whether to take the caller seriously. The other dispatcher signaled that the call had lasted the required time for a trace and they now had the location of the caller and dispatched a patrol car to the residence.

—

Sergeant Bill Walker, a twelve year police veteran, took the call. He was only a couple of blocks away when it came in. He quickly turned the patrol car around and headed for Patricia's house.

As he turned into the neighborhood, he slowed his patrol cruiser down. He pulled over to the curb about a half a block from the house and double checked the address with the dispatcher. He shut off the vehicle and grabbed his helmet by the leather chin strap, lifting it from the holder near the floor board. He exited the squad car and crouched next to the vehicle while he put the helmet on. He took a long deep breath and released it slowly. *Domestic calls are the worst,* he thought.

Bill thought about the limited information he had available concerning the developing situation at the house. All sorts of thoughts raced through his mind, but realizing that there was no time to waste, he jogged toward Patricia's house. He stayed away from the streets, skirting the shrub lines and hugging as close as possible to the protective covering of the neighboring houses. He slumped down beside the corner of a neighbor's picket fence. Patricia's house seemed quiet.

He crouched beside an evergreen at the edge of the lot, carefully studying the back of the house. All of his training and experience were being called upon. He thought, *No neighbors coming out to gawk. That's good. Sure wish I could see movement in the house. I would love to know the lady's position.*

He could see into the middle of the house through the patio door, but the curtain was open only a few inches. His angle of observation was very poor, yet he decided to take the risk and make his move across Patricia's yard. He sprinted alongside the chain-link fence to the house. He planted his lead foot and flattened himself against the side wall. With his breathing rapid and pulse racing, he reached for his service revolver, a .45 caliber that he owned. He felt the cool textured leather and unsnapped the flap. He placed his hand around the grip, withdrew the weapon, and held it tightly in his right hand. He checked the safety and then cautiously moved toward the window.

Bill took a quick look through the window. It was an

empty bedroom. He inched his way to the next window. The rough red brick pulled on his jacket as he shuffled cautiously ahead.

Meanwhile, Patricia was looking out the front window, still talking on the phone.

"Listen and do as I say. I can turn this gun on somebody else just as easily as I can shoot myself," she said, trying to sound tough.

"Ma'am … Patricia … I believe you. I'm here, and I'm listening for as long as you need me."

"Hey, I don't believe you, but you better believe me." Her voice trembled. "I've got a confession typed out. Make sure somebody gets it. This is important. This letter has some valuable information. Do you understand?"

"Sure, Patricia. Could you kind of summarize the letter for me, so that I'm sure I understand what you mean?"

"Get real. Let me tell you where I am."

"Ma'am, we've run a trace and notified the closest officers. They should be there shortly to help you."

—

With the revelation about David still fresh in his mind, Robert knew he had to take action. He wasn't sure what he had to do, but he knew he had to save Patricia. Robert rushed from his mother's house, jumped into his 'vette, and sped away. Tears streamed down his face. He could barely see the road. *No time to waste. I can at least make one wrong right.*

—

Outside of Patricia's house, Bill Walker stood perfectly still, peering into the window. For the first time he saw the caller. Patricia was seated in the rocking chair. Her attention was clearly funneled toward the front of the house. She was still talking on the phone.

The police dispatcher was sweating heavily. His chest felt constricted. He took slow deep breaths. "Patricia, you've got to tell me how I can help you."

"You can't help me. Just make sure I'm buried next to my son."

"You don't want to end it now. You sound young with a lot of life ahead of you. Nothing can be so bad to want to take your own life."

Patricia chuckled. "You have no idea what you're talking about. Sometimes life's just not worth living. I'm through talking now. Goodbye."

"Patricia, wait!"

Walker kept watching Patricia. She laid the phone in her lap. She grabbed the rifle and flipped it around, pointing the barrel at her face. She touched the tip of the cold steel to her nose sliding her right hand down the barrel and moving it toward the trigger. Walker watched anxiously. "Oh lady, come on, don't do it!" he whispered. "Pick the phone back up. Come on, pick it up." Walker breathed a short, deep sigh as he watched Patricia pick up the receiver again.

"Atta girl."

"Who am I talking to?" Patricia asked.

"Mike Compton, ma'am."

"Well, Mike. Desperate people do desperate things."

"I know. I hear a lot of that," Mike answered. "Patricia, don't do something stupid."

There was a pause as she thought.

"You're stalling. I know it, you know it," she said.

She was absolutely right, and Compton was frustrated, but he continued. "I need to know more about your family. And then you said something earlier about other murders. Hey, if there is a killer on the loose, we need you alive as a witness. You will not do me any good dead. I know what I am talking about. It is hard to convict somebody on circumstantial evidence, so stay with me, and let's talk."

"I have no family that would want me. You do your investigation according to the information in my note. You won't have any problems. Doctor Robert Vanhouse is a dangerous man."

"So that's his name!" Compton tried to pretend that the name was the major evidence he needed. "Look, even if you're guilty of a crime, we can get you a negotiated sentence. I beg you to think this out. We can plea bargain. Maybe you're not guilty of any crime worth imprisonment."

"Look, Mike, I have thought it all the way through. Goodbye."

—

Robert approached the house doing nearly sixty miles per hour through Patricia's neighborhood. He slammed on his brakes, the tires squealed, and he made a sharp turn up her driveway. He then made a hard right into the middle of the front yard. Robert jammed the stick shift into first gear and opened the door all in one frantic move. The car rolled another few feet as it sputtered and lurched forward to a stop.

Sergeant Walker heard the screeching tires. He assumed it was his backup. *Geez, fellas! Why don't you just startle her into pulling the trigger!* He remained at the window, observing Patricia. If she made any sudden moves, he would have to move in.

—

At the side window, Bill watched Patricia hang up abruptly. She quickly felt for her heartbeat with her left hand, placing her middle three fingers on her chest and then moving them slightly until she found the perfect spot. She moved the rifle with her right hand, propping the stock on the coffee table and pointing the barrel at her heart. Awkwardly, she placed her right thumb on the trigger.

—

Robert scrambled up the steps and nearly yanked the screen door off its hinges. Somehow it stayed intact. He crashed through the front door and yelled, "Patricia, don't! I love you!"

Startled by the sudden noise from a familiar voice, Patricia reflexively jerked around toward the sound. The rifle barrel followed her movements, twisting in Robert's direction.

Sergeant Walker could wait no longer. He brought the barrel of his gun back and hit the window. Shards of glass exploded into the room. The curtains parted, knocking over a plant stand. The Boston fern crashed to the floor, scattering potting soil. A jagged edge of glass ripped through the meaty part of his right hand just below his thumb.

"Freeze! Police!" he yelled as he took aim at Patricia.

"No!" Robert sensed that the officer was going to shoot. He dove at Patricia. The sudden charge by Robert further confused Patricia and she jumped. Her rifle discharged. The bullet ripped through Robert's leg.

Sergeant Walker automatically fired his service revolver at the source of the rifle shot. His bullet missed Patricia but found an unintended target, lodging in Robert's chest.

Blood ran from both of Robert's wounds. He rolled to face Patricia. Their bodies tangled and fell to the floor.

"Forgive me!" Robert pleaded. Patricia saw a tenderness in his face she had never seen from any man.

"I ... I love you," Robert stuttered.

"Oh, Robert," Patricia sobbed. "I ... "

Robert smiled. His chest heaved. He took a deep breath and moaned, "I love you so much. I don't deserve your love. I've ... "

"Shhh. Don't talk. We'll get help." Patricia attempted to call on her nursing skills to stop the bleeding. Sergeant Walker assisted. It seemed futile. Robert was losing blood at an alarming rate.

Robert knew that his life was ebbing away as each beat of his broken heart pushed more blood onto the carpeted floor. He only had minutes to make things right, and he was grateful for the chance.

"I'm responsible for many deaths at the hospital," Robert began.

"Not my Anthony," Patricia blurted out. It was the first thought to enter her mind.

"No, I didn't kill your baby, but I could have done more to help him."

Patricia collapsed in sorrow. Robert continued, "I have to get this out. I have to tell somebody. Injections usually," he gasped. He began to pass out. Patricia attempted to coax him back.

"Injections…"

"Yes, injections. Bonnie Rowden and three to four others." He closed his eyes. Patricia pulled him closer.

"My mother," he screamed. "I killed my own mother. Couldn't stand to see her suffer. What have I done?" He coughed. "I didn't want to hurt anybody, and I hurt everybody."

Robert gathered what little strength he had. He opened his eyes and placed his hand gently on Patricia's cheek. "I love you. Will you forgive me?"

"I can forgive you," wept Patricia. "Robert, I can't stop the bleeding."

"An ambulance should be here any second, ma'am," Walker interjected. He grabbed a towel from the kitchen and wrapped it around his bleeding right hand. "I already had backup on the way."

Robert took a very deep breath, deep enough to utter his last words.

"Do you love me? Tell me you love me." He closed his eyes. His body shook then went limp.

The words came as a whisper. They came late. "Yes, Robert, I love you." Patricia leaned over and kissed Robert's forehead. She wept uncontrollably. She rocked his lifeless body back and forth.

Sergeant Walker calmly tried to pull them apart. "I'm sorry, ma'am. You'll need to let him go now." He waited patiently, allowing her to grieve for a few more minutes.

"Ma'am, you'll have to let him go. The paramedics are here."

Now Walker had no choice but to separate the two lovers. He guided Patricia to a chair.

The paramedics came in and began their routine. They immediately saw that no life-saving measures were necessary.

"He's done," mumbled one of the paramedics. The other attendant moved to Patricia's side.

"Miss, were you injured? You have blood all over you."

She looked down at her soaked blouse. Some of Robert's blood had already dried on her arm. "I'm fine," she said through a handkerchief Sergeant Walker had provided.

"Nobody can be fine after going through all this. Why don't you let us take you to the hospital? There are people there who can help you. They will check you out and give you some medicine to help you sleep."

"No! I am fine. Just leave me alone, please." Patricia was leaning on one hand and wiping tears from her face with the other.

Sergeant Walker sat down opposite Patricia. "Miss, normally I would need a statement from you, but since I witnessed much of the incident myself, I can wait until tomorrow. Just promise me you'll be at a phone number where I can reach you."

"Sure. Where am I going to go?"

Patricia leaned back in the living room chair and watched the beehive of activity. Lights flashed as the police photographers took pictures of the scene. Policemen combed through the living room looking for shell casings and bullet fragments in the walls. They were especially meticulous with their investigation because an officer's weapon had been involved. One of the detectives found the blood soaked suicide note and placed it in an evidence bag. Two investigators for the medical examiner's office looked closely at the body to determine which of the wounds were fatal. Soon they loaded Robert's body into their van and departed. Not long afterward, the rest of the force left. All but Sergeant Walker.

"Ma'am, can I take you somewhere?"

"No, I'll stay here. I don't have any place to go."

Sergeant Walker handed her his business card. "Well, if you need anything, anything at all, you give me a call."

"Thanks. I'll be okay."

16

CHAPTER

Three days after Robert's death and the day before his funeral, Lieutenant Steele called the hospital.

"Dr. Murdock?"

"Yes, I'm Murdock."

"Lieutenant Steele here. This whole puzzle seemed to fit together pretty quickly. I'm still waiting on some minor details and some autopsy reports, but I can tell you what I know as fact, and I'll tell you what we expect to find out. We were able to access some old army records. It seems Robert had a very traumatic time in Viet Nam. The army discharged him. They let him go rather than having him return to combat. They suspected that he put down some of his comrades in order to prevent his own capture. They could not prove it, however. The army lacked conclusive evidence. I do know for sure that Robert witnessed his twin brother get killed in action during that same battle."

"That would be tough to deal with," remarked Murdock.

Steele continued, "Here is the real shocker. It seems Robert killed his own mother. We had the body exhumed, and toxicology reports showed high concentrations of morphine. The body was positively identified as Mrs. Vanhouse through X-rays and dental records. She was wrapped in plastic. Inside the plastic a syringe was recovered that tested positive for morphine. We pulled a few partial fingerprints from the barrel of the syringe, and they were positive match for Robert."

Murdock look stunned. "That's horrible. I thought I knew him. I never suspected him at all."

"Don't beat yourself up about it. A lot of people didn't suspect him, including me. But let me continue. One of our officers witnessed Robert confess to killing people by injection. I strongly believe that our investigation will prove this to be true. It takes a little time to exhume bodies and get the reports back from the medical examiner. There's a lot of tests to be run and a mile of paperwork. In this particular instance we have several bodies to deal with, so it's going to take awhile for all of the pieces to come together.

I also had a very interesting talk with one of your staff psychologists, a Doctor Jeff Hibbitts."

"What did he say?" Murdock asked.

"Well, the two men were apparently long time, close friends. They went to high school together. He said Robert had recently dropped by for advice. The doctor said Robert was troubled by some dreams he was having. He saw no indication that there was any big problem. Robert rejected the use of sleep aids, so naturally the psychologist thought it was no big deal."

"Oh my, I didn't see it coming either," Murdock said. "Now that I think about it, Robert seemed a little ragged looking, and he had come to me about a dream also."

"The psychologist suggested some hypothetical reasons why Robert may have acted as he did," Steele said.

"What would that be? I would like to know."

"He theorized that Robert was unable to separate his dreams from reality or maybe he was compelled to act out his dreams in real life. He speculated that Robert may have had a multiple personality disorder. He just didn't have a chance to formally diagnose it."

"Well, certainly the mind is a complicated, strange machine. Robert's actions were so opposite from his perceived character. He seemed so gentle. He loved to laugh and tease. He kept so many of us in good spirits."

"There's more. We found some transcribed hospital reports at the mother's house. In the margins of the reports were handwritten notes in red ink saying simply 'suffering.' That word appears next to all of the recent deaths at Hall Park General. Our handwriting analysts have determined that they were written by a left-handed person. Hibbitts told me that David was left handed and Robert was ambidextrous. Hibbitts theorized that Robert's dual personality was so complete that he even imitated David's handwriting."

"A regular Dr. Jekyll and Mr. Hyde," said Steele.

"So it seems. Thanks for the call. I'd like to have a complete report of the investigation once everything is done."

"I understand. I figured you'd want a copy for the hospital files."

"You bet. Keep in touch." Murdock gently hung up the phone. He was shocked, amazed, and saddened, but relieved it was all over, or at least everything but the funeral.

—

The Wells' station wagon had done more than its fair share of road time recently. In addition to the normal routine of family life, there were new excursions required of the old car. Since coming home from the hospital, Rebecca was now required to return to the Hall Park General three times a week for dialysis treatments. On the morning of Robert's funeral, the vehicle coughed, sputtered, and reluctantly started.

"Thought I was going to have to get out and push," remarked Brent.

"You think this heap will get me to the funeral?" asked Rebecca.

"Once I get her started, she's usually good for the day."

"Well, I'm holding you to that. It sure would be embarrassing to get stuck out there at the cemetery."

"Alone? I thought you were taking old what's her face."

"I'm going to pick up Patricia. We became friends through this mess, believe it or not."

"She does need a friend, that's for sure."

"Well, I agree, and I'll be picking her up as soon as I drop you off at work. We'll have some time to visit before I drive us to the funeral."

"I wish you could have found a way to leave Alicia at home."

"I couldn't find a sitter. Besides, Patricia would love to see the baby."

"You know you really shouldn't be holding her in the front seat."

"I know. You sound like my mother."

"Well, hey, I just got you two out of the hospital. Do you think I want to check you back in because of an accident?"

"All the more reason to pay attention to the signals!"

said Rebecca while motioning ahead and jamming her feet into the floorboard.

———

Patricia eagerly welcomed Rebecca and her baby into her house. She hugged Rebecca and then kissed Alicia on the fingers and cheek. Then she rushed off down the hall, saying, "I'm just about ready."

"That's an interesting choice of attire to wear to a funeral," Rebecca yelled down the hall.

Patricia stuck her head out of the bedroom door. She was putting on an earring.

"Oh, I know. I thought about wearing some dark-colored dress, but then I got to thinking. This was Robert's favorite outfit. He loved this dress and earrings. He often commented on how nice I looked in it. So I said why not."

Even though Rebecca thought it proper to wear the darker colors of the mourning, she smiled and said, "It's cute on you. I can see why Robert liked it so."

"See? It's really pretty nice." Patricia ran her hands up and down her sides as if she were showing off the grand prize on a television game show.

"If that's what he liked, then by all means," said Rebecca. She stepped into the bedroom and took a seat in a chair.

"I miss him so," Patricia said and sighed. "I hope I'll do okay at the funeral. Do you have any tissues? I don't own a handkerchief."

"I have an extra." Rebecca pulled one from her purse. The women moved to Patricia's living room and played with the baby. It was a nice distraction.

—

It was a warm, June day in Oklahoma. Small town funerals tend to draw large crowds, particularly with the mild weather. This one was no different. People came from all around the community. The story had been front-page news in the *Hall Park Herald*. Rumors about Robert circulated throughout the hospital, some true, some not. Of course, Robert had no remaining close relatives. The hospital staff was his family, and they came out in force to see the funeral service. Some came to pay their respects to the memory of a man they knew as pleasant and funny. Some came as a means of expressing their sorrow for a young doctor who had lost so much. Still others came as friends of Robert Vanhouse. They did not excuse what he had done, but they needed to be there nonetheless.

Keith Murdock and Elizabeth Shircliff chatted briefly at the graveside after the service.

"Well, Elizabeth, who would have ever thought such a cordial, compassionate man could ever have committed such crimes. I'd known him for years."

"Oh, Keith, I'm just as shocked as you," Shircliff responded. "I really admired Robert. He always made me laugh. He checked up on patients when they weren't even his responsibility. Patients he may have seen only for a short time in the ER. He helped keep life upbeat for so many of us."

"Upbeat," Murdock said. "It's interesting you chose those words. He kept us upbeat, and yet from what I understand he just beat himself up. Lieutenant Steele's investigation uncovered a little information about Robert. He had suffered from battle fatigue and the traumas of war. Evidently it marred him for life. He coped until a few months back. Do you know Jeff Hibbits, our staff psychologist?"

"Yes, I've met him a few times."

"Robert approached Hibbitts about some dreams that were troubling him. As I thought about it, I remembered Robert coming to me about a dream he'd had recently. Anyway, we just didn't know."

Keith paused. A tear trickled down his cheek. He brushed it away with his hand.

"I don't know if we could have prevented any of this." He looked directly into Elizabeth's tear-swollen eyes. "One other thing. I owe you an apology, Elizabeth. I was terribly wrong in questioning your integrity and medical skills. Forgive me."

"Oh, Keith, you were just trying to do your job in a stressful situation. Of course I forgive you."

They both looked back to the grave. It was quiet. A soft summer breeze ruffled the spray of flowers standing next to the gravesite.

A backhoe operator squirmed impatiently on the seat of his Case tractor over by the tool shed. He pulled a cigarette from his shirt pocket. He could tell this was going to take awhile. He was hoping everyone would leave quickly so he could fill in the hole and go home. It was not that he didn't feel compassion for the people involved; it was that his son's little league baseball game started soon.

Elizabeth tossed a daisy onto the coffin.

"Keith, let's go. It's over. It will take some time to heal, but it's all behind us now." She was relieved to be cleared of all suspicion and to know the spike in the mortality rate at the hospital was not her fault. It was due to the actions of one man. The two returned to finish out the day at the hospital. Hopefully it would be a routine day.

Rebecca and Patricia lingered behind after the brief burial ceremony. They were the only ones left in the cemetery. Rebecca cradled her newborn in her arms. The little girl was wrapped in a pink blanket and had a matching pink cap on her head.

Patricia was struggling to regain her composure. She had tried to remain stoic, but she just could not hold back the feelings she had for Robert, even with the terrible things he had done. Rebecca turned to face her.

"Patricia, I can't imagine the pain you have been through. And I know this won't help, but Brent and I talked. We want you to be the godmother of little Alicia."

Patricia just broke down and wept. "Rebecca, you are so kind. I'd be … I'd be honored." She choked on the words. Patricia stroked the baby's head and smiled. Alicia just looked back at her and wiggled. Patricia struggled to speak. "I have been thinking, too. I know you need a kidney transplant because of the poison I gave you. This seems so hollow, but if we are compatible, I would like to donate one of mine. I followed your chemistries in the hospital, and your blood type is the same as mine. I think there's a good chance we are compatible."

Now it was Rebecca's turn to cry. She wrapped her free arm around Patricia's neck. They held Alicia between them. Both sets of tears sprinkled down onto Alicia's blanket.

"All this is so overwhelming. I really did love Robert," Patricia stammered. "I … I really … really loved him."

"I know. I'm so sorry. I'll be here for you. It will be okay; you'll see. Things will be different," Rebecca said. She let Patricia lead. She realized her friend needed to grieve. She handed the baby to Patricia. "Here, would you like to hold Alicia?"

Patricia's lips almost curved into a smile. "I would love to."

Patricia carefully cradled the tiny infant and instinctively rocked back and forth. The baby cooed and Patricia grinned. It was a good feeling. A feeling she hadn't felt in a long time. Patricia looked at Rebecca. Her cheeks still glistened from the oceans of tears.

"I think I'm ready to go now." Patricia pivoted and walked slowly toward the car. She clutched the Wells baby to her chest. She repeated what Rebecca had said moments ago. "I'll be okay. Things will be different." Just then she froze in mid-stride.

"Are you all right?" asked Rebecca.

"Would it be okay if we went by Anthony's grave?" asked Patricia. She pointed to the northwest. "It's just over there."

"Of course we can," Rebecca said.

The two women walked together, Patricia still holding little Alicia Wells. Once at the grave of Patricia's son, she got down on her knees.

"Hi, Anthony. I've got someone for you to meet. Patricia held up Alicia's tiny head. "This is Miss Alicia Wells. She's my goddaughter. I thought you would want to meet her. Isn't she beautiful? I think you would like her. She comes from a great family." Rebecca stood behind Patricia. Her lips trembled into a smile underneath her fingers.

After a few minutes, Patricia stood up, and the friends once again headed toward the car. As they passed the centerpiece of the cemetery, a towering marble cross, Patricia paused. Rebecca looked at her in a questioning gaze.

"Sorry I stopped," Patricia said. "I was just thinking … I'll be okay." The twenty-foot tall structure stood on a six-foot pedestal.

"That's so pretty," Patricia said. "I hadn't noticed it before." She silently read the inscription on the base: "In the way of righteousness there is life, and in its pathway there is no death" (Proverbs 12:28).

"It is beautiful, indeed," agreed Rebecca.

"Yes, I think things will be different for me," Patricia proclaimed.

The women walked beyond the monument. The shadow of the cross passed over them.

listen|imagine|view|experience

AUDIO BOOK DOWNLOAD INCLUDED WITH THIS BOOK!

In your hands you hold a complete digital entertainment package. Besides purchasing the paper version of this book, this book includes a free download of the audio version of this book. Simply use the code listed below when visiting our website. Once downloaded to your computer, you can listen to the book through your computer's speakers, burn it to an audio CD or save the file to your portable music device (such as Apple's popular iPod) and listen on the go!

How to get your free audio book digital download:

1. Visit www.tatepublishing.com and click on the e|LIVE logo on the home page.
2. Enter the following coupon code:
   f709-6128-dbf4-a6e8-7237-22db-5f38-fc10.
   Download the audio book from your e|LIVE digital locker and begin enjoying your new digital entertainment package today!